KU-616-632

OVERDUE BOOKS WILL INCLUL
VERY. DAM GE TO, OR LOSS OF, B
E BORROW

LLYRO
BRANCH
Ph. 9415

DATE DI

09. N

14. [

2. N

JAN 89

**COMHAIRLE CHONTAE ÁTHA CLIATH THEAS**
**SOUTH DUBLIN COUNTY LIBRARIES**

---

**SOUTH DUBLIN BOOKSTORE**
*TO RENEW ANY ITEM TEL: 459 7834*

---

Items should be returned on or before the last date below. Fines,
as displayed in the Library, will be charged on overdue items.

British Library Cataloguing in Publication Data
Dillon, Eilís
   Citizen Burke.
   I. Title
823'.914[F]        PR6054.I42

ISBN  0  340  25617  6

Copyright © 1984 by Eilís Dillon. First printed 1984. All rights reserved. No part of this publication may be reproduced or transmitted in any form or by any means, electronic or mechanical, including photocopy, recording, or any information storage and retrieval system, without permission in writing from the publisher. Printed in Great Britain for Hodder and Stoughton Limited, Mill Road, Dunton Green, Sevenoaks, Kent by Biddles Ltd. Typeset by Hewer Text Composition Services, Edinburgh.

Hodder and Stoughton Editorial Office: 47 Bedford Square, London WC1B 3DP.

# To Phyllis

## _Author's Note_

Father James Burke is an historical character. Little seems to be known about him other than his birth in Ireland, his education at the Irish College in Bordeaux, his abandonment of his ministry for farming, his part in averting the famine in Bordeaux and his subsequent defence of the Irish College, in which he succeeded with the help of the revolutionary Ysabeau. I am indebted for this information to Dr. Richard Hayes' book *Ireland and Irishmen in the French Revolution* (1932). In the absence of any other information about Father Burke, I have felt free to invent his subsequent career. He played a small part in my novel *Wild Geese* (Hodder & Stoughton, 1980).

E.D.

# PART ONE

# _1796_

## 1

"MARCH 12, 1796. COLLÈGE DES IRLANDAIS, BORDEAUX.

"I have just finished inspecting my defences for the fourth time today. It is about five o'clock. None of the city clocks are on the same word. No one seems to repair them now. I have no communication with the enemy. All I know is that they have received my letter saying that I will oppose the taking over of the College till death. My defences are all in good condition, with no sign of their having been tampered with in any way."

Father James Burke pressed his back against the hard back of the desk chair. The decision to keep some sort of journal had been taken not in fear that he would forget a single moment of his present crazy existence but to punctuate the long, uneasy days. It was bitterly cold. From the high window of the Rector's study, in which he was sitting, he could see the sentinels on the roof of the Fort du Hâ huddling in their cloaks and tramping vigorously to keep warm. Clouds whirled across the sky, grey edged with white, blowing in from the Atlantic, almost certainly bringing more rain.

The dingy room was the warmest in the house, the only one in which the window and the door fitted well enough to keep out the whistling draughts that ran like little animals all over the rest of the building. Even the mice were not able to get into this room, though they slithered and hopped in dozens through the bigger rooms and through the corridors, especially at night. It was disgusting to tread on them and to hear the appalled little squeak under his foot. Burke guessed that Lacombe had used the study as his office. The big worn desk and the chair were still in fair condition. Surprising that they had not been removed with the other furniture.

9

He shifted in the chair and picked up the quill pen that he had cut with his pocket-knife earlier in the day. Jean-Paul had brought him a handful of crows' feathers with the bread one night. The small pile of paper and the dried-up bottle of ink that had been left in the desk drawers were the immediate inspiration for the journal.

The ink was a faint grey, barely legible. Perhaps he had added too much water. He took another of the quills and stirred up the bottle, feeling the resisting sludge at the bottom soften and move. He read what he had written. Inspecting the defences was a waste of time, since no one was seriously trying to drag him out. Everyone seemed to have lost interest in that kind of violent action. A couple of years ago, a defiant priest would have been a challenge to the mob. Now even the mob was gone. Poor Dr. Glynn, in whose chair Burke was sitting, had been condemned in a few minutes and carted off next day to the guillotine in the Place Dauphine, along with the old man who was serving his Mass and a few women who formed his congregation. Dr. Everard, the Vice-Rector, had watched the execution from the window of a house where he was hiding, and six months later when Lacombe raided the Irish College and took all the priests and students off to prison, he told Burke about it in grisly detail.

"Can't you take example from the courage of this martyr for the faith? His only crime was to say Mass for a few good Catholics in a private house. Doesn't your Irish blood rise up in anger against this tyranny?"

If only he had not mentioned blood – Burke had almost pointed out to the saintly man that it seemed better to keep his Irish blood inside him for future use but Dr. Everard was not a man who appreciated jokes. And it was not a time for jokes. Lacombe was ready for a feast of Irish blood, when Burke's intervention saved them. He never got much thanks for it, rather the reverse. The apostate Burke, they called him. He knew that.

The cold was unbearable. He sprang out of the chair and walked up and down the little room, hugging his arms to his body, covering his hands with the rough peasant cloth of his cloak, presently feeling a little warmth creep down to his feet. He sat down quickly at the desk and wrote, very fast, no longer caring that with this ink his words were almost illegible:

"Dr. Everard was in hiding in a house near the Place Dauphine, not being able to leave the city undetected. On one of my visits to Bordeaux in December of 1793, I was amazed to find him waiting for me in the parlour of the house of some friends of mine where I was staying. His clothes were in rags and his hair and beard untrimmed. He looked like a scarecrow. I scarcely recognised him. He told me that the Irish students and priests who were in the Carmelite prison were in danger of being executed as enemies of the Republic and as British subjects. He asked me to use my friendship with Claude Ysabeau to get them free. I did this. I had helped Ysabeau to get food into the city during the famine and he owed me a debt of gratitude. When the boys were not immediately released I was afraid that Ysabeau would be recalled to Paris before he could redeem his promise and I followed him around on all his village visits, to Bourg, to Blaye, and other places, importuning him to keep his word. He did, and they were all released and sent back to Ireland in an American ship."

He read over what he had written. It was like a prisoner's deposition before his trial. Writing it down in those stilted, bold words, was a relief. It was the bare truth. Ysabeau himself would not deny it. When he saw Burke at his elbow everywhere, he said: "All right, all right, Citizen Burke. I'm doing all I can. Trust me."

An idealist, Ysabeau, though an unholy terrorist. Like the rest of them he never knew when to stop. Rescuing the Irish was one of the few occasions when he was a match for Lacombe, the Robespierre of the Gironde. Lacombe liked that description. He always had his decree from the National Convention ready in his fist and he terrified his colleagues nearly as much as the people he hounded down.

11

Darkness was falling. Burke felt the need to see to his defences again though he knew it was foolish. They were simple, but effective against any but a professional assault, and against that he knew he would be powerless. Sacks stuffed with rocks that he found in the yard were the mainstay, and he had also erected barriers from planks lifted out of the attic floors. They came up easily, never having been nailed into place. Leaning against the heavy main door, with one end under the huge bolt and the other braced against the last step of the stairs, they would not easily give way. The rocks were a godsend. Someone must have meant to make a drain, of the kind that you fill with rocks to let the water seep lower. He had done a lot of that out at the first farm. Saint Jacques d'Ambes. He could not afford to think of that now. Who would think of planting in his way, when he was not there to tell them to do it? Lazy sods. He had not seen the place since the day he was arrested.

Feeling his way downstairs he saw those strange little points of light that seemed to shake from time to time, as if someone had crossed them. He could not discover their source, yet they seemed to contain evil. When he walked boldly up to them, there was nothing, no one. Perhaps they came from the Fort, from the sentinels' torches. There could be no other reasonable explanation, but Burke thought that they might well have a supernatural source. Why they should appear to him he had no idea, unless it was to frighten him from his determination. He was not afraid of demons, only of those so-called soldiers of the Republic. Tigers. Predators. Bandits. Anger was a dead loss. Nothing ever came of it. He could almost feel energy flowing out of him. He had had enough of that. Rage, black rage, they called it. He would have said yellow. It turned the face yellow. It sent a yellow fog before the eyes.

There was still at least two hours to go before Jean-Paul would come. The flag-stones of the ground floor felt cold through the soles of his boots. A pity he had been wearing town boots when he was arrested. The heavy ones that he wore at the farm would have been better here. The scoundrels had taken every ounce of firewood out of the College, and the tools as well. If he had had a saw, he could have cut up some of those planks in the attic and made a fire. Strangely enough, when he was a student in this same College he never felt cold, or if they felt cold the students never complained. Complaints were not encouraged, in those days. No doubt all those young bodies had generated heat, enough to keep the whole house warm. Jean-Paul had kept him supplied with candles so far, but getting them alight was always a problem. The tinder seemed to soak in the damp and often it refused to ignite for minutes on end. But there was no hurry, after all. Nothing else to do.

Back in the study, he found the flint and tinder in the darkness and got the candle lit without difficulty. This was the last one. He was expert now at finding things in the dark. As a boy at home in Ireland he had been the best at playing blind-man, a game which consisted in finding, blindfold, an object which the other children had hidden in the room. The old skill came back to him easily now. A good memory, perhaps, or some invisible machinery, like a bat's, which made eyesight unnecessary.

He set the candle on the desk and gazed at it with intense pleasure, as if it were a fire, then stretched his big, rough hands towards it to warm them. Rough. They were not the hands of a gentleman, nor of a priest. They were the hands of a farmer who has worked his own land, scarred and calloused, with swollen knuckles and broken nails. The hands of a citizen, a brother. During the Terror, hands were sometimes used in evidence though the servants of the condemned often went to the guillotine with their masters. There was no logic in those revolutionaries, no humour. Rage possessed him again now, and he picked up the quill to write quickly:

"Rage and humour seem to me to have this in common: 'Men have it when they know it not.' I find that anger rather than resignation or despair disturbs me most in my confinement. It takes possession of me without my knowledge and is an insidious enemy which could destroy me, since it will certainly destroy discretion.

"Humour seemed to desert the apostles of the Revolution as time went on, though individually some of them had plenty of it. The mob had a kind of humour always – at least they laughed a lot, if that was ever a sign of humour. They shrieked with laughter when they put Madame de Lamballe's head on a spike and raised and lowered it before the windows of the Conciergerie, with all her poor hair flying around her. They thought it was the Queen who cried out in horror every time the wretched thing passed the window but of course she was not there at all. It was the gardener's wife, or the porter's. Tales like that disgusted me with their philosophy."

The candle guttered and he laid down the pen to pinch the wick between his fingers. Philosophy! He could almost hear his father's voice say: "A kick in the arse would do them more good than all the philosophy in France." The French were never as poor as the Irish. In the country at least there was always something or other in the pot, though the better food and the wine had to be hidden when the excise men or their spies were near. When the people around Saint Jacques d'Ambes came to know Burke better, they often opened the trapdoor near the fireplace when he came to visit them, and brought up good bread and ham and wine and eggs which they had hidden in this way – things that were rarely enjoyed by the people who worked the land in Ireland. Burke admired the French for their spirit and ingenuity in beating the landlords.

The cities were different. Paris was by far the worst – houses like rookeries, filthy streets whose stench would keep you at bay if the looks of the inhabitants had not already frightened you off, beggars, street vendors and menders of everything under the sun, a rotting mass of humanity where you could lie dead for days and no one would bother to shift you except to rob your body.

Good people too, of course. There were always good people. Some are good by accident, hardly know what they're doing. Some have goodness forced on them. If he was ever good, Burke thought, that was how it happened with him. His mother pushed him into the Church with the same energy as she often pushed a recalcitrant cow into a field of juicy grass. She knew what was good for him and she was determined that he would get it. She died pleased with herself, and she had reason to be. If Burke had died on the guillotine he might have been certified good too, or if when he had gone back to Ireland he had been hanged for treason by the law there, which would condemn him for being a priest.

His mother had said: "France is the country. Get out there and you'll never have to root in the wet soil of Ireland. You'll be a doctor or a priest and live like a gentleman."

She said it every day until he took the ship from Galway with a bunch of boys on their way to Bordeaux Irish College. That was when he was nineteen, thirty-six years ago. On his last days she wept and wailed as if he were already drowned at sea or hanged but she cheered up when he was ready to go and said he would surely come back some day and help to make old Ireland free. That could have been her main object in sending him off, he thought, but one could never be sure what was in her mind. A large part of it was the wish to get him out of the way so that his older brother John could have the farm.

The Burkes were always a little better off than their neighbours, with a better landlord and a patron with a business in Ennis, four miles away. The Blackwells were powerful people, and Burke suspected that it was Mrs. Blackwell's idea originally that he should go off and get educated. Indeed it was she who paid his fare. Whenever his mother went to Ennis market, she visited Mrs. Blackwell and they sat for half an hour in the parlour over the shop. James had been present on several of these occasions but his future was never discussed in his presence. Women – when they put their heads together they were invincible.

He had a vision of hell two nights ago, while he was lying in the dark on his heap of sacks, afraid to waste the candle.

15

The sacks reeked with the smell of the potatoes they had contained. They came from the same stock that he had found in the vegetable shed next to the row of latrines in the yard, on which he had drawn to form his barricades. The sacks had never dried out properly and the cold and damp ate into his bones. Candles were getting scarce. Jean-Paul said he might not be able to get any more. In that case two thirds of his time would be spent in total darkness. This thought came to him before the vision, which however was bright and full of light. Hell should be murky. Dante's hell was full of swirling mists and vague shapes, mysterious mountains and rocks and half-seen figures curled into strange attitudes by their torment, cries of pain and shrieks of despair making an endless tumult. Burke's hell was broad daylight, a big, clear valley which he must cross forever, walking painfully, with difficulty, carrying a bag full of some abominable things which he could not identify. His sins, no doubt. These symbols were built into him – the weight of our sins – he had often and often used that one in his sermons. He was walking on a crooked path, and there were other people walking too, all carrying bags. They passed a knot of men fighting, while others baited a bear with some little snarling dogs, urging them on with obscene shouts. Down in a deeper part of the valley, a crowd was watching a man and a woman and their children being guillotined. It was not a dream. He was wide awake. Even when he stood up and walked around the room, he could not rid himself of it until it was ready to go. Then there was darkness. The Irish hell is cold – the cold stones of hell, he remembered, or the cold stones of pain. When he had gone over the details of the vision again and again, he was quite certain that Louise was not in his hell.

Jean-Paul must make some candles. Darkness could break his nerve. There was always plenty of tallow. He must be told that they were not to sell it all. Burke himself had set up their trade in everything with Bordeaux. Their peasant greed might have induced them to sell even the things that they needed. They adored money. Still Jean-Paul never left

16

him hungry. Now that the Terror was over he had more courage.

When there is danger, Burke had seen, the French peasant behaves as circumspectly as a rat or a rabbit, shrinking back into his burrow, putting forth a cautious head from time to time to see if all is clear. Jean-Paul had come back one day from Bordeaux in a state of almost laughable fright, having seen a peasant guillotined, though he had watched unmoved while dozens of aristocratic heads were cut off. A peasant, a poor man! He could never understand it. Then someone told him that the peasant had sheltered an aristocrat in his house, and after that Jean-Paul had put poor Charles Lally and his silly wife and their half-grown children out of the attic where they were sheltering, and they were soon picked up and guillotined. Hard to forgive him for that. Lally was an honourable name in France, if there were any honourable names left. Burke was not sure that he would have trusted Jean-Paul now, if things had not quieted down, or indeed if there were anyone else to trust.

But he was good-hearted essentially, like most of the Garonne peasants. When he was the sacristan in Saint Jacques, he was honest and reliable. Then when Burke gave up the Church and went to live altogether at his farm, Jean-Paul came with him as a labourer and remained just the same.

Burke asked him once: "Don't you have any qualms about following me, a priest who has deserted the Church to be a farmer?"

"It seems to me that you deserted the Church to save your neck," Jean-Paul said calmly. "If you were still down there, do you think you would be alive today? Those wolves would have got you long ago."

Burke argued with him:

"It was not just to save my own neck. Taking the oath made me safe enough for a while but I could see it was not going to last. I had to think of my flock. The wolves coveted my house to live in, my church to make into a factory or a store. They thought I was rich."

He said: "Yes, they thought you must be rich, with that big house and the poultry-runs, and a chicken for dinner every Sunday."

"And the bones of the chicken for the rest of the week."

"They didn't know that. You were able to buy a farm. Then you bought two more. That proved you are rich."

"Yes, yes. I got the first one cheap. I went into debt to pay for it. Then because I had one I was able to get the others – to him that hath, much shall be given."

They were sitting in the kitchen at Saint Jacques d'Ambes, eating dinner at noon, when this conversation took place. Jean-Paul's mother was serving the soup, thick with beans and carrots and with rings of fat floating on top.

Burke said, leaning back in his chair to avoid her ladle: "I felt that my parishioners respected me more when I was one of themselves, when I was no longer standing up over them telling them how to behave. They saw that I was supporting them in their struggle for a better life."

The mother said: "That's true. I heard many a one say it, that you're one of ourselves now and that you'll look out for us all."

Jean-Paul was chewing his beans impassively, his jaws giving them all their attention. Burke never really trusted the mother but she did his housekeeping at Saint Jacques and he used her sometimes as a means of receiving or conveying information. According to Jean-Paul, she went to the farm-house every day still, and it was she who spared the bread and cooked the eggs and meat that formed the rest of his diet. The food came wrapped in cloths that were cleaner than Jean-Paul would have thought necessary. Once she had even put in a little pat of butter, knowing how much he liked it.

He had indeed looked out for the peasants, his flock, his parishioners or whatever relationship they bore to him now. Some of them were even his tenants, since some of the land he had bought up had been the property of displaced aristocrats. He worked that land, and produced food and made his neighbours improve their marketing methods.

18

The wretched authorities in the city seemed to know little or nothing about farming. Burke became a hero to both sides.

He picked up the pen again to write:

"You can never make laws for farmers. You either pay them for their produce or you do without it. They will eat it themselves, or hide it, or sell it illegally to the highest bidder, or not grow it at all. Over thousands of years, governments have tried to force farmers to grow more food and hand it over to the cities but it has never worked. That was our position. To my neighbours I was a great man, a powerful man, who had travelled to Paris and had fine friends there, who spoke English and French equally well and was not afraid to talk to the gentry. Being a friend of Count Lally of Saint André de Cubzac was a mark against me in those early days but after he was dead that was brushed aside. Friendship with the great new aristocrats, especially Ysabeau and Tallien, more than outweighed my other alliances. Farmers have no real understanding of politics and never will have.

"An aristocrat is essentially someone who governs by virtue of an accident of birth. Both Claude Ysabeau and Tallien were low-born and they governed for that very reason. The world upside down. Tallien's father was maître d'hôtel to the Marquis de Bercy and Tallien therefore knew how to live like an aristocrat. He loved the opera, for instance, and fine suppers with candles on the table and good silver and glass. Our turn now, he said. He learned a great deal from Madame de Fontenay, his mistress. She is a beauty, jet-black hair like silk, bone-white skin, not the type that appeals to me. An aristocrat – I think Tallien liked her better for that. I was close to Claude, but he would never tell me where he came from. He reminded me very much of the young shop-boys I used to see in Ennis when I went to market with my mother. A small-town man, probably. They were the new aristocracy, in some ways as intransigent and grasping as the old one, though not idle. I thought that they would do well when things calmed down but I was wrong.

19

"My peasants could make neither head nor tail of their new masters but their chief interest was the land. They were interested in knowing, as Rousseau said, what master's saddle they would have the honour to carry next, but only insofar as it affected the land. I understand this feeling, though I never let them see how much. In Ireland the landlords would never go down to the fields and muck with the men. I did it here, and they respected me for it, as well as because I could handle city people. They felt in their bones that I would not cheat them of their profits as I was one of their own number."

Who was going to read all this? No one, probably. Writing it down had the odd effect of making him feel a little warmer, or perhaps it was his proximity to the candle. The moving flame was delightful to him. From time to time it seemed to yawn with pleasure in itself. The tallow was too soft. It might not last until Jean-Paul came. He never came before seven. That first day, when he entered the building with Burke, he stayed for a few hours helping to set up the barricades, and then left by the back way. He would climb over yard walls, he said, reaching the river by a series of back streets which he would note well for future use.

Burke said: "You'll come back, then?"

"Of course. You have nothing to eat. You'll need bread and eggs and wine, if you're going to do as you said."

"I'm going to do it."

"Well, then. Do you want to be starved out like a fox?"

"You might be followed. They might see how you get in over the back wall. I can't defend the back."

"I'll be careful."

Jean-Paul was young, in his early twenties, not yet married, though he had selected his future wife and was sleeping with her whenever he got a chance. Men are supremely confident at that age. Tallien and Ysabeau were the same at first. Their henchmen too. The energy, the determination of them! Burke scarcely remembered being like that, physically at least. He had a fellow-feeling for

20

them in the matter of their single-mindedness. They descended on Bordeaux with their little army two and a half years ago, September 1793, like a pack of wolves, as Jean-Paul had said. The people seemed to despair at once. They gave themselves up – the Mayor and the various notabilities of the city – Burke could never understand it. They had muddled along for years without thinking and now they muddled their way to the guillotine. They had an army of their own, composed of members of the leading families of Bordeaux, and a large battery at the gates, yet they opened up to seven hundred young men with only two guns. They allowed the guillotine to be set up permanently in the Place Dauphine, though a few cannon-shots fired into the closed ranks of the revolutionaries as they passed through the rue du Faubourg-Saint-Julien would have scattered them. Worse than that, when an order was published saying that all arms were to be handed up at the Château-Trompette before midday, they scurried to obey, though they could have made better use of the same guns by defending their city.

It was Lacombe who cowed them into helplessness, with his loud, domineering voice and his barked orders. He was the leading spirit from the Committee of Public Safety and General Security within the city, which actually sent for help to carry out the aims of the Revolution, and he was top dog until Tallien and Ysabeau arrived. Then he had to climb down a few steps but he was always able to make them believe in his importance as the link between the outsiders and the city. They needed him.

For all their appearance of efficiency, the People's Representatives made terrible mistakes from the beginning. The very day they arrived, they caused the famine. God knows why they did not see what they were doing. They posted notices – they were fond of that way of doing things since it spread the word of what they wanted very quickly. A tax on food, of all things, in a country which had started a bloody revolution because of the high price of food. Burke was in town that day, seeing what was to be seen, and he paused to read one of the notices. Prices fixed and the death penalty for infringement, and a small tax on every bite sold. The answer was simple: no more bites were sold. Then they began to guillotine the bakers who refused to bake bread at those ridiculous prices, and with such wretched materials. The merchants with the big granaries hid their wheat and oats, hoping the prices would return to normal. Grocers who closed their shops when they ran out of food were guillotined. The peasants were afraid to bring in their produce to sell at the market.

Burke could not keep away from the city. Every day he rode in and stabled his horse at the far side of the river, then walked across the bridge to see what was happening. There was always plenty to see, and everywhere one went the roll of the drums from the Place Dauphine battered the ears. Disgust gradually replaced the original exaltation.

Yet Burke's head still tingled with the memory of the first days of the Revolution, when a clean, fresh wind seemed to blow from Paris across the whole world. Everything would change. There would be no more oppression, no more masters, even the ridiculous pomposity of the Church would be swept away and honesty and reason would reign. Reason took a peculiar form, however. One day soon after the People's Representatives arrived, he saw the Goddess of Reason parading through the streets, some poor prostitute dressed in a cope and wearing a bishop's mitre, surrounded by a howling mob of the citizens of Bordeaux also wearing vestments stolen from the cathedral and from the city churches, accompanied by carts carrying reliquaries and church plate and carved wooden statues. Following them, fascinated, he saw them pile all these treasures in the Place de la Comédie and burn them to ashes. That day a worm began to gnaw at him, his new faith was destroyed as if it had never existed and some fighting spirit that had lain dormant began to revive.

A day or two later he came into the city again and went straight to the College. As soon as he stepped into the hall he knew he was too late. It was full of strangers, young men in red revolutionary bonnets moving furniture, running up and down the stairs as if they owned the place. Wondering whether he should make a run for it, he saw Lacombe come out of the students' refectory and knew he was trapped. Lacombe looked him up and down, then said: "Who are you? Another priest?"

"Citizen Burke, a farmer, from Saint Jacques d'Ambes."

"I know you," Lacombe said. "You were the curé there. I remember you when you taught in this very College."

Burke remembered too. Lacombe used to bring mended shoes from his father's cobbler's shop in the old days. He had had a diffident look then but he had put all that behind him. His voice was loud and strong, and he seemed to have learned a new language composed largely of clichés.

"Come to see your friends, have you? They're all down in the Carmelite convent, prisoners of the people."

"All?"

"All who were here when we came, forty students, five priests, all enemies of France, spies for the English – "

Though his hands had begun to sweat with fear Burke said contemptuously.

"The Irish? Nonsense, citizen. The Irish are all on the French side."

"Foreigners, British subjects, all spies."

Trying to sound casual Burke asked: "What will become of them?"

Lacombe made an unpleasant chopping gesture with his right hand, watching Burke closely at the same time.

"Enemies of the people, citizen. I know you've taken the oath." Burke's relief must have shown on his face because Lacombe laughed. "An honest farmer, that's what you are now."

Burke said: "Yes. That's what I am now, and as I'm here I want to ask you what you're doing about feeding the people. I never saw such a sorry look on a city as this one has at the moment. Those bread queues, and the digusting stuff they get for their money, sticky, black – you wouldn't give it to a dog. You'll have the whole place rotting with disease if you don't do something soon. Winter is coming on."

"What can we do? Those thieves won't give up the stuff. Anyway, it's not my business. I'm only concerned with purging France of traitors. Go to Ysabeau and Tallien. They're the administrators."

"I don't know them."

"I'll give you a note. Come this way."

Feeling like a mouse following the cat Burke walked slowly into the room from which Lacombe had come. It was set up as a court. The long refectory tables were placed in a semi-circle and behind them there were seven chairs for the judges. Burke recognised the improvised dock as the pulpit from the chapel. Lacombe went to one of the judges' tables and spoke to a young man who was writing there, and who looked up inimically at Burke as if he thought he was already condemned. A minute later Lacombe brought him a document on which had been written a few words of introduction, and Burke was free to leave, sweating, clutching this talisman in his hand.

Tallien and Ysabeau were living in the Hôtel d'Angleterre. Burke walked through the silent streets, not a carriage to be seen, only the shuffling queues at the shops and an occasional pedestrian hurrying along on some essential business. These seemed to keep close to the walls as if they feared to show themselves. Burning with his mission, Burke demanded to be shown into the room where the two young men were in anxious conference.

It was after midnight when he got back to Saint Jacques d'Ambes. They received him brusquely, but Ysabeau quickly changed his manner when he heard that Burke had come from Lacombe and that he was able to help them. They drew up a plan on Burke's advice, calling on all the farmers to support the Revolution by bringing their produce into the towns twice a week, a safe conduct guaranteed and proper prices paid for everything. No threats, Burke insisted.

"You want those farmers alive, not dead. Crops have to be planted and husbanded or you'll have nothing next year either. These are skilled people, like the bakers and millers.

You can't send a bunch of soldiers into the farms to do the work."

"It was stupid to execute the bakers," Tallien said. "They were more useful alive."

Ysabeau said venomously: "The Republic can't tolerate any disobedience. A patriotic tour might bring the farmers to their senses."

Burke said: "If you go on a patriotic tour, as you call it, and set up the guillotine in my villages, you won't see a cabbage or a carrot from that area for the rest of the winter. I'll go on a different kind of tour and get better results."

Ysabeau glared at Tallien, but not at Burke. Then both turned to listen to him. Them and their 'patriotic tour'! That might do for the towns. Tallien was the milder of the two, at that strange meeting, but Burke knew that he was one of those limbs of Satan who had gone into the prisons in Paris and butchered fifteen hundred men, women and children in September of last year. How had he looked then? Now he kept trying to make his rather pretty face look strong and far-sighted. Ridiculous fair curls surrounded the edges of his military hat, which was covered in shiny cloth and had a tricolour plume. He wore a cross-belt with a sabre on one shoulder and a long silk tricolour scarf on the other. Everyone in France had learned to fear these symbols. When he was allowed to leave them at last, Burke felt as if he had spent the day with two tigers in a cage.

The candle sent up a tall flame that smoked vigorously at the point, then it died down suddenly and went out in a puddle of stinking tallow. Within a minute the pitch darkness turned to grey. He stood up and felt his way to the door. He could not stay in the study a moment longer. It was a mistake in his present predicament to recall those days so clearly. Tallien – he almost seemed to be there, in the room, with his boy's face and his silly hat. They took all those clothes away from him when he went to the guillotine with Robespierre. No pity to be wasted on them: they themselves had had the Queen led out with a rope around her neck, like an animal. Ghosts, demons, darkness. On the threshold,

Burke turned back and made the sign of the Cross towards the empty room, a sign of exorcism, a sign of pain.

Ysabeau complained to Paris that Tallien was weak and had him recalled to his death but Burke remembered that Tallien's compassion for the people was the thing that had averted the famine. Ysabeau saw dimly that his own policies were disastrous but he had become like a killer sheepdog. Day after day he fought against Burke's plans, day after day he had to be convinced again that it was necessary to be lenient, even conciliatory, to those who had food supplies if he wanted to save the people of Bordeaux. In the end he admitted that he would never have adopted Burke's policy unless he had been forced into it. For four weeks Burke never slept in his own bed. He rode all over the district, showing written promises, making firm commitments with farmers, guaranteeing prices, sleeping in filthy inns or in farmers' kitchens, sometimes in Bordeaux when he came back to report progress. It was on one of these visits that Dr. Everard came out of hiding to ask him to save the students and priests who were still locked up in the Carmelite convent. Every day a dozen people were summoned to the People's Tribunal and never came back. Soon it might be their turn.

In a blazing fury Burke went to Ysabeau, banging his great fist on the desk and shouting: "Here am I parading the country, doing all your work for you. Get those boys out of that damned prison at once or I won't move another step for you."

Ysabeau said: "That's Lacombe's business. Why don't you go to him?"

"Lacombe's business is butchery. A fat lot of good it would do me to go to him. It would only draw his attention to them and they'd be nearer than ever to their end. You must go after this yourself. You're his superior, aren't you? Don't tell me you're all equal. By the holy God above us, I'll draw down curses from heaven on you if you don't get them out of there."

"Still a priest, citizen?"

"Still an Irishman. I've worked for you as if this were my own country – "

"All right, all right. I'll do it. Give me time."

"Do it now. There's no time to waste. Do it now."

Ysabeau was lucky to be still alive. One of Tallien's crimes against the people was his part in the September massacre, which discredited the Revolution. Something of this idea may have occurred to Ysabeau. He did go at once and get the Irish boys out, and the priests too, and chartered an American ship to send them safely back to Ireland. Burke saw them before they left, starved and unkempt and covered with some skin disease that they had picked up in the prison. They were herded into a warehouse on the Quai des Chartrons waiting for the boats to take them to the ship. Dr. Everard, always a gentleman, introduced Burke as their saviour and those brats actually turned their backs on him. All ready for martyrdom, were they? But they were only boys, after all, and they saw only black and white. He had gone over to the enemy. That was enough for them.

## 2

SHUFFLING CAREFULLY DOWNSTAIRS, WITH A HAND ON THE thin iron banister, Burke heard the mice scuttling in the hall below. He stamped with his feet to frighten them and worked his way along the passage towards the kitchen. A smell of stale food still hung around, though no one had cooked there since Lacombe and his family had left. This did not smell like College food – too much onion. The College food was excellent, for students and priests alike. That was one of the reasons why Burke continued to teach there twice a week after he went to the parish of Saint Jacques d'Ambes. Latin was his subject, one which almost anyone could have undertaken, but he loved his connection with the College, and it gave him rights at special banquets and feast days when all the plate was brought out and dinner was even better than usual. Lacombe had gone off with the plate – perhaps he had it still, or had sold it on behalf of the nation. He was no thief, whatever else he was. It might still be possible to get it back.

The kitchen used to be the warmest, most cheerful room in the house. Now it was the coldest. The sun never reached in here and since the great fires no longer blazed on the double hearth a skin of damp always lay on the flagged floor. The last chef was a Basque from the mountains near Saint Jean Pied de Port, and he was always bringing in cousins of all ages as helpers. There was a boy named Michel, whose job it was to mind the new roasting jack that Count Lynch's father had presented, and to clean the copper pots. He used to play football with the students whenever he got a chance. They 'had all disappeared back to the mountains at the first sign of the Terror.

Burke found the back door and ran his hands over the three heavy bolts that held it shut. They slid back with a grinding squeal. He never kept Jean-Paul waiting to be let in, in case he had attracted notice and been followed. Besides, there was an intense pleasure in leaving the defences unbarred for a short while, as if he could walk out quite safely at any time he liked. He took his only outdoor exercise now, pacing up and down the flagged path from the back wall to the door, then from the vegetable shed to the woodshed, placing his feet cautiously so as not to be heard. The nearest neighbours were across the lane and at this time of the evening it would be sheer bad luck if someone happened to notice him. Besides the citizens of Bordeaux seemed to have learned some lessons in the last five or six years, and one of them was to mind their own business a bit better than they used to do.

This was a poor occupation for a farmer, pacing a prison yard. He felt the muscles of his knees come to life and stretch as they did when he set out to walk his land. That had always been his father's Sunday entertainment, as if he had to make sure the fields were still there. Every blade of grass was known and recognised for its importance in the battle against the landlord. All conversations seemed to concern whether or not the rent could be paid, whether or not the lease would be renewed, whether or not the landlord's son would be better or worse than his father when it came to settling questions of rent and leases. The tenants watched the growth of that youth with trepidation, from a friendly child taking walks with his English nurse to a surly schoolboy with a foreign accent and finally to a full-grown man who brought over English friends for the hunting and rode arrogantly over the land that was in theory his but in fact contained the precious crops on which the lives of the tenants depended. Burke's brother, who rented the farm now, wrote lately to say that no one had been to the big house for several years, and that there was a rumour it was to be sold.

A sound beyond the wall sent Burke padding lightly to

the yard door, his skin crawling with terror. He stood there, ready to flee back into the house. The cathedral clock began to strike seven. He had to wait until it finished to hear Jean-Paul's signal, two short knocks, then three and two again. Half way through the strokes of the clock he almost pulled back the bolt in his anxiety, but better sense prevailed and he waited, almost afraid to breathe, until the prearranged knocks came. Then it seemed that the bolt made a sound like thunder as he worked its heavy handle up and down. Tallow – a candle rubbed on all of the bolts, if Jean-Paul had brought enough candles. It was the first question he asked him.

Jean-Paul said: "Yes, yes, I brought three. My mother is making some more."

He was a skinny, wiry man with a long head and protruding teeth, a shock of black hair and skin like a Spaniard's. Even when Burke was the curé, Jean-Paul had never treated him with much respect, yet he seemed to have formed an attachment to him which gave him a sense of responsibility for Burke's safety. He accepted Burke's present mad behaviour as easily as a sheepdog would do. He walked ahead now, opening the back door familiarly, as if he had been doing it all his life, felt his way into the dark passageway and made for the stairs. Burke found the bolts and pushed them across, then followed Jean-Paul upstairs.

He had lit one of the candles and stood it on the desk by the time Burke arrived, and had opened one of the cloth bags that he carried.

"The cold in here! I've brought you some wood, not much but it will take the chill off for a while at least. This place is like a tomb."

While he lit the fire with dry chips which he had not forgotten to include, he chattered.

"I have bread and a bottle of wine and some hard-boiled eggs and a piece of chicken, and a drop of plum liqueur, and there is a letter from Ireland and one from Paris as well."

"Where? Where?"

"Quite safe, in with the bread. You're always wanting

letters. No one has ever written me a letter and if they did I'd burn it without finding out what was in it. Letters bring nothing but trouble."

"How do you know, if you've never had one?"

Burke enjoyed using his voice, noticing that it had gone hoarse like the unused bolts. Jean-Paul turned from the hearth to look at him as he answered with contempt.

"I know a few people who have had them and they always brought trouble."

The letters would have to wait. Burke knew from experience that Jean-Paul would never allow him to concentrate on them. Better to enjoy them later, now that he had the certainty of some light. He asked: "How are things at the Château? Has anyone come out from Bordeaux?"

"Not a soul. My mother thought someone might come to put locks on the doors as they used to do a few years ago but no one at all has come."

"Anything been stolen from the house in Saint Jacques?"

"No. They know we're watching. No one will touch your property until you get home. When are you coming home?"

"I don't know."

"It's a mighty strange thing. If I were arrested and put in gaol, like you, and then let out, the first place I'd make for would be home."

"This used to be my home."

"That's true. But it's a cold home. Why do you care about it?"

"It belongs to my country."

"France is your country now."

Dangerous ground. Burke said: "Yes, France is my country. But I have a duty to Ireland too."

Jean-Paul had lost interest. He scarcely believed in that other country of Burke's though his manner suggested that he knew it bred peculiar people. He was taking the food, wrapped in a clean napkin, out of the second bag and laying it reverently on the table. Food was sacred to these people, each pinch of herb carefully considered before it fell into the

31

family soup-pot, days and days spent in preparing a stew of pork and beans that would be eaten slowly, every bite savoured as if it were the last in this life. Burke enjoyed his food but he knew he would never be able to take it so seriously. Still he exclaimed with delight at the things that Jean-Paul had brought and sat down to eat them with proper signs of appreciation. He offered Jean-Paul an egg, but he refused.

"I promised my mother that you would eat it all. Well, I'll take a piece of bread and some wine. Bernadette got the bread. She would find bread where there never was any."

He had brought a bottle of the best red wine, heavy and with a tang that remained as an aftertaste. There was only one glass, and now and then Jean-Paul took a sip from it, each time picking off small pieces of bread to accompany it. Burke sat in the desk chair and Jean-Paul knelt close by. He squatted back presently and rummaged in the food-bag, taking out two crumpled letters. In the yellow light of the candle Burke saw that neither was from his brother. Peering closer, he recognised old Lady Sophie Brien's angular hand-writing on one. He picked it up, and Jean-Paul said: "That came from Bordeaux. The other was on the Paris coach this morning."

Perhaps he should adopt Jean-Paul's philosophy and burn the Irish one. There could be no good news from Mount Brien. The very sight of the folded paper, with its lump of sealing-wax on the back, was enough to send a jet of acid memory tingling through him. Sophie's last letter was several years ago, reprimanding him sharply for his crime first in taking the oath as a constitutional curé and then in abandoning the Church for farming. She was illogical in that. If the oath was a crime, then the abandonment of it was not. She had received accurate information, probably from André de Lacy on his trip to Ireland with Rabaut de St. Etienne four years ago. She even knew that he was the first priest in Bordeaux to take the oath. A long time before that, fifteen years, there was the letter about Louise. He picked up the other letter, then laid it down again. They would have to wait.

The fire had begun to warm the room and a sense of well-being made Burke push his huge body back in the chair and say, as he lifted his glass: "To your health! No wine on earth like Médoc. Your mother is a good provider."

"She wants to know when you will come home."

"When I win this battle."

"That might take a year."

"When I win or lose it, then."

"You're needed at home."

"Nothing to be done about that. I was lucky to get out of prison so quickly. Have you heard any news of the others?"

"Oh, yes, I heard that they let most of the Irish-born out but not the priests or the English. I have your books."

He was rummaging again, this time in the sack in which he had brought the wood. In dismay, Burke saw him take out two books, a small, thin one and a larger one, and lay them on the table. What devil, or instinct had led him to pick out the sonnets of Ronsard, of all volumes?

Burke said sharply: "Those are not the books I asked for. The black prayer book, and a thick leather-bound book by Descartes – "

Jean-Paul fixed his big brown doggy eyes on him reproachfully and said: "You know I can't read."

"Well, that's why I described the books. Or you could have asked Mademoiselle de Rochechouart. These are good anyway. I'll read them. The days are long."

"Of course."

But he was offended. At Saint Jacques d'Ambes Burke had offered to teach him to read but the offer was refused. Too late, Jean-Paul said, and besides he did not have the mental capacity. He would never need to read, and French was a difficult language, one he rarely used. That was true enough, since the language of the Gironde was certainly not Burke's kind of French but a mixture of Basque and Spanish and French that only the people of the area completely understood. Burke had picked up some of it, but he used

33

French in all his dealings with his workmen and tenants. They would have considered it a kind of insult for him to have used their language, even if he could have done it with confidence.

He asked conciliatingly: "Is the tobacco showing yet?"

"Very nicely. The rain was just right. We'll be transplanting in a day or two. They're a hand high already, some of them more. I wish you could be there to see them. Jacques and Martin did the harrowing."

"And the lambs?"

"Only one gone, and I don't think it was a wolf. I'd have found the carcase by now – I've walked every inch of the district and I found one, but it was too long dead to be ours. I think it was a human wolf. That's the only thing that has been stolen and it would have happened even if you were at home."

"Of course. I know it's not your fault. Everything is as well looked after as if I were there."

Suddenly Burke shivered, his shoulders shaking. Jean-Paul said anxiously: "Why did you do that? Are you getting sick?"

"No. Not at all. In Ireland we say that someone must have walked on my grave."

"We say that too. Or that a ghost passed, the ghost of a priest."

The casual, joking remark was unfortunate. Soon afterwards he made ready to go and Burke almost got to the point of appealing to him to spend the night. But it would have had only bad consequences. Jean-Paul knew it was his business to get home, to take care of the farms and to bring back some food the next evening. If any such request had been made he would have suspected that Burke was weakening.

But he had the candles, and the letters. They would provide diversion, until it was time to sleep. Tonight at least he would be warm. Jean-Paul laid the last of the wood on the fire and said: "I think you need a fire as much as you need food. I'll bring some more wood tomorrow."

"In Ireland we say that a fire is one-half of life."

"Ireland, Ireland – thinking of Ireland is what has got you into all this trouble."

He folded his two cloth bags neatly and led the way downstairs. In the yard the wind was biting cold, trapped in a downward draught with a few heavy drops of rain. Burke said:

"I'm afraid it's going to rain."

"Not until I get to the stable," Jean-Paul said, after an expert's glance at the sky. "Too much wind up there. I may even get home before it. Pangloss always makes good time on the way home."

"You always ride Pangloss or Abelard."

"I've kept Abelard at the stables these last few nights, in case you decide some night to forget all this and come home."

"Have they asked at the stable why you come so often?"

"Not a word, but they could get curious after a while. I'll think of a good story."

The noise of the wind hurling itself against the stone walls of the College covered the screech of the bolts. Back in the study, Burke collected the droppings of the candle to grease them. It would occupy some time in the morning. Tomorrow too he would ask Jean-Paul to bring a hammer and saw and some nails, so that he could begin to repair the worst of the mouse-holes. A cat would be a good idea too – why had he not thought of that before? A cat would sit by the fire with him, lie on his bed of sacks, keep the mice down. A cat must come. There were always plenty of them around the farms. He had never had a house-cat in France, though there was at least one in every Irish family. Little predators. Making off with the chickens and ducklings. Tormenting the women with their thieving. Providing proverbs and stories for the children – the King of the Cats, the Cat that turned into a Witch, the Black Cat that was really the ghost of the orphan girl's dead mother. Ghost cats. Ghosts.

He sat down quickly and picked up the Paris letter. Claude, still alive and well in Paris, still grateful for the commonsense advice that had saved his bacon. It should hardly be necessary to tell anyone that when a peasant brings in two sacks of flour to sell in a starving city, it is a mistake to guillotine him for hoarding flour. Word gets around – so simple, they were. Burke had liked Claude Ysabeau the better of the two, from the first moment they met, though his reputation was more unsavoury. He was lucky to have got away when he did. Tallien's power in Bordeaux was one of the things that ruined him, in the end. A pair of murdering fools. Yet Burke was pleased at the beginning of Claude's letter:

"Of course I have not forgotten you. That would be impossible, you did so much for the Revolution during my time in Bordeaux. I am glad to be able to give you any help that I can but with the army setting out for Italy soon, it is difficult to get the powerful people to listen."

They were going to fight Austria and Italy now. Nothing was too hot or too heavy for them. Austria wanted revenge for the death of the poor Queen, their princess. The old Empress, lamenting her daughter, but partly blaming her for what had happened, might have settled for some kind of apology, but there was none forthcoming from the revolutionaries. The courage of the young was terrifying, almost admirable in its way. The soldiers were half-starved and half-naked but they would fight like devils in Italy, for the lovely loot that they would get as a reward.

There was so little respect for law and order that Burke had scarcely believed the document he and the others drew up in prison would get any attention at all. Nearly three weeks ago, February 23 it was, one of the soldiers guarding the prisoners remarked that the Irish College had been sold. He even knew the price, thirty-six thousand livres. It was going to be a tobacco factory, he said. Everything was over and the contract signed. Peter Lynch, with lawyer's caution, asked if the contract had yet been delivered. Not yet, the soldier said. He knew about it because his brother worked in the Directory. Because of the war, the property of British subjects was nationalised, so it was all perfectly legal. Burke felt the blood rush to his head but he had the sense to say nothing until the soldier was gone. Then he and Lynch and two other Irish prisoners who were lawyers got together and prepared a petition to have the delivery of the contract postponed until the question of the legality of the sale could be investigated. Between them they wrote out an impressive document.

They sent it out by the very next visitor with instructions to take it straight to the Directory. The following morning a note came from the President of the Directory ordering the release of Burke and Lynch and the two others, but Eric Palmer, the Englishman who had also signed the document, was left behind. His house, his vineyard, his horses, everything was gone, but as he said philosophically, at least he was still alive and his wife and children had been allowed to leave the country.

On the same day, Burke wrote a long angry letter to Claude, telling him about his arrest and his fears for his own property, as well as for the College:

"If France does not behave intelligently about Irish property, she will make an enemy of the one country in Europe from which she could expect help, and which has always been friendly to her. This would be a disaster."

He was putting words into Claude's mouth, arguments to be used with the Minister in Paris, but after the letter had gone off he feared that Claude's pride would prevent him from using those arguments. It seemed not to be so. Claude wrote:

"I have put your point to the Minister, that since the proceeds of the sale of Church property are designated for aid to the Revolution in Ireland, it is not logical to sequester or sell Irish property in France on behalf of the nation. I have also said that it would be a poor return for all the help you gave us in our difficulties if your personal property were touched. I told him that it was disgraceful you have been imprisoned and that he should give orders forthwith to have you released."

They had not had to wait for the Minister's instructions

there. It was funny to think of Ysabeau chiding the Minister for ingratitude towards those who had helped on the Revolution, when one thought of the end of Tallien and Robespierre and Arthur Dillon and thousands of others whose main mistake was in getting too close to the fire. Ysabeau gave no information about himself but it was clear that he was still surviving well and moving in high company.

The day of his release, as he was leaving the prison, Burke was accosted on the steps by a stranger who had been waiting for him. He was a heavy-set, middle-aged man, shorter than Burke but still a good height. He moved lightly and quickly in spite of his girth, and Burke after his weeks of privation envied him his air of well-fed vigour and certainty.

He called out loudly: "Citizen Burke!"

"Yes?"

Burke's clothes were creased and dusty, the other's neat and smooth, with a clean white collar and stock. His voice was a squeak of fury.

"You won't get away with this. If you think it's a question of who gets in first, I have friends in high places too. I bought that property with good money and I'm going to keep it."

The tobacco manufacturer, of course. Burke said:

"The sale was illegal."

"Legal, illegal – who is talking about law? We have new laws now. New laws, and a war with England."

In his fury he could no longer speak clearly and he turned away spluttering, striking at the air with his silver-headed cane as if he would have liked to use it on Burke. He had the wrong accent for a cane like that. Loot, probably. Who gets in first – in that moment Burke changed his plans. When Jean-Paul came for him to Mr. Lynch's house, instead of going home he went to the College, opening the heavy door with his own key. That proved he had rights. Then he told Jean-Paul that he would never leave it until its return to the Irish was guaranteed. He wrote a letter for Jean-Paul to deliver to the Directory, and since then he had heard nothing

38

from that quarter. Ysabeau's letter was the first sign of progress.

The wine was making him drowsy. That first evening, when Jean-Paul had left him alone with the ghosts, there was no wine to give him courage or make him sleep. He had sat up on guard most of the night, hearing feet and whispering voices all around him once darkness had fallen. Tonight the sounds were recognisable, so familiar that they were almost comforting, the whistle of the wind as it passed the corner of the house, the scratch of a weed that had managed to get a hold in a gutter and had fallen partly down, so that its dried stalk sometimes touched the glass of an attic window.

He saw that the candle was burning low and he lit a second one in its flame, then placed both candles side by side on the desk. For a few minutes he would have a double light, until the first one went out. This cheered him out of all proportion to its importance and he sat for a moment of pure delight, watching the two brilliant little flames bowing to each other in the draught. This was the moment to open Sophie's letter. He slit the seal carefully, knowing how she would cross and recross the writing so as to get as much as possible on to the single sheet. He read the first words almost in fear, as if she were present, berating him for his failures. It was a pleasant surprise to find that the tone was polite:

"Dear Mr. Burke."

That was an improvement on the last time, when she had begun:

"Sir, you have disgraced your country."

She wanted a favour. It was not immediately clear what that favour was, and she said that she was also sending someone from Ireland to perform it, or to help it on. Then he realised that she wanted her grandson, Robert, to go home. She had no idea of how much injury she had done to that whole family. The very suggestion of it would astonish her. Glancing quickly through the letter he saw that she still thought of herself as their saviour, the only person who had a proper sense of how the family should survive, the only one who knew who was to blame for all its misfortunes. Never herself, of course. His eye fell on the words '*Nostalgie de la boue*'. That was how she described her son Maurice's marriage to Fanny, a woman of the people to be sure but more than good enough for that sot, who in any case had taken his son's girl for his mistress and ruined her, given her a baby that died. Then Lady Sophie had tried to prevent Robert from finding the girl and marrying her. And Robert's young sister, Louise – to this day old Sophie never blamed herself for the fate of Louise, whose tragedy was even worse than Robert's, since she had deserted a living child when she ran away from the old roué that the family found for her as a husband. Burke was supposed to have prevented that marriage. It was one of Lady Sophie's grievances against him.

In a sudden fit of fury, Burke beat on the desk-top with both fists, so that the candle sputtered and rocked. He hated that woman, hated her. He said it aloud, then stopped, frightened at himself. Yet there was satisfaction in expressing in words something that he had kept out of sight for years. As with everyone else, she thought that she had done him immense favours. In fact she had ruined him just as surely as she had ruined her own family. Here in the semi-darkness, free from all interruption, there was plenty of time to analyse her methods. He remembered La Rochefoucauld: "Humility is the true test of Christian virtue; without it we retain all our faults, though they are cloaked by pride, which conceals them from others and often from ourselves as well." Pride, like all the French aristocracy. Pride so deeply ingrained that it was never questioned, not even by those who suffered most from it. Though many in her household resented Sophie's certainty of superiority, the fact that she herself believed in it so utterly kept them from questioning her right to it. Fanny, the unsuitable wife, was terrified of her.

Still, Burke could not help remembering that Sophie had not wanted Louise to be sent to France with her brother. In fact she had put up quite a fight – her only granddaughter, the only member of the household with whom she felt at ease – but her son Maurice insisted on it, and Sophie knew that Fanny was really behind the plan. Sophie had asked Burke to intervene – Burke of all people! For all her sophistication, she seemed to have no idea of his feelings towards Louise.

Now for the first time it struck him suddenly that she might have known, and have chosen to ignore it. To her Burke was another servant, though he was the chaplain to Mount Brien Court and the tutor of Louise and Robert. Even at this distance, anger mounted in him again as he recalled the position into which she had forced him.

Sophie sent to Ennis for him when he was on a visit home to see his father for the last time. He rode all the way up to Mount Brien in answer to her summons, fifty miles, because it seemed the polite thing to do and he supposed that she had some messages for her cousins in Paris. She received him in her own sitting-room upstairs, looking him over as if he had applied to her for the position that she had already arranged for him. She ordered up cake and wine for him, then broke the news. The Archbishop of Narbonne had settled with Burke's bishop in Bordeaux that he was to stay in Ireland, live at Mount Brien and teach the two older children.

Burke gazed at the old lady sitting upright in her chair by the window, her face well out of the glare of the late autumn sun. She had placed him so that the light fell on him. He stood up and moved into the shade, noticing that she was displeased at this.

He said: "I must get back to my parish, my teaching in Bordeaux. I can't stay any longer. I came only because my father is dying."

"I know. I've explained all that to the Archbishop. He thought it would be a good thing for you to minister to the people here for a few years. We need you badly."

A few years – she said it quite calmly. He was needed here, it was true, since the laws against priests were fierce. He would be protected at Mount Brien. He was trapped, and he knew it. Archbishop Dillon of Narbonne was a cousin of Sophie's. There was no escape.

At first he had not tried to escape. He had all the instincts of a good priest in those days, before he lost his innocence and became the scoundrel that he was now. He beat on the desk-top again, then laid down his fists and looked at them in alarm, as if they had done this without his leave. It was a dismal story, the thirty-eight-year-old priest falling in love with his fourteen-year-old pupil. It had come on him gradually, like a sickness. The boy, Robert, was no intellectual, and Burke despaired of his task at first. Then he discovered that Louise had a first-class brain, instantly comprehending everything he put before her, making her older brother look foolish over and over again.

Still there was no ill-feeling between them. They were like two exotic birds, slender, blonde, rather small, utterly different from their three little half-brothers who took after the Brien side of the family. Sophie was very proud of the older two, treating them like heirs to a throne, an attitude which drove their step-mother, Fanny, to fury.

Burke had not taken all of this in for a while. All he knew was that the clever little girl more than made up for the slower-witted boy, who was nevertheless by no means dull. He was not interested in geometry and Latin and Greek but Sophie said he was to be filled with knowledge so that he would not cut too poor a figure when he went to the Sorbonne. That had been decided a long time ago. Sending Louise to Paris with him was a later idea.

Gradually Burke found that Louise was never out of his mind, waking or sleeping. He dreamed of her, he thought of her incessantly, at first deliberately, for the sheer pleasure of it, then obsessively in a kind of nightmare in which he was barely aware of what was happening to him. Her lips were pale, barely pink, broad in the centre, then curving suddenly down to the merest line where they joined her delicate cheeks. When she bent over the table in the school-room, sometimes she pressed her lips together, creating a new line that was narrower in the middle and that sent the sides running upward. Her hands were long and fine, like Sophie's. She had a habit of touching her lips with the left one when she was thinking out a problem, then laying it down, palm upward, as she reached the solution.

When he realised what was happening to him, Burke was scandalised. He thought he was past the age for this. After thirty, they said, you were safe. The fire died down. Priests began to make jokes about carnal love, or to speak seriously about methods of dealing with it in their besotted parishioners. Separation was the first recommended remedy.

Burke went to Sophie and said: "I had better get back to my real work. Anyone could do what I'm doing here. I should be teaching in the College in Bordeaux."

She had her answer.

"The priest who has taken over your work temporarily is better qualified than you are, Mr. Burke. I'm sure you won't mind my pointing that out. Your parish work in France is being well done by a Frenchman, also probably better than you would do it, since after all you're a foreigner."

"These children don't need a Doctor of Divinity to teach them Latin and mathematics."

"Indeed they do. The teacher should always be as highly educated as possible. If they lived in France they would be taught by the most eminent philosophers. That's how we do things there, as you well know."

"It's not proper work for a priest, teaching."

"You speak as if it's your only work. Until you came, the people hadn't heard Mass for several years. They're delighted to have you here. It means the whole world to them. Don't tell me you're afraid, Mr. Burke."

"Of course not."

"I'm glad to hear it. This household has never been molested. If someone informs on you, we'll hear about it in time and get you out of the country safely."

Burke thought: "Or else you'll go to my hanging in Galway and sit in your carriage praying for me until I'm dead."

43

Gloomily he went on with his work, his mind and body absorbed in the dreadful fascination that Louise exercised over him. At eighteen, when he renounced the world and went to Bordeaux to start his studies for the priesthood, he had privately renounced his addiction to poetry also. Now he began again, composing verses in Greek and Latin and Irish and French, experimenting with new verse forms and using old ones in the wrong languages – sonnets in Irish and Latin, quantitative verse in French, Greek laments and ballads in the Irish style, forcing the words to fit the oddest rhythms. Their subject was always Louise. Her name sang in his ears all day long but he never once wrote it down. He knew that to do this would be the final lunacy.

# _3_

BURKE SAW THAT THE MOMENT HAD COME AT LAST WHEN HE could write her name. With a sense of delectable evil he opened the desk drawer slowly and took out his little hoard of paper. He had put it away carefully, before going down to let in Jean-Paul. Drawing it towards him, picking up the pen, dipping it in the ink, writing the name, was a complicated act of love. It was there, for the first time. He looked at it. She existed, a light, a sun, a blazing fire. He had created her. It was good not to have done it until now, so many things had happened to both of them in between. Carefully moving the candle aside, he leaned forward and kissed her, the writing on the page, the golden girl, for the first time.

At that moment it seemed to him that she was in the shadowy corner of the room, barely visible, as she had been once after dark, only a single candle lighting. It was in the big schoolroom at Mount Brien Court, with its wide table and benches, prepared for some long-ago family with far more children than this one. He had gone there to fetch a book and had found her, studying. She had not expected anyone to come and she leaped up from the table in fright when he marched into the room. It was the moment when he could have taken her in his arms and kissed her, and babbled out all his lust for her, and been thrown out of the house in disgrace. Instead he said: "What are you doing?"

"Learning the Ronsard sonnet."

"Say it for me."

"I don't know it yet. I will by tomorrow."

He saw that she was afraid of him, and no wonder. When

45

Robert was stupid or idle, Burke would shut him up to study, saying that he would not release him until the task, whatever it was, was finished. This meant that he had to shut in Louise for her failures, too, very rarely indeed. Otherwise some hint of his madness might appear.

He said: "No hurry. I think you know most of it already."

Tentatively she began:

*"Comme on voit sur la branche au mois de mai la rose,*
*En sa belle jeunesse, en sa première fleur,*
*Rendre le ciel jaloux de sa vive couleur,*
*Quand l'aube de ses pleurs au point du jour l'arrose."*

Reciting it with her, he brought her to the end of it, her soft voice forming the words with precision while his eyes were fixed on her pale, angelic lips as they moved, graciously, slowly, penetratingly. After he left her he tried to draw the vision back to him, seeing again how the curve came and went. Madness or sin, depending on how you looked at it. Appealing to Lady Sophie to rescue him was useless after that, since wherever he went Louise would be present, as she was with him now.

He lifted aside the sheet of paper on which he had written her name, placing it at the exact edge of the pool of candle-light. Then he looked at the last words he had written earlier. His relationship with the peasants – "I was one of their own number." He began a new paragraph:

"Jean-Paul has just been here, with wood for the fire and two letters. He is still sympathetic though he obviously thinks I'm mad. He says that all is well at Saint Jacques and that his mother goes to the house every day. He mentioned Bernadette but I did not answer him or scold him. How could I, since I live in sin myself? He might have asked whether I am going to marry Jeanne soon. I find his company refreshing, he is so simple about things like this. I wonder how long it would take to make him devious and sophisticated, if his family benefited from the revolution and became rich, owned houses and castles and could afford to marry aristocratic heiresses. Four generations might do it.

"The letters were from Claude Ysabeau and from Lady

Sophie Brien. Claude is trying to help me in my present impasse, Lady Sophie is making trouble, as usual. She still believes that I have influence over my pupils, as she calls them. She wants me to go to Saintes and persuade Robert to go home to Ireland. Otherwise, she says, the house will be brought down forever. She writes of her three grandsons, Fanny's children, as if they were interlopers. They have no French blood in them, she says, though of course they have hers. Hubert, the eldest, is twenty-six, and she describes him as a great hulking lout who walks with his head down like a bull and makes advances to the governess, Rose French, who succeeded me as the boys' teacher. Why is she still there? The youngest boy must be in his twenties. Ireland is always like that, hordes of servants who do no work and eat up the family's substance.

"What would Lady Sophie think of me now, if she could see me, sleeping on a pile of sacks in a corner, with a three-weeks' beard, fighting a private war against the city of Bordeaux? She would probably approve. If I am dragged out and guillotined, she would approve even more. Even for a woman who saw public executions as a girl in Paris, she seems insensitive to what is happening here. I think she is not able to envisage it as it is. How could she? We lived through it and could scarcely comprehend such casual slaughter. Lady Sophie even allowed herself some gratification when her old enemy, cousin Charlotte in Paris who was the cause of Louise's misfortunes, was guillotined with a crowd of other useless aristocrats.

"And still I can hardly blame her, when I remember the excitement of the first months of the Revolution. She must have approved of a lot of it though she is a dyed-in-the-wool aristocrat herself. It was the aristocrats who invented the Revolution, in fact, drawing-rooms of women talking idealism and philosophy. Everything was to be changed for the better. We knew it would not happen easily. One man would be as good as the next. There would be no more oppression, no more rich landlords grabbing the earnings of the poor and wasting them on entertainment and clothes,

47

there would be justice for all, no more *lettres de cachet*, no more whispering into the King's ear. There would be no more kings, or only those who knew their place. It was a new dawn, a heavenly prospect of peace and justice. What we got instead was a monster, a whole nation intoxicated with blood, exalted by it, invigorated, exhilarated. Just as some men need to be bled from time to time, it seems to me that the human race feels the need of periodic bleeding.

"It has eased off now but there are still some who miss the thrill of the drum-rolls, the hush that preceded the arrival of the tumbrils, the curiosity to see who of one's friends or neighbours was to be sacrificed this time, the slow climb of the victim up the ladder, the powerful figure of the executioner, like God, going through his ghastly ritual, the hope of further delight if the victim cried out or refused to play the game, then the great moment when the head fell neatly into the basket below and the body twitched in agony. They may yet have their fun with me. I fear it. Now as I write it down I have increased my load instead of lightening it. I have just manufactured a nightmare.

"I wonder if this writing is a hint from God that I am near my end. If I am, it must be by the guillotine, since I am perfectly healthy. They say that dying men want to tell the story of their lives to anyone that will listen. We have a proverb in Ireland: My own story is everyone's story - *Mo scéal féin scéal gach duine*. It could mean that all human stories are much the same, or else that no one wants to tell any story but his own.

"Why do I write that last sentence, as if this journal is to be read by strangers? No one will ever see it, except God who sees all. Still I have written some things that I hope even God will not understand. That is blasphemous. God knows all, even the hidden depths of my iniquity. I took that in at an early age and have believed it ever since. He watches over me sadly. 'I am a worm and no man.' That was Saint Paul, who was a man and no worm. Isolation could send me out of my mind.

"A while ago I wrote that Lady Sophie was the prime cause of my sin. It is true that she placed me in daily contact with a delicious young girl, as if I were a eunuch. She introduced me to the gentlemanly life of Mount Brien Court so that I longed to own such a piece of property myself. Do I really believe that my sins are her fault? I took to that life like a duck to water. If she was to blame, I was certainly a very willing victim. La Rochefoucauld has something to say about me too: 'The heart always out-wits the head.' And: 'Not everyone who knows his own mind knows his own heart also.' Sententious bastard. But the truth is often sententious, axiomatic. If I had paid more attention to La Rochefoucauld and to my prayers – where would I be? Dead, probably. Not a useful line to follow.

"My thoughts are becoming confused. This writing is meant to clarify them, not to excite them to hysteria. The basic facts are that I have abjured my priestly calling to become a landowner and I live with an aristocratic lady who has fallen on hard times and is glad to have me to take care of her. It was a long time before I began to sleep with Jeanne. My neighbours would not give me much credit for that, if they knew. She was the owner of the Château, my second purchase, or her father was, the Count de Rochechouart, until they took him away. I found her hiding in the cow-sheds when I bought up the place. I let her stay. For a while she watched me in terror lest I might think I had bought her too. Then she watched me in terror lest I might not be interested in her at all. Poor soul, when I finally went to her bed my fantasies were all of Louise. That must be the greatest sin in the calendar, far worse than any of my other sins.

"All the same, by sleeping with Jeanne I was hoping to exorcise the devil that has ridden me for years. She is a good creature, pretty in her frightened way. I don't know her age – about twenty-four I think. They say her father used to beat her. She jumps and stutters if I speak to her suddenly. No wonder, since her whole family was guillotined, but I don't

49

think that is the reason for it. She seems afraid of life rather than of death.

"She does everything she can to please me, so that in spite of my hard work I live elegantly in the evenings. My day begins at five in the morning, when I ride out to see to my three farms, and twelve hours later when I get home, she has prepared a meal and set it out in the dining-room and is dressed in her best to receive me as if I were her husband. After dinner we sit in the drawing-room while I read the books that I brought up to the Château from the first farm, and she does her embroidery. Most of the books from the Château libary were stolen. At nine we go to bed. So I have a double life, bean soup with Jean-Paul and his mother at noon and roast chicken with Jeanne in the evening. That fate seems to be written for me.

"It would be a great injustice to Jeanne to marry her, though I think she would be willing enough. I sense that the Revolution is over. Those are the saddest words I have ever written. All this will pass away like a shadow, and girls who have married renegade priests from Ireland will be ostracised by the returned aristocracy. What then will happen to the renegade priests? In Ireland they will be remembered from generation to generation as rats, jackals, the damned. People like to condemn. God does not. If those who will condemn me had seen the things that I saw, they would be more restrained.

"Making excuses again. No one is to blame but myself. I could have written to my bishop and said that I was exposed to excessive temptation of the flesh at Mount Brien, and he would have rescued me, set me a massive penance and turned me out to grass in a parish where there were no women under sixty. Does anyone cut off his right hand? I lived on and in my sin, but I never gave scandal then. I think I was such a figure of fun that no one ever suspected me. I have never learned to dress elegantly, not even when I can afford good clothes. The first evening with a new suit, perhaps, I look neat and well-brushed and gentlemanly but then something happens. The suit expires, gives in, knows when it's beaten. It shudders as I put it on, so that wrinkles spread from side to side, never to leave it again. My hair will take no shape no matter how I brush it, and when I wear a wig it always slips sideways and makes me look ridiculous. I had the wit not to try to change. That would have been noticed, all right. Nothing more ridiculous than an old man sprucing himself up to look young.

"I thought of myself as old when I took Louise and Robert to Paris in 1780 but I was only forty-one then. To them I seemed seventy-five. On the ship I watched my darling darting about everywhere, taking care of her maid who was seasick all the time, chatting to the young Kerry sailors in Irish and to the only French one in French, as easily as if she were their brother. With me she was polite, edging away from me to escape as quickly as possible when we met on the little deck. It was so obvious that she feared and disliked me that I ended by spending most of the voyage in the cabin. Then, in Paris, I made an attempt to warn her of the dangers but she was all ready to fly into the air with the flocks of parrots that surrounded her. I left her sitting at the table in her room in Charlotte's house, studying geometry, but already I could see what was going to happen to her.

"I was right. Before the end of the year they had married her off to that old goat, Armand de La Touche from Angers. Lady Sophie wrote to me that I should go to Hautefontaine and put a stop to it. They would never have listened to a seedy old provincial abbé. I didn't even attempt it."

The truth. He would write the truth. No one would ever read it. Once it was written, the devil might leave him. But there was a story he remembered, told to warn chatterboxes, of the king's barber who learned in the course of his business that the king had horses' ears. Terrified of telling his secret to anyone, he whispered it to the wind, and when the corn came up and swayed in the wind it sang: "The king has horses' ears, the king has horses' ears."

*Tell, tell, tell.*

A demon was at his elbow. There was still another candle but if he used them all tonight, there would be hours of darkness between sunset and the arrival of Jean-Paul to-morrow. He wrote quickly:

"I could have gone to Hautefontaine. They were all staying there with Madame Dillon and the Countess de Rothe. I could have appeared like a vision of judgment, in my black wrinkled suit, and warned them all of death and damnation. They might have listened to me. They were afraid of God. I could have told them He was watching them. There was time. Lady Sophie wrote to me well in advance. She wrote a vicious letter when I did nothing. She thought I was afraid.

"That was not my reason. I thought, if my Louise marries an old man he will die, and then I'll get her. So deeply buried in my soul, I barely knew the hope was there. But I did know it, I remember the sense of relief and satisfaction I experienced when I heard from Lady Sophie that the bride-groom was already in his sixties. If he had been young, I might have raged off to put a stop to it."

Burke read what he had just written, appalled. So that was it. He had never recognised it before. He would have seen it, sooner or later. One cannot entirely stifle conscience. What was conscience? The voice of God telling man that he is doing wrong. That is it, in a nutshell. But the conscience can be toughened, Burke always warned his flock, by hard usage and by habit. The truth can be obscured. Saint Paul says: He that contemneth small things shall fall by little and little. Contemn – to scorn, from the Latin *com* – thoroughly, and *temnere* to scorn or despise. Etymology was no cure. He had abandoned that girl for the ugliest of reasons, ridiculous too. What hope had he that she would ever look at him? Another truth occurred to him, even uglier than the first. He wrote:

"Mixed with my lust for her was some element of con-tempt, for her ignorance, for her youth, for her being a woman, for her physical beauty. On a still deeper level there was envy, leading almost to hatred, of her background among wealthy aristocrats and her instant success with them."

The seven deadly sins were represented here. Anger? That is part of envy. Gluttony? Part of covetousness. If you had one, you had them all.

Burke stood up, realising that this was the first evening he had felt warm. The gaol was warm enough, since there were so many prisoners and they were allowed to make a wood fire in the evenings. He recalled the day of his arrest – he could scarcely believe it. A party of police came to the Château for him. They had orders to arrest all British citizens and when he shouted that he was Irish they showed him his name on the list they carried. Someone in the neighbourhood had given it to them, he thought, but they would not say how the list had been made up. They probably did not know. They gave him a moment to speak to Jeanne, who was hovering about like a frightened hen, and he gave her any instructions that occurred to him and told her to send Jean-Paul in to visit him in gaol. At least he knew where he was going. But he had no idea how many hours or days of his life were left. His arrest could be a sign that a new wave of terror was about to begin. The blood fever had died down but the guillotine still stood there and at any moment the fever might flare up again.

He went to the hearth and put the last log on the dying fire. It sent up a long flame at once, then settled down to burn steadily. Louise. She was in Como, with her husband, André de Lacy, the man she ran off with when she left old de La Touche. Married now, of course, since the old man was dead. Burke was present at their first meeting, in Ireland. He saw André watching her, with the unmistakable, goggle-eyed adoration of love at first sight. Fate, or coincidence, or God threw them together again and again, until he took her away with him to America. Old Sophie was behind that move too, Burke suspected, for all her moralising. She could make any villainy fit her conscience.

Burke could not help liking André, though he detested his youth and energy and charm. Those Frenchmen of Irish descent thought a lot of themselves. It was true that they were working for the freedom of Ireland, travelling the country organising the Irish to rise when the French would land, going back and forth to the revolutionary army with information, trying to extract promises of help from them – a bunch of heroes, in fact. Burke would have despaired of Ireland long ago, only for them.

*Tell, tell, tell*, said the demon. *Do you really care about Ireland?*

Yes, of course I do. Why else am I here, in the dark, with the mice and the damp and the smells?

*Why don't you go back?*

I have gone back, I've brought messages and sheltered Frenchmen on the run – I've worked for Ireland all my life.

*That's all in the past. When you get out of here, would you leave your three farms and your pretty Château and go back to pull your forelock to the Irish landlords?*

I'll never pull my forelock to anyone.

*Your father used to go down on one knee to the landlord and call him 'Your Honour'.*

I never did that.

*Your brother did.*

He was expecting to get the farm.

*Would you have done it for the farm?*

That's not a fair question. One reason I came to France was to get away from the landlord and the farm.

*Not to be a priest?*

That too. One can have several reasons.

*Jean-Paul says you're a Frenchman now.*

You have to be Irish to understand the pull of that country.

*Perhaps he understands you better than you do yourself.*

Examination of conscience was a large part of the priestly training. Dr. Glynn quoted anyone and everyone in his classes – "Know thyself" – "To thine own self be true" – find thyself out in all thy mean little sins – the priests went to the guillotine asking God's forgiveness for a thousand peccadilloes that God had not noticed. Burke's God was a different personality altogether. He was liberal and kindly. He thought of his people as sheep and lambs, wandering sheep and weak, witless lambs. He believed in justice.

54

Dr. Glynn had spent a long time questioning Burke about his vocation, not only when he first came to the College but over and over again afterwards, almost until the day he was ordained.

"Are you sure you will serve God best in the priesthood?"

"Quite sure, Father."

"Have you thought of all the things you will never have, a wife, children, a home of your own? The servants of Christ have no place to lay their heads."

Better not make any jokes.

"Yes, I've thought of that."

"Have you the strength to go through with it? It's not an easy life."

"God will give me strength."

The cliché didn't satisfy the older man. He almost looked angry.

"God helps those who help themselves. There are many other things you could do."

"This is all I want."

Unless his father gave him the farm, and as the younger brother he had no hope of that. It had been arranged with the landlord for years that when the lease was renewed it would be in John's name. He would not stay at home and act the servant-boy to his brother. He had had enough of that, with his father. Glynn looked at him doubtfully still but Burke had all the answers and there was no way of finding out what were his deepest thoughts. Besides, he meant exactly what he said. He was willing to make those sacrifices. He believed in God. God would help him. It would be all right.

It would have been all right, only for Louise, and the Revolution. After he became the curé, Burke was happy in the little house by the church in Saint Jacques, occupying his days with Mass and confessions and marriages and visits to the sick and dying, filling in his spare time with the obligatory recital of the liturgy of the hours, and with his garden and his chickens.

Gradually the chickens became an obsession with him. He refused to leave their care to his housekeeper. He began to breed good egg-layers, consulting all his neighbours about their experiences and putting these together with his own. He bought clutches of the eggs of good yearling layers, insisting that the male bird should also come of a good laying strain. This was a new idea, but as Burke pointed out, breeding of all animals should follow the principle that both parents are important. Watching his chickens grow became the most interesting part of his life. He tended them and gave them comfort as if they were race-horses. The water must always be clean. Their feed must contain greens as well as grain. Sea-shells must be scattered to provide them with lime. The hen-houses must be swept and fresh straw put down every day. The nesting-boxes must have clean hay. The laying hens must have exercise. He kept a record of the number and weight of the eggs and of his profits, and was triumphant when his notes proved that he had succeeded.

Then he took to riding off to visit farmers who were expert in the diseases of poultry. Instead of being disgusted by the variety and details of these, he would enter into long conversations with the women who had charge of the poultry and note their advice on feather-eating and egg-binding, and fowl-pox and bumble-foot and a dozen other plagues that befall chickens. He applied his knowledge, and soon was so successful that he was obliged to run a weekly clinic for the benefit of his neighbours. At some point he began to realise that he dreamed of chickens and cocks and hens day and night, that all his mental and physical energy was spent on this new enterprise.

Burke pressed the logs together with his boot, making the last two chips flare again. Slowly he walked back to the table, and wrote:

"My epitaph should be: 'He gave up the cure of souls for the care of chickens.' They were my downfall. I starved myself to feed them, then ate one of them every Sunday. Is it any wonder that a little, fine-boned girl was repelled by me? She probably saw that my proper company was chickens. I became parsimonious, saving my egg-money like a farmer's wife, piling it up and counting it now and then, converting it into gold louis when I went in to Bordeaux, quietly increasing my hoard from month to month and from year to year. How many years? Seven or eight, at least. It was a slow disease. I took to asking the farmers about sheep and cattle prices, and costings in their tobacco plantations, and methods of harvesting and selling grain, whether it was best to sell the whole crop to one miller or spread it out among two or three and play them off against each other. The farmers came to welcome my visits because I was full of good advice, not about their souls but about money.

"I didn't care about money for its own sake, though I believe this is possible. I know now what I was doing. I was saving to buy a farm. My years in Ireland with the Brien household were an interruption but they were not enough to put me back on the path of holy poverty. Rather the reverse – I learned a great deal there, from watching how Sir Maurice managed his land. He was a good farmer in those days, though he went to pieces afterwards, according to Lady Sophie. She says in her letter today that the land has all gone to ruin and the house is neglected. She is too old to fight Fanny any longer. She wants Robert to come home with his wife, the girl she despised so much long ago, and put the estate back to its former glory.

"While I was away in Ireland, my chickens died and my garden went wild and my hen-houses rotted. I came back to the kind of ruin that Lady Sophie describes in her letter. I'd like to see her face if I were to tell her of that comparison – my hen-runs and my dingy presbytery with her beautiful house and gardens and home farm and wood and pastures and paddocks. But she has a feeling for land – she would understand that I loved my little patch as she loves her big one. I had to start all over again, find breeders and build coops and save and save and save. The saving was easy, with the example of my neighbours. No one can save like a French peasant. Not a potato-peel is wasted.

"For me, owning a farm was a crazy dream, but the Revolution made it possible. I bought the first one right in Saint Jacques, in my own parish. I made quite sure the owner was dead before I went to the auction. He was a serious man who believed in the king as sent by God, a great church-goer. His wife got off to America. The house was in good order and his men were working, so I thought he might still be alive. Then I met someone who had seen him guillotined. I got the place cheap, because it was the first one to be sold in our parish. People were not quite sure that they wanted dead men's property. My example set them all at each other's throats. After that first one, there were not many cheap farms to be had, but I saved my profits and bought two more over the next five years. The second one was the Château, with Jeanne. The last one was only a few months ago.

"I stayed on in the presbytery for half a year after I bought the first farm, then I moved to the farmhouse. My congregation had disappeared. There was no point in staying, even with my oath to protect me. The farm-house seemed like a palace to me. My old house-keeper, Anna, came with me. She is with me still, a good hen-wife now that I have trained her, and willing to do everything I tell her. As ugly as a bucket, naturally, since that is always required in a priest's housekeeper, but it doesn't seem to worry her. In a way it's a kind of freedom for a woman to be ugly – so many things she need never consider. That is, of course, only if she is poor. If she is rich she has suitors and must reckon with the fact that they love only her money, since they cannot possibly love herself. Not that my parishioners consider love much when they look for a wife. The matter is too serious for that.

"When I walked the farm for the first time, I was like a bridegroom on the first night of his marriage. I cannot describe the sensation. It was perhaps like being born, or like discovering a new continent. The sun, the sky, the clouds, the grass, everything looked different, was different. I wanted to swagger, and run, and roll over and over like a boy. Jean-Paul came with me, as pleased as if the land were his, a smile the width of his face and his eyes lit up with pure pleasure. It was April, and the vine leaves had begun to grow. Jean-Paul stopped to touch one now and then, and to observe that they had been perfectly pruned. I had bought the stock with the farm, and we went to see the cows, twenty-four of them, grazing in a sloping field that was as green as an Irish one. I said this to Jean-Paul and he said: 'There is only one France.'

"I was careful after that not to draw comparisons but they were always in my mind. The lowland was foggy but the cows did well on that. I doubled my herd, profiting from my experience with the chickens in going after the best stock and never sparing money where the return was certain. If my father had been alive I could scarcely have resisted writing to tell him of my success. Fortunately, he was dead, and my mother stopped writing to me after I left the ministry.

"In times of war, good horses are prized like gold. I bought the Château for the limestone land and began to breed horses. I had all the foals born there and at a month old I sent them to the hills with the mares. I sold them well as yearlings. At the same time I collected inferior animals and sold them at a profit to the army. This is still a good source of revenue. I love all my animals personally and have given them private names, all in Irish – my stallion is Fergus. My best brood mare is Maeve. My bulls are Cúchulainn and Fionn MacCumhaill and Conor Mac Nessa – never saints' names. That would be blasphemous. My work horses and my saddle horses have French names.

"Sometimes when I am out alone on the farm, I fancy myself back in Clare, in the nibbled fields, with the clear, pale sky and the wild flowers and the wind from the Atlantic always hurrying by. In a sense I never left Ireland, or I took it with me.

"After I went to the farm, for the first time since I came to France I was really healthy. At night I slept instantly and woke as fresh as a daisy, though my conscience should have been torturing me if it had been properly about its business. Study is not my natural life – at the College I always had haemorrhoids and constipation and bronchitis and rheumatism and swollen feet and headaches. None of those things afflict me now."

Was that his apologia, then? It was the best he could do at the moment. Most men are healthy when they are doing the work they enjoy, or living with the woman they love, or have easily achieved their life's ambition. Self-sacrifice, a hard life devoted to others, intensive study of abstruse and essentially uninteresting subjects are all dangerous to mind and body. God had not meant him for a life of contemplation.

Where did Louise come into this? Was she the occupation of an idle, unhappy mind? Faced with this unbearable thought, Burke poured half a glass of Jean-Paul's plum liqueur and swallowed a mouthful of it. It stung like a wasp, making him cough. Almost at once a wave of warmth began to tingle through him.

The last candle was reduced to half. Soon he would be in the dark, with the fiends. Anticipating the terrors that were to come, he picked up the piece of candle, cradling it carefully with his huge hand, and went to make a last round of his defences. Shadows higher than himself awaited him on the stairway. Tiny sounds could be heard now that the wind had died down, a creak, a shudder, an almost imperceptible sigh. Something flicked quickly out of sight. He stopped abruptly, held the candle until the flame was steady and peered ahead. Nothing but those maddening little points of light, like fireflies. Step by step he went down. Now they were behind him. The skin on the back of his neck twitched. He began to pray:

"O God, who hast created the light and the darkness as a lesson and a protection to us, lighten our darkness with the power of thy heavenly presence. Amen."

God would not be taken in by that. Thou, God, seest me. Have mercy on me, O God, have mercy on me, for I am alone and poor. That was more like it. But rich – he was rich. The foxes have their holes but the Son of Man has not where to lay his head. Out of the depths I have cried to thee, O God. O God hear my voice. Step by heavy step down the stairs, holding the banister. If he were to break his leg on this damned stair, he would lie there until the doors were broken down, or until Jean-Paul managed to get in. Lacombe perhaps would like to starve him out. Surely someone would soon realise that food was being brought to him. Then it would only be a matter of time before they broke in at the back. It was a mistake to swallow that plum brandy before going downstairs. Now he had to visit the latrine, which was by the back door. The tricks God played on man, making his body so conveniently inconvenient. He placed the candle on the floor while he was inside the latrine. It would last until he was finished. When he came out, he stooped and picked it up as carefully as if it were a baby. Tomorrow night he would be more sensible. It was madness to use up the candles all at once. They should be lit one by one, with an interval between in which the firelight would do. The last half of the last candle should be kept for emergencies.

The piece of candle expired finally on the stairs, burning his hand slightly. He had marked where the study door was and he fled towards it with a gasp of pure terror. Inside, the embers made a tiny spot of light. He found his way to the bottle and glass and drank again, sipping frantically so as not to burn his mouth but eager to get the anaesthetic effect of the alcohol as quickly as possible. Still clutching the bottle he groped to his pile of sacks, knelt to arrange them and lay down. Shuffling his heavy body around, searching for a comfortable position, he felt a longing for Jeanne. At this moment he could have been at home in his own Château, in the big bedroom on the first floor, with the remains of a fire of logs still giving off scent and warmth, with Jeanne in her lace nightcap beside him, her head resting comfortably on his shoulder, his hand gently stroking her soft, round breast, her gentle, sweet voice whispering to him affectionately. The explosion in his mind that had brought him into this

61

fortress separated him from all these comforts. God or devil – which had sent it to him? God in a last attempt to rescue him, devil to show him the poverty of the world he had sensibly left behind, God to shock him back to his duty, devil to frighten him out of that duty for good and all?

# —4—

BURKE SLEPT LATE AND AWOKE WITH A HEADACHE. THAT
damned plum brandy. Last thing at night was wrong for it,
and so much. It was a drink you had after making a bargain,
a tiny glass drunk standing, before you set out for home
with your money in your pocket or with your new horses
following in a string. It brought a pleasant muzziness then,
and its effect wore off quickly in the fresh air and with the
exercise.

He heaved himself slowly upright from the sacks, then
stood to look down at them, an unsavoury nest if ever there
was one. He remembered the warm stench of the prison, all
those unwashed bodies, too many of them. At least he was
alone here. The light was grey, an uncivil patch of it near the
window, the rest of the room dim. Still, any daylight was
better than the demon-infested darkness.

Not a sound. The fire was dead ash, flat, as if it had never
burned high. Wood consumed itself almost completely. It
hadn't occurred to him, nor to Jean-Paul apparently, that
the smoke might be seen. No harm if it was. They knew he
was there. The deadlock was unnerving.

Bells – seven o'clock. Time for Mass, matins. He hadn't
thought of that for a long time. It was inevitable, living in
the College where the whole of life had run to the tune of
bells. Saint Eutrope was the Irish church, where they went
to Mass in procession and had all their ceremonies. That was
up for sale too – who on earth would want to buy a church,
and what would you do with it if you owned it? A tobacco
factory, or a granary, or a stable for horses. That was the
Irish experience, the travelling cavalry of Cromwell's army
looking for stabling for the horses and using Saint Nicholas'

63

Collegiate Church in Galway, hay on the altars, oats in the fonts, straw on the floors, the captains' horses in special quarters behind the altar rails. The Galway people would never forget that. Armies are the same everywhere and horses must be stabled.

Opening the door in daylight created no advance fears. He left it open, to air the room which smelt heavily of wood-smoke. A long day to go. An empty house is suspended in time, waiting. It echoed – it had always echoed, nailed boots on the stone corridors and stairs, Irish boys from the country running as if they were out in the fields, until one of the older priests told them they would have to give that up. A warm silence once classes began, smells of cooking, a shaft of sunlight full of dancing dust giving hope of a life outside. All those mea culpas, peccavis, penances – forming the character, the mind. It worked for some. It had only made Burke devious, or perhaps he was so already.

He had not laced his boots and he sat on the last step of the stairs to do it. Not a move in the barricades, but a tiny shaving at one end suggested that a mouse had begun to build in there. It must seem a godsend to him, little spaces and holes ready made, nothing to do but put in the soft stuff to lie on. How he would gallop, indignantly squalling, if they broke down the door.

It was quiet outside now, though street sounds never came through loudly unless the windows were open. Not much traffic in the rue du Hâ and the door was thick and solid. Father Glynn was not fond of the air of Bordeaux. He said it was full of miasmas, mosquitoes, evil smells, noise, distractions. He would have liked to keep the boys perpetually inside, for the good of their souls and their bodies, but fortunately the others had more wits. Burke remembered the choking sense of loss that he experienced when they all turned back to the College after a game of football in the field across the river, especially in spring.

The same grey light had got into the kitchen by the time he reached it. He left its door open to light the dark passage to the back door. He would have to empty the earth closet.

Fortunately its bucket and shovel had been left behind when those blackguards made off with everything else, and a box for the earth that was dropped in discreetly every day. There was just enough garden for him to bury it. The boys were never allowed to use this latrine. It was for the cook and his helpers, handy near the kitchen, a box of earth kept full at all times. That was the scullery-boy's job, poor devil. Burke opened the back door wide to let in some air.

While he was at work with his bucket and shovel he remembered:

Ashes to ashes, dust to dust.
If God won't have you, the divil must.

Ancient Irish wisdom. If he were to be guillotined, he could ask to be buried here, in Irish ground. That would turn the tables on them. *Bás in Éirinn*, a good toast for all exiles. If they agreed, it would be an admission that the College and its precincts belonged to Ireland. Too subtle for them. Their logic had somehow all been washed away in blood.

There was a feeling of spring in the air, a freshness of growth, a few new blades of grass here and there, the moss on the wall a little greener. The swallows were back, shining dark-blue suits and pink waistcoats, all business with their nest-building. Ask Jean-Paul this evening if they have arrived at the Château. They always built under the eaves of the stables where there was plenty of material for nests. Mud was what they liked for the outside but they needed a lining too, wool from a passing sheep, and the oats were convenient food. And Jean-Paul must bring some tools, and a cat. Burke had not forgotten last night's decision. If he had had a cat then, he might not have got the horrors. Jean-Paul would think he was mad but he thought that already. If he had the name of it he might as well have the gains of it. Burke's mother used to say that about someone living scandalously.

He refilled the box of earth, spading it in carefully, his hands happy with the feel of the spade-handle, his arms lifting the little weight as if he were working in a potato-field. Irish potatoes, sweet as apples, Irish cabbage, white all through in summer, rich dark-green in winter, Irish bacon boiled with the cabbage, a feast, a debauch. Burke was hungry.

As he turned to go back into the house he heard a slight noise in the lane. He stopped like a gun-dog, waiting. Someone was there. A hand tried the door, swishing along the jamb, rattling the latch, a fist thumped once idly, or perhaps in anger. Still he waited, lest the man might take it into his head to climb the wall and look inside. Burke measured the distance to the back door. He would not be able to reach it in time. Then the feet passed on.

Back at the house he filled a wine-bottle with water from the tap in the yard, then secured the door and went upstairs. There was almost enough bread to keep him going all day, until Jean-Paul arrived. Bread and wine. He could say Mass. A priest forever according to the order of Melchisedech, even if he was in a state of mortal sin, but that made it another mortal sin. They piled up, one on top of another until they flattened you into the ground. Anyway he had no missal, and there was no point in it. He was finished with all that. The church made such a mess of its affairs, no one in his right mind could stay tied to it. Messing, and high living. They said of old Archbishop Dillon that he would not allow his clergy to hunt, though he loved hunting himself. When the king asked him how he worked that out he said that his sins were the sins of his ancestors but his clergy's sins were their own. A man after Burke's heart in many ways though he did nothing to save Louise when the time came. They would have had to listen to him, if he had deigned to speak. He was probably in on the deal some-how. Had a finger in every pie, they said. And always after money, always needing more.

Too early in the morning to think of Louise. His brain was still fogged with last night's wine and the liqueur. Breakfast was good. It settled his stomach. The coarse bread was chewy and tough since it was no longer fresh. It

66

had a sweetish aftertaste. Bread in France, potatoes in Ireland – the staff of life. The water had a fetid taste, though in Bordeaux it was never the worst. A drop of wine remained in last night's bottle and he poured it into the glass but it was no improvement.

Putting the rest of the bread into the desk drawer for safety from the mice, his hand fell on the journal. Ever since awakening he had experienced an odd sense of having achieved something yesterday, as if he had done a useful day's work. Now he could feel sentences beginning to form, as if he intended to continue with it. Nothing else to do, and it had passed the time as well as clearing his head. It brought in the devils, but they were there already – Lacombe had left a dozen of his own, in case there was any shortage.

Lacombe – Burke had never been able to make friends with him as he had with Claude and even with Tallien. They couldn't understand Lacombe either. He seemed to have no soft spots, no point where you were given a clue to his deepest mind. But he had a wife, who was devoted to him, and who promoted all his causes. She was particularly good at spotting women who ought to be brought to trial and Lacombe always gave her charge of them. There were not too many of them in Bordeaux. Most of the women tended their houses and their children and knew nothing about politics. Burke admired Madame Lacombe for taking her place so easily with the men but later it upset him to think of a woman being mixed up in what was really a war. One never gets rid of these ideas no matter how times change.

He lifted out the little pile of papers and dated today's entry:

"March 13, 1796."

He had finished last night with the comment that his health was improved with the farming life, that the scholar's life had never suited him. That was an admission of failure, for an Irishman. In that country, since prehistoric times the poet and the seer were regarded as a class apart, with rights and privileges, and with powers that were above and beyond the capacity of ordinary men. Everyone aspired to be a poet

67

of some sort or other. Burke did too – indeed he was a poet, but his body demanded that he be a farmer. No need to write about that again. He began:

"A fair morning with a touch of spring. Last night I was somewhat dispirited but today I am firmer than ever. Nothing will induce me to abandon my position. Perhaps they will come for me today. I hope not, as I have some important messages for Jean-Paul. One concerns Robert Brien. Though I blame Lady Sophie for many things, I think now that she has the right to want him to go home. Everything will be better for the Catholics in Ireland from now on. Pitt has had a fright. He knows very well that the spirit of our Revolution has spread there and that it is foolish to keep ninety per cent of the population permanently in a state of bondage. The new seminary for priests that is being opened outside Dublin proves this better than anything else could do."

Burke looked back on what he had written and paused in surprise. Our Revolution. Jean-Paul said he was a Frenchman now. Could it possibly be true? Would he go back to Ireland now, if he were invited to do so? As Lady Sophie pointed out rather rudely, he was no scholar. But supposing for the purposes of argument that he had been asked to teach in the new seminary, to help to set it up, since he knew so much about the organisation of such schools from his experience in Bordeaux and in Paris, would he have accepted? It was not absolutely impossible that he would have been asked, if he had not flown off the target so thoroughly. Dr. Everard would probably be there, Dr. Glynn too if he were alive. Burke turned his head quickly, to make sure that Glynn was not standing there watching him, that wry, knowing, insulting smile on his face. He had seen through Burke from the start.

Burke picked up Lady Sophie's letter and read it again. That abominable paper and the tight, secretive handwriting, as if she were afraid that someone was listening to her as she wrote – it was a day's work to find out what she was saying. His mother's sister Ellen used to lower her voice to a whisper when she had anything of special interest to tell, so that you literally had to put your head together with hers in order to hear her. Sophie was sending someone else to Robert as well – Katta's son, Colman, of all people. Katta was the former nurse, who still came sometimes to Mount Brien Court to visit, though she lived in a desolate village on the lake shore, miles away. Colman knew some French, Sophie wrote, because he had sometimes joined in the lessons with the older Brien children. He was about to emigrate to America and she had persuaded him to go to France first and urge Robert to go home at once. She was never lost for a plan. And this was a good one. Colman and Robert were like brothers, though their stations in life were so different.

Robert was living near Saintes now, in a house that had belonged to the family of Lucy Dillon's husband. Having survived the Terror, he might well be settling down again to running his little estate and bringing up his children. Burke would send Jean-Paul to say that he should stay where he was. Why should an escaped fly walk back into the web again? There was something evil about the pull of that country. If Sophie knew his thoughts she would never have asked his help in this matter. She said peremptorily that Burke was to go at once and instruct Robert where his duty lay. How could Burke, who had abandoned his duty, be expected to give that kind of advice?

Burke remembered Colman, standing respectfully in the hall, waiting for his mother. Butter wouldn't melt in his mouth – but Robert said he was a regular firebrand, always preaching risings and rebellions. It was no wonder he was emigrating. That kind of man couldn't bear to spend his life bowing the knee to everyone bigger than himself. Burke realised that he would like to meet him when he came, to talk about things in Ireland, to get a good account of the feel of the country.

Better not to develop reasons for getting out of here. That way madness lies.

If he were at home in the Château, by this hour he would have been to the new farm and be on his way to dinner at

Saint Jacques. He had lost a lot of weight on this thin diet. Bean soup with pork would be good now, bread to mop up the gravy, a glass of red wine to help it all to settle. His face was thin too – there was not even a well where he could see his reflection but he could feel the unaccustomed bones under his beard. Later, when the sun was a bit warmer, he would venture into the yard again and splash his face and neck with water from the tap. If they had left any sort of tub behind, he could have taken a bath. Jean-Paul had brought a miserable little towel. For a few moments he contemplated the possibility of stripping naked in the yard and rubbing down with water from the tap, drying himself on that towel, but it would not do. He would catch his death of cold. And he would be terrified of being seen. Bad enough to be hiding in the building but there is no one so vulnerable as a totally naked man. Better stay dirty, for the present at least.

He read what he had written and continued:

"Lady Sophie's letter has brought my mind back to Ireland and its problems. I hope that Robert will not do as she wishes. Mount Brien Court is a fine inheritance, but it can go to one of Fanny's children. They seem to be made of tougher material, chasing the servants instead of seducing the daughters of the down-and-out local gentry. No doubt they take after their mother. Their father is a weak vessel, a bad example to Robert, and would be a hopeless burden on him. And there is Celia, Robert's wife. Her story is too well known. They made a ballad about it:

> O lie with me, said the fine young man,
> And then you may lie with my father.
> He'll keep you close, he'll keep you warm,
> While I'm gone over the water.

"Pack of savages. Robert himself told me about that ballad. But there was pity in it too, appreciation of her tragedy. Robert behaved well towards Celia. Her life is peaceful now. Why should she go back to the place where such horrible things happened?

"It is possible that Robert's father is dead or dying. Lady Sophie doesn't say. She would have nothing more to do

70

with him, after he disgraced the family, though they live under the same roof. Robert should not be swallowed up in that nest of vipers. One can imagine the atmosphere. She gives no information about this Rose French but I can well imagine the complications that she would introduce. Robert would have to be king of the whole miserable tribe."

Thinking about them gave him wind in his gut. Live in Ireland? Not in a fit. What if Lacombe offered to send him back there now? He might ask to be guillotined instead. That would make a change. Most people howled at the thought of death but Burke could imagine worse things.

It occurred to him that rather than give up the College he could burn it down. Jean-Paul would bring him wood. Floors would burn – but most of them were made of stone, the stairs too. No furniture to make a start. The roof timbers would burn, if they were not too wet, and if he could climb up there. There were lots of those floor-boards in the attic. That would be as good a place as any. Old buildings did sometimes burn, even churches. But he would have to be prepared to die in the fire. God had put up with a lot from him. Suicide would be the last straw. It might not be necessary.

He had not been to the attic since he went up there with Jean-Paul to fetch the planks for the barricade. He laid the pen down with distaste, as if it was to blame for his distress, and went out of the room to climb the last, narrowest flight of stairs. It finished abruptly at a small grey-painted door. He turned the handle slowly, as if he feared to find a ring of last night's demons sitting on the floor, waiting for him. This would make a suitable retreat for them by day.

Madness. He flung the door open. Dim sunlight streaked the bare floor. The roof sloped sharply so that the windows were small and low. This was once the library but the plain pine shelves were quite bare. When Burke came in to take possession of the building, it had not occurred to him that the books would have been taken away. The shock of the empty shelves was still clear in his mind. He crossed now to touch them, almost as if he could not yet believe his eyes.

71

It had never been a great library but it contained Milton and Bacon and Swift and Shakespeare and George Herbert, Dante of course, Racine, Corneille and Molière, Homer, Horace, Tacitus, Catullus – everything one would ever want to read was there. The senior students were allowed to use it under careful supervision. There was another library of less secular books in the room off the refectory. That was empty too. This was one of the things that Burke wanted to thrash out with Lacombe. When the College was restored, those books would have to be brought back from whatever hiding-place they were in. He could not believe that they had been sold, nor that anyone would have bought them if they were offered. Lacombe and his kind were not much inclined towards books in any language.

Leaving the door open, Burke walked to the far end of the long room. The boards moved under his feet, loosened by the removal of those that he had taken downstairs to make his barricade. They were wide, soft pine, untreated, grey with use. There had never been enough money to finish the library properly, though a long table was presented by the O'Neill family about ten years ago, with a dozen chairs for the readers. They were gone too. Dr. Glynn had been proud of them, the only decent pieces of furniture in the library, mahogany, leather-covered with gold tooling. They changed the appearance of the room completely. Not much hope of getting them back.

Burke had to kneel in order to see out of the window. By twisting his head he could look down at the street and into the square beyond. People were moving about down there but it seemed that they were all passers-by, shopping or going about their business. Someone came into the rue du Hâ and stood for a moment, gazing along the street. Then he turned back into the square. No reason to suppose he had anything to do with Burke. It was a waste of time being up here, since he could not see directly to the front of the College. A crowd could be gathered there at this moment, preparing to break down the door.

As he straightened up he saw, lying on the narrow sill,

72

almost invisible against the white paint, a tiny circle of white. Altar bread. So this was where they said Mass in the last terrible months before they were forced to leave the building altogether. Dr. Everard was told that he and Glynn had better get out while they could, that they had been named as anti-revolutionaries who had refused to take the oath and were exerting an evil influence on the other inhabitants of the College. After they had gone, Mass continued until they were all arrested – what more likely place for it than here, with a lookout at the window? They certainly would not have used the chapel downstairs.

This could be a consecrated host. He tried to remember at what hour of the day or night the arrests had taken place but he could not recall that Dr. Everard had mentioned it. If it was early morning, if there was a flurry of excitement during Mass, during the distribution of Holy Communion, the tiny piece of bread could have been dropped by mistake, lying there unnoticed ever since. Was this why the ghosts had led him up here? He turned around furiously as if to yell abuse at them. There was nothing there, no one but a silly old fool afraid of his own shadow.

Softly he picked up the piece of bread, held it for a moment in finger and thumb, unspoken words running through his head.

"*Domine, non sum dignus ut intres sub tectum meum, sed tantum dic verbo et sanabitur anima mea.*"

Then he placed the bread in his mouth and swallowed it quickly. That action might cost him an eternity in Hell, according to some experts. It did not seem possible to Burke that the inventor of the universe could have such a petty, vindictive mind but it was largely believed that he had. Still, he had to have a sense of humour to make some of the animals as he did. Snakes, for instance, and monkeys like little old men, and elephants and giraffes. Bears. Hard to believe in some of them.

He walked soberly to the door, remembering his first reason for coming up here just now, something to do with the idea of burning the whole building down. He would never do it, not for any reason whatsoever, not even if he had to leave it to that scoundrel. For ever and a day it would be a holy part of Ireland, even if it was turned into a livery stable, an inn, a tobacco factory.

The emptiness of the library had upset him more than anything else about the College, a desecration as painful as the desecration of a church. Blasphemy – he was incorrigible. But he protested to the all-seeing God that he did not will these ideas: they happened to him. The ridiculousness of everyday things appeared to him like visions, bishops and cardinals and eminences of all kinds in funny hats and gaudy cloaks, covering their mental nakedness, behaving like kings and expecting to be so treated. It was true, as Dr. Glynn suspected, that he should never have been a priest.

Closing the attic door carefully, he went downstairs. He had an odd sensation of having been up there for a long time. The day still stretched before him, empty and useless. The other book – back at the desk, he opened it at random but he was in no mood for Voltaire's cheery scurrilities. Why had that fool not brought Descartes? Burke could recite the beautifully ironic opening passage of the *Discours de la Méthode* from memory, since the first days at Saint Jacques when he kept it beside his bed and meditated on a few sentences before falling asleep:

"Good sense is the most readily shared thing in the world; everyone thinks himself so well provided with it that even those who are hard to please in every other respect never feel the need of more than they have of this quality."

Slouched in his chair, his head on the desk, he awoke in the early afternoon realising that he had slept for several hours. He remembered getting back here, thinking of Descartes, sitting down – he must have done all those things in a reasonable way. His mouth felt nasty – only one cure for that. A hair of the dog that bit him. He saw the bottle where he had left it, beside the dead hearth, still half full. Jean-Paul had the right idea there. When things got bad enough with him, the cure was to drink himself into a stupor. Burke had never done that but he had never before been set about

74

on all sides as he was now. Better not lose the last of his wits. A glass was enough. It went through him like a battalion of ants, running down his arms and legs, crossing and re-crossing his chest, sending shots of delicious warmth up the back of his head, clearing his mouth of the disgusting taste of last night's excess. There could be worse things than to remain gently drunk during the whole of his time here, not enough to make him do anything foolish but enough to keep his heart up.

He corked the bottle firmly and went downstairs, chewing on the last of the bread, his thought anxiously running ahead to count the hours until the next bite would come. By the front door he heard a clock strike three. Instantly his mood dropped to one of despairing sanity. Four hours still to go. Another clock struck, then another – two more hours of daylight, then the darkness of the pit. His stupidity in using up the candles amazed him. It was a warning that other, more important mistakes were possible. The remaining time in daylight should be spent profitably, at least, though he could not help feeling pleased that he had escaped for a few hours in sleep.

He found that he detested the efficiency of his barricade of the front door, it shut him in so securely. He left it at once to inspect the refectory windows. They were high, covered with a thick coating of dust both inside and out, with stone frames and panes too small to admit a man's body. Never-theless he had pegged the tiny piece that could be opened in each with a sliver of wood, six windows on the street. This was where the busy judges had sat, where Burke himself might have been arraigned to stand trial. Had they brought Dr. Glynn here from the Maison des Orphelins where he was first imprisoned? Odd that Burke had not asked Dr. Everard about that. If they had, it was the refinement of cruelty. It all happened after Tallien was gone. His successor was Jullien, a ruthless devil, devoted to the cause. It was he who handed over Glynn to Lacombe, as President of the Military Tribunal. By the time you reached him, it was all up with you. Poor, good, upright, saintly man.

The chapel windows were high and narrow too. The room led off the refectory and after a silent meal the students went in there for more silence and prayer. Some of them throve on it. Burke had always found it painful, yet here he was, silent as an egg all day long. Some holy man or other remarked that the one thing you fear is the thing above all that God will send you. No wonder He has so few friends. It was Saint Teresa who said that, very witty. The chapel gave him the creeps. He saw that all his little pegs were in place and left it quickly.

The wind had risen again and was hurling drops of rain on the glass as he passed back through the refectory. He knew now what he wanted to do. He marched upstairs, with his heavy farmer's tread, each step a firm thump as if he were in a ploughed field where his foot might catch at any moment in a rough spot. The journal – he would write it down. *Scripta manent*. Nothing like the learning. Writing it down would be as good as an oath. He dipped the quill with great care, as if to emphasize this solemn occasion, and wrote:

"I have just been to the attic that used to be our library. It is a sad place now. On the window-sill I found a Sacred Host and disposed of it by swallowing it, as was my duty. I had no way of knowing whether or not it was consecrated but I could not take the risk. The shock was great. It has brought back terrible memories, questions, anxieties which I thought I had put behind me, though my presence here at the Collège des Irlandais should have told me how my mind was tending. When I came it was mainly out of a feeling of outrage at the ingratitude of the city in touching the property of a friendly country, whose representative – myself – had done it such great service. I now find that other ideas have begun to grow in my mind, or perhaps were there already, unknown to me. It is seven years since I abandoned the ministry. Either the excitement of the times affected my judgment or else I was simply too weak to fight the temptation of owning land and working it with my own hands. I incline to the second explanation. I think now that I was ready to abandon the Church at the first prospect of becoming a landowner. That is all past history. Today I have come to a decision.

"Whenever it is possible, when our bishops come out of hiding or when they are allowed to return to their bishoprics – if there are any of them still alive – I will go to mine and reconcile myself with the Church. There are plenty like me. I will be welcomed back like a lost sheep, a dirty, foolish, wandering, unreliable, disgraceful sheep but good mutton for all that. In hard times even sheep must stick together. With this resolve firmly in mind, from now onward I solemnly intend to live as a priest should."

There it was, in writing. No more Jeanne. No more thoughts of Louise, no more hopes of some day possessing her – had he ever had such a hope? If he had, it was idiotic, a dream, an embarrassing fantasy.

How would he live without her? He heard her voice, clear and childish, recite:

*"Ainsi, en ta jeune et première nouveauté*
*Quand la terre et le ciel honorait ta beauté,*
*La Parque t'a tué et cendres tu reposes,*
*Pour obsèques reçois mes larmes et mes pleurs,*
*Ce vase plein de lait, ce panier plein de fleurs,*
*Afin que vif et mort ton corps ne soit que roses."*

He had sworn to part with all that. It was there in writing. Even if it were not, he knew that he was finished with that ruinous side of his life. Once he saw the ridiculousness of it, it was gone. It had lasted so long only because he had never confided it to a soul. He should have, in Confession. He should have said: "I am obsessed with a young girl, my pupil." He could never bring himself to perhaps knowing that he would instantly have been exorcised of it. He had wanted to keep his little mean sin as long as possible.

Dangerous thinking. If he were not careful he would be back where he started. He re-read his resolution. It was nicely expressed. Can a man be cured suddenly of a sickness like this? Perhaps it was the grace of God. The fear of God is the beginning of wisdom. Fear for his skin, more likely, fear of death. Yes, he was afraid of death. All sensible people

77

are, even when necessity forces them to face it. It seemed that what he had learned since he had incarcerated himself was that above all he loved his land, his farms, his three houses.

Would he be obliged to renounce them too? He doubted it. The wish for property was never regarded as the equal of sins of the flesh. To renounce his land would be appreciated as a saintly, praiseworthy act but not at all necessary to salvation. Henceforward his whole comfort would be in the simple, natural creations of the good God, horses and sheep and cornfields and money in the bank. These are public things. Love for another human being is private and therefore dangerous. If it is allowed to be perceived it is ridiculous, inexcusable, an outrage, a failure of intelligence, sentimental, romantic nonsense. In oneself it is the mainspring of life, the reason for existence, the light that shines in the darkness. The sooner Jean-Paul brings that cat, the better. Flowers in pots too, and perhaps a makeshift bird-bath. Birds came into the yard sometimes.

The light faded gradually, the rain closing in and cutting off the daylight before its time. He watched the window anxiously, savouring the last moments when it could be said to be still daylight. Then the abominable night fell. He was tempted to feel his way down to the hall in the last moments, to make sure that he reached it safely, but he knew there was no need. By this time he was familiar with every step. It would be colder down there and he would have to sit on the stairs.

While he could still see, he poured a glass of the plum liqueur and it comforted him for a few minutes. He filled the glass again, holding the neck of the bottle in the circle of his finger and thumb to make sure that not a drop spilled. He held his hands around the glass to warm it, so that the scent rose to his nostrils. Scent of turf-smoke, his mother making bread at the table, her hair scented too, chestnut brown, not a sign of grey. A gentle, oval face, with long eyelashes, soft grey eyes, a saintly face.

Always got her way. She had appalling difficulties and

78

she disposed of them in the same way as she disposed of him. A middle-aged man, almost an old man, getting angry with his mother – it was ludicrous, especially as she was dead. Some memories of her would never die, no matter how he trod them into the earth. She never looked him in the face, that he could remember. She was at the table, bent over her bread, she knelt on the hearth repairing the fire, she stood with her bucket of feed for the hens and ducks, her voice high and clear, calling them to her, her back to the house and to him. When he came in from the fields she rapped out an order to him without turning her head. Even when she struck him, she avoided his eyes. Never look in the eyes of the damned. More ancient wisdom.

In this house of ghosts it was dangerous to think of her. Can the dead see the thoughts of the living? Some believe they can, else how could ghosts hold conversation, since they rarely speak? There was a singing in his ears, a new disturbance, a sort of humming, very unpleasant. Another glass – then he would hide the bottle. Jean-Paul would notice at once how little was left.

A flare from the Fort du Hâ warmed the window-pane for half a minute. What were they doing up there? They had plenty of prisoners still, poor devils, both men and women. He had never allowed Jeanne to come to Bordeaux. Out of sight out of mind, though no one seemed to be interested in finding her. But as long as that infernal machine stood in the Place Dauphine, someone might feel an urge to use it.

Burke lurched to his feet, holding the edge of the desk to steady himself. Jean-Paul had not mentioned Jeanne even once, and Burke had not asked after her because he feared to begin an unpleasant conversation. The same thought may have been in Jean-Paul's mind. Though he was a fervent revolutionary, or said he was, he had never commented on the fact that she was an aristocrat. He would have said if she had been arrested. Burke was certain of that. He would ask about her this evening, how often Jean-Paul had seen her, how she was managing the farm without him, whether he

79

had been taking the early vegetables to the market for her with those from Saint Jacques. That would be an easy, natural way to approach the subject.

He put the bottle to his mouth and took a long swallow. Funny how his throat no longer burned. Must have become accustomed to it. He corked the bottle tightly and knelt by his disgusting bed to bury it among the sacks. A bottle in bed is better than a wife, some would say. He began to laugh but his own voice uttering those peculiar sounds upset him. Man is the only animal that laughs, though monkeys smile. When they make laughing sounds they are angry or anxious. He fell on all fours twice while he was trying to stand upright, then succeeded, pausing for a moment to make sure he was steady before moving back towards the desk. He sat heavily, almost missing the chair, bruising his thigh, and remained there for a long time without moving. Drunk. The idea that Jean-Paul might find him like this was intolerable. The singing in his ears was louder. Perhaps he would soon be deaf.

Where was the towel – where had he put it? On the desk, of course. He found it with wandering fingers, clawed it towards him, clutched it tightly. If he dropped it on the floor he would never be able to pick it up in his present state. He straightened himself deliberately, breathing deeply. Instantly it seemed that an explosion went off in his head but it was clearer afterwards. He moved slowly towards the door and went out on to the landing, his troubles too pressing now for him to have patience with demons or visions. He found the banister, felt his way down, clung by the wall until he reached the back door, manipulated the bolts and got it open. A blast of windy rain struck him viciously, making his forehead ache. Just what he needed. Leaving the door open and the wind swirling inside, he stepped out into the yard and turned his face to the rain. Madness. He was going mad. This was how it happened. Next thing he would be jumping up and down and singing, all alone in the rain. More deep breathing, a splash of icy water from the tap on his face. Bells, damnable bells everywhere. Half an hour to go, or was it an hour? He had not counted the bells, though they were so important to him.

There was more light out here than in the house. The rain was bitterly cold but he could feel it restoring him to sanity. He walked cautiously towards the yard door, then back to the house, back and forth many times, his feet gradually steadying, his head clearing. A long, cool drink of Irish spring water would be heavenly now, the grass around the well a shining, juicy green, the hawthorns in bloom, meadow-sweet and honey-suckle thick by the low stone walls. Tears mixed with the rain on his face. Maudlin drunkenness, the most despicable kind. He wiped his face with the towel. Bells again, the sound carried peculiarly by the wind, seeming to fly high in the air, then to drop suddenly. Seven o'clock.

At the yard door he waited, as quiet as a cat. There he was, always on time. Burke felt tearful again, then squeezed his hands angrily on the towel. The knocks came, a little sharper than last night, as if he were agitated. Perhaps someone was coming into the lane. Burke worked on the bolts – he had meant to grease them to-day but had fallen asleep instead. They groaned and squealed but the noise of the wind covered the sound. He pulled the door inward. There were two figures. Braced for an attack, he slackened in a moment, realising that the second one was a woman. Out of his sick, stupid mouth came one word:

"Louise!"

Fortunately Jean-Paul was stupid too. He said: "Get a move on, Mademoiselle. She forced me to bring her, citizen. I told her you would be angry but there was no stopping her."

It was Jeanne, of course, peeping at him from under the hood of her cloak, bent under the weight of a huge sack that she was carrying. He seized the sack from her as Jean-Paul pushed her into the yard, forced the bolts back into place and led the way silently to the house.

81

# — 5 —

JEAN-PAUL REACHED THE DOOR FIRST AND WENT AT ONCE INTO the greasy kitchen to light a candle. He turned accusingly to Burke:

"You waste the candles. You have been in the dark. That's disgusting."

"Yes."

"High time you got out of this rat-hole."

"That reminds me to say that I want you to bring a cat when you come tomorrow night. This place needs a cat. Pick one of the quieter ones and put him in a strong bag."

Jeanne said: "Oh, my God!"

He had revealed at once that he was drunk though it was the thing he had most wanted to conceal. He probably smelled like a distillery too. He turned to Jeanne saying: "It was good of you to come. But it's dangerous. I told Jean-Paul not to allow it."

"I don't take orders from servants."

She said it contemptuously, unconcerned that Jean-Paul was too close to miss it. Burke put out a hand as if to stop her, then said: "Upstairs is warmer."

Again Jean-Paul led the way, Burke heaving the sack that Jeanne had carried, obviously loaded with blocks of wood. Halfway up he said: "How did you manage this?"

"Swinging and lifting. We took turns. I've got strong in the last few weeks. I've been working the land."

"Ploughing?"

"Not quite. Following the men and telling them what to do."

"On foot or on horseback?"

"Both. I know now why you get so tired. The men are

82

lazy – they do nothing unless they're told, then they do it badly unless you're watching them."

This time he held her back by the arm and whispered: "Jeanne, for God's sake stop talking like that. Don't you know you're in their hands?"

Now he had frightened her. She said: "I know no other way to talk."

"Then be quiet."

"I miss your help."

"It won't last forever."

He remembered his oath, written out so carefully. She was finished, poor, ineffectual, harmless Jeanne. He would not leave her until he was sure she was safe. He could compensate her with the Château, which had been in her family so long that it was like a limb to her. She was learning to farm. She would be able to carry on without him. But immediately, before this pious notion had time to take hold, he began to shrink from it. The Château would be wasted on her. She would be trapped into marriage with some peasant in no time, some greedy, ambitious lout who would covet her property and be willing to take her with it. Better to set her up in a corner of the huge building, in that set of rooms over the stables, or the bigger ones over the laundry. She could act as a housekeeper, keep an eye on the place when he was busy elsewhere. But if she were there, the bishop would not allow him to live at the Château at all, not even in another part of it. She would be considered a temptation, as indeed she would be on cold winter nights when the wind wailed across the flat soggy land with a lonesome sound and the bed-curtains shivered in the draughts. And he loved the Château. He felt at home there, the blood of his Norman ancestors responding to its spaciousness, the oppressed Irish part of him gloating over possession of a great house, even in a foreign country and without the regiment of servants that would have accompanied it in Ireland.

Jean-Paul lit the fire, his back to them even when Burke placed some logs from the bag on the hearth. His stooped, curved body was skeletally thin, and this, combined with his angular face and wild shock of hair, lit up by the yellow flames of the fire, gave him the look of one of the fantastic figures from Burke's vision of hell. Jeanne seemed unaware of the strange picture he made. She was busy at the table opening one of the other bags, taking out bread and a chicken and a bottle of wine, which she placed carefully in the middle of the desk. The sight of the bottle revived Burke's spirits, though he was crafty enough not to refer to it. She had taken off her cloak, and there was a soft, inviting curve to her body which he had scarcely noticed before. She began to cut up the chicken with a new precision, as if to show that she had really gained skills in his absence.

He said: "I miss our evenings at home."

"So do I."

"Why did you come?"

"To make sure you're all right. Jean-Paul said you were shivering. He said you're getting sick."

"It's not true. I'm as strong as an ox."

"Well, that's good. I have other reasons."

"What are they? If you want me to give up my fight, it's no use. I'm not leaving here until I win."

"Don't shout at me. I haven't asked you to give up anything."

He had never seen her angry before. It was an interesting change. Her insipidity had always bored him, so that even as he said he missed their evenings at home he knew that what he missed was the fire, the dinner, his books, his accounts, his new plans for goats and chickens and ducks and pigeons. When he looked up from these occupations his first glance was never for her but for his Irish setter bitch Banba, spread out on the rug before the wood fire, every feather elegantly in place, her gold-tipped ears slack, her paws twitching now and then as she dreamed of chasing plover and snipe with him over the marshes. Even when she was in pup she bounded along, flying over the tops of the reeds, her tail like a little sail, her feminine elegance apparent in every turn of her body. She was too independent to watch

84

him as Jeanne did, the anxious look turning into an apologetic smile when she caught his eye.

He asked sharply: "How is Banba?"

"The pups were born yesterday. She's all right."

"You should have told me at once. How many?"

"Eight. Five of them are red, three black but they look well."

"Are they feeding?"

"Perfectly, even the small one."

"Which colour is the small one?"

"Black."

"Thank God."

Red was what he always wanted. He had had her sent out from Ireland and had bred her several times with a strong black water-dog. Though none of the pups were as fine-boned as she was, they all had her speed and style.

"Mr. Burke," Jeanne said in English, "I am going to have your child."

His hands made fists before he could stop them and he lunged towards her. She sprang back with a squeal. Jean-Paul turned his head to stare at her. Burke forced his hands down slowly, almost casually, saying: "Are you sure?"

"Of course I'm sure."

God was laughing. This will teach Burke to think he can sin strongly and repent strongly. It was a real joke, Burke breeding horses and dogs and chickens and calves and goats and every creature that walked on two legs or four, then being amazed to find that he was in the same boat himself. Repenting, vowing to give up the lusts of the flesh when he was almost too old to enjoy them any longer, making a mockery of the laws of God – this fate of his was built in with his sins. She was watching him fearfully, one shoulder lifted as if she was ready to make for the door if he attacked her again. He had indeed attacked her, though unsuccessfully. He would not forget that. He dropped his big hands on the table and looked at them saying quietly: "I wouldn't have touched you. I got a shock."

"Why should you be angry with me? Do you think it's my doing?"

"No."

"You're the wise one – the old one – "

Her English gave out then and she signalled towards Jean-Paul to indicate that the conversation could not continue in his presence. He was listening. One could almost see the cock of his ears, like a dog's, his head on one side and his hands gone quiet, still holding a block. Perhaps he thought they were plotting against the Republic – why else would they use the enemy language? They watched him silently as he laid down the block and turned completely around to face them. The fire was burning nicely, the hearth no doubt still warm since yesterday.

Burke began to move towards the desk, even saying: "Well, time to eat. I'm starving, after this day's fast."

Jean-Paul said: "Citizen Burke, now you will have to marry her."

"What!"

Jean-Paul raised his two hands as if to ward him off, saying: "Don't threaten me. I'm giving you good advice. It has been noticed that you're not in a hurry to be married. That could mean that you still have hankerings after the Church. It's not my idea – it's what they say in the wine-shop."

"What the hell do I care what they say in the wine-shop?"

"It would be sensible if you did. Those are the people that rule the world now."

"When did you hear this?"

"Today. They're interested in your siege. And now after what Citizeness Rochechouart has told you, they'll be watching."

"How do you know what she has told me?"

Jean-Paul shrugged and gave him a pitying look.

"There is only one thing she could have told you that would make you angry enough to strike her. Your bitch has pupped, things are going well on the land, she has

86

brought you your dinner – what else could she have to tell you?"

Jeanne said bitterly: "Shut up and get on with your work."

"Mademoiselle, I'm on your side."

He turned back to the fire again, giving Burke time to send her a warning look. She faced him, her lower lip stuck out defiantly, like a hen defending her chicken from a dog. He was the dog, also the father of the chicken. It was unthinkable. He was hungry, he longed passionately to begin on that food.

Jean-Paul said, pushing the logs together with his foot: "Things are going badly since you went away, not at the farms but with the fodder for the army horses. They're saying in the city that you have turned traitor. They say you're more interested in this old heap of rubbish than you are in the success of the war in Italy."

"I'm not running the war in Italy. What has that to do with me?"

"You're the organiser for collecting the fodder. The farmers have begun to hoard the hay again, hoping the price will go up."

"God damn them for a bunch of greedy bastards!"

"That's the way to talk. Now you don't sound like a priest. But you're the only one that can say a thing like that to them."

"I'll skin them, I'll crucify them!"

"You can do nothing as long as you're in here. They say there will be more wars, horses and fodder will go sky-high. They're not anxious to sell their horses either but that's not really your business. Fodder and food for the market are your responsibility."

"I gave my orders. I told them exactly what to do. Why are they not doing it?"

"Now you're talking like a priest again. You should know that people don't do what's right, unless it's in their own interest."

"It is in their own interest."

"You'll have to go out and tell them so."

"I told you, I won't leave here until it's agreed that the College is Irish property."

"They might take your farms – that has been said too."

"Have you been gossiping about me?"

"I have a pair of ears and I use them. Would you prefer not to hear these things?"

"No, no. I'm sorry. Go on."

"At the stables just now there was a man from home, asking me where I was going with the lady. He asked if she was running away. I said she was going to visit a sick friend and he winked as if he knew who that was. If I know anything he has already sent word to someone or other that she is in Bordeaux."

"To whom? Where would he send word?"

"How the devil should I know? His kind always has a string of curiosity-mongers like himself. They collect information like a beetle collecting dirt."

"What else happened? What else?"

"I'll tell you if you stop swinging your fists at me. If a man in Saint Jacques did that to me he would never see tomorrow."

"All right. Go on."

"If you were married to Mademoiselle Jeanne here, living in the Château, they would do everything you tell them. They wouldn't have a leg to stand on."

"How?"

"Can't you see? They have always taken orders from the Château."

"That's all finished."

"I couldn't say this in any other company, but I can tell you that it will never finish. As long as one man is taller than another or has bigger balls – excuse me, Mademoiselle – there will never be equality in this world. The people in Saint Jacques know you're their boss and they won't move a toe for anyone else. Come home for the love of God, marry your woman and be done with it. This is only an old ruin full of mice - a cat is all that's needed here, as you said yourself. A wife and children in the Château is

88

what's needed in Saint Jacques and in every village in France."

"I can't do it. I swore an oath."

Jean-Paul spat in the fire contemptuously.

"You've been swearing oaths ever since I've known you. What's the good of oaths? You know as well as I do that when we're dead we're buggered. I want a chicken in the pot in my kitchen, not in some pot in the sky that I may never see."

Burke knew that there was a desperate appeal in this. Was anyone ever before faced with such a dilemma? The way of the transgressor became a nightmare when the sinner tried to reform. Oh God, may I repent but not yet – that was Saint Augustine. He was in much the same fix, living comfortably with his concubine and her children until his mother came along and made him leave them flat. Burke's mother would do the same, always able to poke her nose in between a man and his conscience. God forgive me – a good woman, dead too.

He said: "Give me a little time to think. I don't know enough of what is going on. Why did she have to come herself?"

"A message like hers has to be delivered personally."

Jeanne said, in that new bitter tone that he had never heard her use before: "You talk about me as if I were a dog or a horse. I haven't agreed to marry you. Is your conscience so tender all of a sudden? I hadn't noticed that it was like this until now."

"Pour me some wine, for the love of God, and let me think!"

There was silence while she filled a glass for him and laid out the food she had brought, on a cloth. He could feel their eyes on him while he ate, like a couple of farm boys watching a temperamental bull. He champed forcefully, crunching the bones of the chicken to get out the last sliver of meat, splashing more wine into his glass and swallowing it with a mouthful of bread. If what Jean-Paul said was true, the people were already beaten. The golden age was over, the big-wigs were back in the saddle, orders would be rapped out and the workers would run to obey as they had always done, as they had done when the orders came from peasants and workers like themselves. The idea of democracy was a myth once conscience became public property. Then the thick-skinned took over and directed the minds of the rest. Where did this leave Burke? Jean-Paul saw clearly that his first duty was to the living, in his own villages. Burke recognised now that if he walked out of the College to reorganise the farmers he would be a hero once more in the cause of the new France, doubling the prestige he had gained when he bearded those two demons of the Revolution in their hell at the Hotel d'Angleterre. It was very tempting. He was bone tired, frightened of the dark and the dirt and the lonesome nights and the impasse he had created. More frightening than all these was the fact he recognised, because of his newly acquired insight into his measly past, that he was gripped by a kind of mystic excitement at the thought of his child. It was something entirely primitive and painful, strong as a hangman's rope. He turned quickly to Jeanne and touched her unyielding arm.

"Pour me some more wine, like a good girl."

Strange that he had noticed a change in her before she told him her ghastly news. In ordinary circumstances, whatever those were, this would be the perfect moment in her life. She was surely hating him for destroying it, distrusting him utterly, seeing deep into his mean, narrow mind.

She said as she filled his glass: "I have other news for you too. You have some visitors from Ireland."

"Oh, God. Who are they?"

"Don't worry. I haven't told them the story of our lives. There is a man and a woman. He looks as if he ought to be her servant but they probably sleep together." Was it he who had made her so coarse? "Her name is Rose French and he has such an Irish name I can't remember it."

"Colman Folan?"

"That's it. He's tall and thin and well dressed but he has the face of a peasant."

"He is a peasant. I know him."

"There is a third one who is obviously a gentleman. Perhaps they are both his servants, though I never before saw a gentleman travelling with a woman servant."

"Who is he?"

"Edmund Brien – I got that much but he speaks such bad French that I can't make out what he's saying. He understands me better than I do him, especially when I speak slowly. I can't take care of all those people – the woman is useless though we brought in good food specially for them. She doesn't seem to like anything we cook, not even the bread. I tell her it's the best we can get but she makes faces and sulks and says things under her breath to the man Colman."

"He speaks French?"

"He thinks he does but it would make the hens laugh to hear him."

So much for Lady Sophie's classes. What misfortune had brought them so soon? Her letter had suggested that it might be a month or two before they would appear but the letter had been slow in coming. And Edmund Brien had not been mentioned at all, nor Rose French, who was suspected of leading on the older boy, the heir to the throne.

Jean-Paul smirked and said: "Good news, you see, citizen. You must be delighted to have visitors from that wonderful country of yours."

"How many people know they are there?"

"Everyone from Bordeaux to Saint Jacques – they asked their way at every cross-roads. We knew they were coming hours before they appeared."

They were both watching him with open derision. He drank gloomily and held out his glass for more. Jeanne filled it, standing close by the table. He realised that she had not sat down since she came in and he stood up quickly and offered her the chair. He knew by the way she sank into it that she needed it badly. While he was reflecting that she should have had the spirit to demand it she said: "I was beginning to wonder if your manners would ever recover."

He returned her glare with interest, the thought flashing through his mind that if he was fated to be a husband he would not consent to be the hen-pecked kind. Hens – he would never get away from them. He felt a belly-laugh rise up in him before he could stop it and a moment later Jean-Paul laughed too, then said: "Thank God. I thought I'd never hear you laugh again."

Jeanne leaned forward suddenly to grab the wine-bottle but Burke forestalled her, saying as he refilled his glass: "Don't worry – wine won't do me any harm. It was the plum brandy that did for me last night."

The face she made reminded him of Sophie and he said: "Did the Irish people bring any letters?"

"If they did they haven't given them to me. Edmund, the gentleman, says his half-brother lives in Saintes. I said he must be in a hurry to go there but they say they will wait until you come. I said that might be a long time and Edmund said they might go to Saintes and come back again. They behave as if they had a right to stay as long as they like, to come and go as they please."

Burke said: "That's the way in Ireland – all one big family."

"What am I to do with them? The young man, Edmund, seems to think I'm some kind of servant. I don't know how to explain things to him. It's dreadful having three foreigners in the house who can hardly understand a word we say to them."

"What can I do? I'm not going to lose all these weeks of my siege for them."

He could stay here until they went away – there is a good side to everything.

Jean-Paul said: "Write them a letter. Tell them they must go to Saintes, that you can't take care of them now with all your other responsibilities. Tell them you're a Frenchman now." He was at that again. "I'll take them the letter and I'll make sure they know what it means."

"No. That is impossible. Their family are patrons of mine."

"You don't need patrons."

"How long have they been there?"

Jeanne said: "Since yesterday, but it feels longer."

Burke said accusingly to Jean-Paul: "You didn't tell me last night."

"I hoped they would go away. Citizen Burke, are you going to keep the young lady in this dump for the night? Where will she sleep? On that heap of rags in the corner? Or would you like to fix a bed on top of the desk?"

Burke roared: "Keep your nose out of my business!"

"Think it out. A donkey wouldn't do what you're doing now. The answer is simple. If you won't write a letter, leave the barricades at the front and we'll all go out by the back way. I get back over the wall and bolt the door from the inside and climb out again, and we go home to Saint Jacques and do our thinking in peace. And you can dispose of your visitors."

There was sense in it. He had Ysabeau's letter to shake under the nose of anyone who interfered. The prospect of getting out into the fresh air was so sweet that he had to treat it with great suspicion. One mistake now could lose the whole war. Another glass of wine – generals on the battle-field live on the stuff. It gives courage, insight, clarity of vision. He shook the last drops out of the bottle, enough to fill the glass halfway. Make it last. Jeanne was nibbling at a chicken-leg. Women in her condition are always hungry but they shouldn't touch wine. What did she think of him? She certainly gave him no loving looks that he could see at this moment. And she should, since he had rescued her from death and taken care of her for a long time. All over France there must be women in her condition as a con-sequence of being rescued by blackguards like himself. Wars are all the same. Horses and women get it in the neck.

He said carefully: "If I were to go out now, I could come back by the same route tomorrow. Is anyone watching this place?"

Jean-Paul said: "They're not exactly watching, but they're taking notice. No one wants to be the first to chase you out.

93

They have no orders from Paris yet. Wine-shop talk. There isn't much happening these days and you're a convenient sensation."

Burke emptied the glass in one long swallow, then looked at it in dismay saying: "Only one bottle? You were going to leave me with a thin night."

"There is another," Jeanne said, and rummaged in the bag.

"Don't give it to him," Jean-Paul said sharply. "He needs all the wits he's got."

"He says he's well able for it," she said, handing it to him calmly.

"There's a devil in the bottle, as you say yourself," Jean-Paul said. "Give me a drop too before I lose my mind."

Burke generously let him drink the first glassful, then refilled it quickly for himself. Jean-Paul wiped his mouth with the back of his hand, saying: "What are we going to do?"

"As you said – go out by the back way, home to the Château and think it all out in peace."

"Remember, if you do that you can't blame me afterwards. It's your own decision."

"Why are you getting nervous now? You've been urging me for weeks to leave this place. Now you come up with good reasons and a good way of doing it, and the next thing you seem to have changed your mind."

"I haven't changed my mind. You'd try the patience of a saint. I only said you needn't blame me if something goes wrong."

"Nothing will go wrong. Don't you agree, Jeanne?"

"I think you should get out as soon as possible and come home. I don't see that you're doing any good here and you're needed at home."

God help her, she felt quite safe. But he saw now that she was the reason why he must abandon his defence of the College. Once people had begun to talk about him, they would think of her and wonder about her position. Someone might think it would be as well to get rid of her. If Irish property was to be seized and sold, as was done with the College, then the Château could become public property too, since it belonged to Burke.

*Aha! So that is why you have been defending the College.*

The demon had appeared from nowhere and was perched in the corner of the room, just outside the candlelight. Burke put up a sweaty hand to ward off the sight of it, shouting:

"No, you imp of hell! That never occurred to me until this moment and if it had it would have made no difference."

Jean-Paul said sharply: "Get that damned bottle from him."

Burke was too quick for them. He filled another glass, drank it and filled it again before they took away the bottle. Jeanne looked frightened. He said: "It's all right. I get confused from being alone."

"He's in the rats," Jean-Paul said. "I told you not to give him any more. I've seen it coming on for the last few nights."

"The rats?"

'The jigs – call it whatever you like. He's seeing things. Put him sitting down. Get the things together."

While she gathered up the remains of the meal and his books, and while Jean-Paul was kicking the fire apart and stacking the remaining logs to one side of the hearth, Burke sat watching them quietly. They were breaking up his home, evicting him. He had grown into this room, seen it change and become familiar. The things he had written here would stay with him forever. The diary – he lurched to his feet to get it from the drawer, a few miserable pages covered with greyish scribbles. He rolled them up and pushed them into his pocket. Suddenly the demon said:

*Keeping them to show to God when you get to the other side? You're leaving here but you needn't think you'll get away from me. I'll be with you all your days, even to the consummation of the world.*

"Blasphemer!"

*Yes, it's my trade. The woman is watching you, listening to you. She is mine, I think. I might trade her after a while if I don't find her interesting enough. Louise would be a good exchange. The Church founders on sex, not on philosophical points.*

"Begone, Satan."

*I would have expected better from you. That's old-fashioned. And if you remember, it didn't work the first time. I took you up to the pinnacle of the temple and showed you all the farms of the Garonne. Neat trick, isn't it? When Dr. Glynn was climbing the scaffold they read him out pieces of news about the success of the Revolution.*

"It's a good Revolution."

*Excellent, from all points of view, including mine. Give the people what they want and they'll come to me like homing pigeons.*

"Boaster! Liar!"

*Be careful. I don't like rude sinners.*

Burke began to mumble to himself: "*Te Deum laudamus, Te Dominum confitemur. Te a eternum patrem omnis terra veneratur, Tibi omnes angeli, Tibi coeli et universae potestates* – What next? Oh, God I'm forgetting, *Tibi cherubim et seraphim incessabili voce proclamant.* He's gone, by the hokey he's gone, the little bastard."

Jeanne's voice crying broke in on him somehow and he turned to her saying: "I'm all right – just been in here too long – you're right, it's time I came home. It is not good for man to be alone."

The demon flashed back for a long moment to glare at him with flat grey eyes, then disappeared. Burke rubbed his hand along his forehead and stood up. They were ready to leave, Jean-Paul swinging one of the bags, Jeanne carrying the other, folded. She was a pitiful sight. By a great effort he managed not to stagger as they went towards the door. His hand in his pocket held the roll of papers – what to do with them would be another day's thinking. Jean-Paul carried the candle, holding it high to light all of their steps. The banisters were a comfort. Slide each foot forward, feel each tread and there was no danger. In the hall the mice scuttled. Burke felt like weeping, as he had done last night. Straighten the back, inside and out. No way of locking the back door except from the inside with the bolt. He would have to risk leaving it open, rely on the back gate being locked. Jean-Paul was working the bolt, the dry metal squeaking and squawking like a flock of seagulls. Never did that job with the candle-grease. The gate was open into the blackness of the lane. Jeanne was the first out, then Burke, then Jean-Paul handed his bag to her and went back inside, closing the door behind him.

The hands on his arms were such a surprise that at first he could scarcely believe in them. He shook himself as a dog does after coming out of the water. The grip tightened and there were voices, one calling for a light, two or three men struggling to hold him, Jeanne giving tiny yelps as if she had not the breath for anything more.

Burke roared: "Get your paws off me, you bunch of louts. I'll knock the whole lot of you into kingdom come."

The light flared and there they were, policemen, five of them, one holding Jeanne by the arms, two trying to restrain him, and one with the torch.

"Put that torch away from me before you burn my eyebrows. What do you think you're doing?"

The fifth man said rapidly: "We charge you, Citizen Burke, with sheltering Citizeness Jeanne Rochechouart and hiding her from the jurisdiction of the people of France."

"Rubbish. This woman is my wife. I have every right to shelter her."

Shocked back to sobriety, Burke suppressed the yell of fury that rose up in him as he saw Jean-Paul straddle the wall. That scoundrel, Burke would never have believed it of him – why should he have done such a thing? The torch was turned on him, the light from below showing up only his head and shoulders, his hair blown in the wind and his mouth open ludicrously as he took in the scene below him. Jeanne had stopped yelping and was standing as close as a frightened child to Burke. He put his arm around her and held her to him.

The policeman who had spoken before said: "How long has she been your wife?"

"Long enough for her to be carrying my child, and if

97

she miscarries because of you, you'll pay for it with your skin."

"I'd advise you not to threaten me, citizen."

But he was taken aback, all right. He looked up at Jean-Paul, not asking who he was – further proof that it was he who had ratted. Who else knew that Jeanne was coming here tonight?

But Jean-Paul was chattering: "Of course she's his wife – if you come out to Saint Jacques d'Ambes tomorrow you can see the certificate in the Mayor's office. We all know about it – a year ago last January, we had a party that went on for two days until everyone was plastered. Citizen Burke, I told you that man at the stables was getting curious."

"All right, all right."

Better to shut him up before he shot off too much information. Burke guessed that the raid had not been sanctioned. The police often conducted these in the hope of being congratulated but perhaps they were beginning to regret this one. What was that story about his marriage being celebrated a year ago last January? And the proof, if these busybodies came out to look for it – his ruin was only postponed for a day. Jeanne clutched his arm and buried her face in his cloak, meaning, perhaps, that she was not going to deny Jean-Paul's statement. If it was a plot between them, they were risking their silly skins. He would eat them all before breakfast.

The talking policeman said: "Why are you coming out by the back way at this hour of the night?"

"I might ask you what you're doing in this lane at this hour of the night – spying on me? Why shouldn't I come out? Have I been sentenced to stay in the College for life? I'm going home to my own farm-house with my wife, by your leave, if you'll get out of my way. You can't hold me, and if you did you might find yourself regretting it tomorrow morning."

My wife – how easily it rolled out of him. Burke liked the sound of it, though it was the biggest joke of his life. But she was his wife in God, in charity. Every privilege has its concomitant responsibility or to put it another way, everything in this world must be paid for sooner or later. Now to get home as quickly as possible and plan the next move. The certificate of marriage could be squeezed out of the Mayor with threats and cajolings but it would have to be arranged this very night. If they wanted him to get the farmers to cough up the fodder, this would be a small price to pay. They knew no one else could do it. After he had settled the question of the certificate he would ride out and encounter a few of the big ones that talked the loudest. They would have half of the work done for him by the time he reached the smaller ones. Pack of little bastards – thinking they could become chevaliers of commerce before they were able to count up to ten.

And those Irish people – at the Château – suddenly he roared: "Get out of my way. Do you think I have all night for palaver?"

Jean-Paul slid to the ground. The policemen looked at each other uneasily, then the one who carried the light spoke for the first time:

"We'll escort you to the stables, citizen. It's dangerous at this hour of the night."

Burke said blandly: "Thank you. One of you could carry a couple of bags."

"Certainly."

So he marched along the lane at the head of the procession, Jeanne clutching his arm, Jean-Paul at the other side, five policemen and a torch to bring up the rear, thus making it clear to all and sundry that James Burke was the leader of the band.

# PART TWO

## _1797_

# _6_

Rose French said:

"I found your diary quite easily. A silly place to hide it, behind the desk in the rent-room. It was the first place I looked. But all your hiding-places are silly, obvious. Not that you could hide anything from me forever. I find everything eventually. It took me a long time to get the key of the wine-cellar but I've had a good supply for months now. I know where you keep your hoard of gold money, and your list of unsatisfactory tenants, and your careful plans for next year's planting. Stupid, that is. Why hide such things, when you discuss them freely with all and sundry at every opportunity? Everyone gets a tuck in the stomach when you begin, especially at dinner-time, when we should be relaxed. Disgusting details of horse-breeding are not for the dinner-table. Your Jeanne does her best to stop you but you're such an egoist that you brush her off like a fly and go right on with your talk, talk, talk."

Her voice had risen. She stopped. All her life she had been told that her habit of sitting alone in her room, talking, was dangerous, immoral, even a sign of insanity. Talking to herself, her mother and her sisters called it, but she never talked to herself. All of her speeches were addressed to someone in particular. She often talked to Burke, that great bag of meal. Punch him in one place and he bulged in another. When Rose sat, expressionless, her hands folded in her lap, answering yes and no as befitted her station, she could cheerfully have kicked the guts out of him. His head seemed stuffed with hen-food and hay and beets and tobacco and all kinds of grain. No room there for anything that didn't either come out of or trot on the ground. Mud-coloured, all through.

But the diary contradicted some of that. It was hard to believe there was so much fire in him. She read it many times, each time replacing it exactly where she had found it. There was no way of knowing whether or not he looked at it himself. He certainly seemed to have no time. Back from the farms in the evenings, after dinner, he played with the baby for a while, then sat in his work-room with the door open while he did some accounts, finally coming back to the drawing-room and reading one of his heavy books while Jeanne chatted with Edmund and did her embroidery. No embroidery for Rose. She was having no more of that.

Even after a year in his house, Burke's feelings towards Jeanne remained a mystery to Rose. He seemed at least as much attached to his dogs. In exactly the same tone as he used to summon them, every night he would say to Jeanne: "Come along, now. Time for bed."

Then she would look at Edmund, fold her work and put it in its basket and stand up slowly and follow Burke out of the room, with a series of movements that matched in time the movements of the dogs as they stretched themselves and rambled towards the door. No one invited Rose to go. For all she knew, they would not have cared if she spent the night sitting silently in the drawing-room. Once she had tried staying on, to see what would happen, just sat there after he had extinguished the candles and there was no light but the flame of the wood fire, on its last legs. Jeanne had looked back at her doubtfully but Burke said in one of those half-whispers of his that were obviously intended to be heard: "Leave her to sulk, if she wants to. She'll come when she gets over it."

Pretending an absent-minded yawn, Rose stood up and followed them. When Burke teased her like this it was almost a relief. At least he knew she was alive. There was every reason for him to notice her. She was a handsome woman, though some might think that at thirty-six she had one foot in the grave. Compared with Burke she was a child – he must be nearly sixty. Rose had pale gold hair that curled beautifully and pale, unfreckled skin, a perfectly oval face, long, narrow, aristocratic hands and feet, a slender, sinuous body which moved flowingly as she walked. She studied herself often in the glass in her room, to make sure she was not deceiving herself, as poor Nellie Fahy at home in Rocklawn used to do when she tied a red ribbon around her spherical body and imagined it made her look enticing.

Rose knew she was exquisite. She knew also why she was left while Nellie could go out and pick up a man with a flick of the finger. Nellie was free because she was nothing. Rose was hamstrung because she belonged to poor Catholic Irish gentry – six sisters, three brothers, brought up in a wreck of a house by a silly mother and a dispirited father whose sedgy farm and sheep-bitten pastures could barely make a living for them. Nothing for it but to make governesses of all the girls. Her older sisters went off one by one and came back for their annual week's holiday looking meaner and thinner, and with noticeably shorter tempers.

When it came to Rose's turn, she went to Mount Brien looking and feeling like a lady but in two shakes the old bitch of a grandmother had asked her: "And the rest of the family, my dear? Your brother is in Castlebar now, I believe?"

No more to be said. The shop in Castlebar had put paid to all their chances. That bright boy, Tom, not content to be a hungry gentleman, by going into trade with the two younger brothers, had ensured that their sisters would go hungry for life. They could marry businessmen, Tom said, but no businessman would have one of that type of lady, with their embroidery and their singing and their flower-gardening and their miserable taboos about clothes, hair, table manners, and all the things that touch the body. Businessmen liked their wives to look like ladies but they also wanted them to be able to do a bit of scrubbing if required. As for associating with the lower orders, the tenant farmers' sons and the labourers, the very idea made the French sisters shudder. After old Lady Sophie Brien had asked her question, there was no hope of a *coup de foudre* at a ball – there was no hope of a ball.

105

It was a pity that Rose loved singing so much. The happiest moments in her life came from the use of her strong, clear mezzo-soprano voice, well-trained by Mama who had had good lessons when she was young, before she married into the miserable Frenches. Mama would never sing now. She had turned into a bitter old pill, with time. Rose, watching with the sharp eye of the youngest member of the family, saw how it happened, the last bits and pieces of her wedding china broken, her last silver spoons stolen or worn out by use in the kitchen, her inlaid rosewood work-table scratched and chipped by the visiting dressmaker who would have been kept to the linen-room if she had not been the remains of a lady too.

Alone in her bedroom, the sacred refuge that she enjoyed since there were only three sisters left, Rose sang:

"It is not that I love you less
Than when before your feet I lay,
But to prevent the sad increase
Of hopeless love I keep away."

One sunny spring morning when she was sixteen, she had gone through it several times and was glorying in the obvious improvement when beastly Tom opened the door a crack and said: "Is that hard to sing?"

Delighted with his interest, elevated by her own power and success, Rose fell head-first into the trap, answering: "Not at all. It's very easy, once you get the phrasing right."

Too late she saw the ugly gleam in his eye. He shouted: "Well, it's damned hard to listen to!"

Then he banged the door shut and left her in a state of quivering rage from which she never quite recovered. That was her first death. The joy of singing was gone for good. She became aware that she was the butt of jokes from the scullery to the drawing-room. Tom saw to that. Why did he do it? A general hatred of life at Rocklawn – he was never tired of enumerating its horrors, almost as if he thought the rest of the family was unaware of them. Who could fail to detest the basins set to catch the drips in the attic, the cracked stove in the kitchen which the blacksmith refused to mend any more until he was paid, the broken pane in the landing window, damaged by a wind-blown bird many years ago, the fearful winter damp and cold when they all sat huddled around the turf fire, quarrelling, sparing the candle as long as a flame would rise on the hearth, loth to go to their icy bedrooms while hating each other's company almost to the point of murder? And the hunger, barely assuaged by the disgusting meals of boiled poultry or half-cooked game and the eternal potatoes, with damp bread from the broken stove – these were the best that Nellie could do, and Mama was too much of a lady to know how to cook.

The second death came soon afterwards. Watching the blood ooze from the pigeon breasts one day, Rose laid down her fork, revolted, and said: "Let me do the cooking. I know I could manage better than this."

Tom burst into a loud laugh, then said: "I can see you gutting the chickens and ducks and making giblet soup of the gizzard and neck."

"Nellie would do those things for me."

Mama and Papa sat silent. Jemima and Maria, that pair of vipers, joined Tom at once in baiting her: "Nellie is going to work for you now. You could train her to be a lady's maid."

"She could brush your gorgeous hair."

"She could draw your bath."

"She could trim your toe-nails."

"Mama, please!" Rose knew she was breaking down. "I only offered to cook, for all of us. I know I could do it. Please let me."

Mama said offhandedly: "Why not? It could hardly be worse than this. You always had a vulgar, practical streak in you. Perhaps you will be quite good at it."

The others sniggered but Rose felt she had triumphed. She went straight to the kitchen, instructing Nellie who was willing and friendly for the first day but who then began unaccountably to snigger in the exact manner of the two sisters upstairs. Rose was bewildered, until she discovered that all three of them were conniving at destroying her efforts, sometimes in quite ingenious ways. They watered the soup that she had carefully boiled and left ready on the stove at night, so that it was sour next morning, they dropped slugs into the cabbage as it went to the table, they closed the dampers on the wretched stove so that it smoked the pastry that she had laboured over so long, they put a chicken's head inside the duck that she had put to roast.

At this Nellie turned against them and said: "Miss Rose, can't you see what they're at?"

"No."

When she heard, she went to Mama who laughed and said: "Where's your sense of humour?"

"Were you aware of it?"

"Don't question me in that tone, Miss. I'm your mother. Yes, I knew what they were doing. I thought you were a fool not to see it at once."

Alone in her room Rose made a short speech to Mama:

"Two can hate. You hate me. I would be a fool indeed not to see it. I don't understand it but there is no need. I swear by the God above us that I will get out of this house as soon as I can and never come back."

By the time, five dreadful years later, that she was summoned to Mount Brien to be governess to the three small boys, she had learned to smile noncommittally in every public situation except funerals. With the children she was more free, but as they grew older even this relief was denied to her. Children, she found, were perfidious, perhaps because of their weakness. And none of them cared a fig for music.

She told some of this to the Frenchman that she called Rabbit, on the second night that he came to her bed. The first night she scarcely spoke at all. She had been aware that he was watching her, all evening long. More than three years ago, in 1792, he arrived at Mount Brien with André de Lacy, Sir Maurice Brien's son-in-law, and they went into conference in an upstairs room with various men who came specially to see them. At five o'clock they came down to dinner, and she saw Rabbit gasp with delight at the sight of her. He made no secret of it, staring like a starved animal at its dinner, a *coup de foudre* without any doubt. Now and then she gazed back at him as they sat formally in the drawing-room, lifting her eyes deliberately from her damned embroidery. The old lady was more animated than Rose had ever seen her, hanging on the Frenchmen's words as if she were listening to God. Otherwise she might have seen the invitation in Rose's glance. With all her strength Rose was saying: "Have me if you want. I'm ready. Come to me. I want you."

Her tongue moved silently behind her closed lips. Hours later, in her room at the top of the house, cluttered with the throw-outs of various bedrooms and sitting-rooms, she stood in the middle of the floor and waited for him, talking to him softly.

"I saw you watching me. You're a long way from home. We're two of a kind and the same age. I know you have no wife. Don't be afraid. I'm waiting for you. The door is open to light your way. You saw me, the only one to go up the last flight of stairs. Use your head. Go into your room, shut the door, and when the house is quiet you can do what you like. Come, come, come! What are you waiting for? Are you another of those fools that visit this house? Politics and wars and plots and revolutions are all they care about. I'll call you Rabbit – my rabbit. I don't care a rattling damn that you're no beauty. I'm beauty enough for two. I'll be quite satisfied with you."

Even now, in Burke's Château outside Bordeaux, Rose remembered with joy that delightful period of waiting for Rabaut to come to her room. He came, though she had not really believed he would, and it was not quite as easy as she had imagined. But she was a fast learner and her Rabbit was delighted with her. Afterwards, dazed, she lay on her back and saw him through a fog, staring at her as he had done downstairs.

He said: "You beauty!"

She closed her eyes. That was not what she wanted to hear. She had not spoken since she heard him moving softly along the corridor, just opened the door wider and went back to stand in the middle of the room. He seemed to understand that there was no need for her to speak. After a long time she said: "I knew you would come."

"I knew you would welcome me. You have never had a lover before."

She doted on that word. She said: "No. My life has been too narrow."

"Rose, Rose French, you are a perfect rose."

Did he love her? He didn't say so. Perhaps it was never said. She loved him, madly, pitilessly. He was her life-blood, her heart-beat, her salvation. With some sense of caution she refrained from saying these things but she described a little of life at home in Rocklawn and the reasons why she stayed on at Mount Brien though the children were grown up.

She said: "I have no other home but this."

"I thought you were a cousin, a relation."

"No. They keep me out of charity."

"My poor Rose."

So he came to her again, once, before they had to go away. He tried to make an excuse to stay. She heard him say he wanted to see Colman Folan again, the son of the old family nurse, a shepherd now and a conspirator like the rest of them, but André de Lacy said there was no need. On the second night she told him how she hated most women, with their wicked tongues and their conniving and man-oeuvring. Perhaps that was a mistake. Perhaps it turned him against her.

On his last morning he asked her to take him to the kitchen garden to select a peach, warm from the high stone wall. The gardeners took no notice of them. He held her hand as they walked between the box hedges – surely he loved her then. She could sense it in the way he moved each of her fingers in turn, as if he were trying to record them in his memory.

He said: "Rose, I will come back. It will be next year. Can you wait for me?"

"Yes, I'll wait."

That was an easy promise, since she had no other prospects.

"If anything should happen you would write and tell me."

A baby was what he meant but there was no reason why she should not write to him anyway. No answer – not a single letter, unless old Sophie apprehended them as they came in. But Rose searched every nook and cranny when the old bitch was out for her walk and never found anything. She listened but his name was never mentioned in her presence.

That could be deliberate. Rose suspected that Sophie knew of her infatuation though she never said so openly. After Rabbit went away with André, trotting down the long avenue with their servants following, Rose was overwhelmed by her pain. It was like a sickness. She sat perfectly still by the window for hours, almost as if she thought he might come back. When she was summoned to dinner she sent a message to say that she was ill. Inevitably Sophie appeared to find out what was going on. She took one look at Rose and said: "You had better stay in your room for a few days. I'll send up your meals."

So she was an ally in covering up the sordid little drama of the deserted woman with hopes of marrying a fly-by-night soldier. Rabbit never wrote, not even once. Why should he? She was easy game and he could have her again any time he came back. But he did not come back either. There was plenty of talk of André, the son-in-law, but Rabbit had completely vanished. There was no one she could ask. Colman, perhaps, when he came once a month to pay in the money from the sheep, but Rose could not bring herself to speak of Rabbit to him. She and Colman always sat in the lowest places at the table. Having Colman in the dining-room at all was a bone of contention between Sophie and her daughter-in-law, Lady Fanny, but Sophie always won such battles easily. He was a child of the house, she said, and he was to be treated as such.

Rose could easily have asked him casually: "Have you ever again heard of that Frenchman with the peculiar name – Rabaut? Has he been in Ireland lately?"

111

She knew it was impossible. Besides, she made a point of not speaking to Colman during meals. He was a servant; she was not. Any fraternisation would rather lower her than raise him, though no one called her a servant.

She had been quite right. She was in constant danger. Even Burke, that renegade priest, that lecher, that father of a bastard child, that pinch-penny peasant turned lord of the Château – he lumped her among the servants in his diary. Chasing the servants, he said of Hubert's supposed advances to Rose, though it seemed that Sophie had called her the governess. She had heard nothing good of Burke in Mount Brien, as she could quickly tell him now if she wanted to. She said softly:

"You have a nerve to call me a servant. You should just hear what they say about you. When you wrote that in your diary, you were planning to repent of your sins, to make your soul, as they say in Ireland. That didn't last long. You're an idiot about that child, and your Jeanne doesn't care a curse for you, as I could tell you if you ever asked me. What do you think she does all day, while you're out on your rounds? Surely you don't imagine that she sits here waiting for the dear father of her son to come home? She's no fool, your Jeanne. The sight of you using her father's rooms and playing squire on his land drives her wild. She only puts up with it because she has no alternative. Without you she would have no roof over her head – she would have no head. That's all you want, you great lout – a good, obedient dog. Perhaps you wouldn't be too concerned if you knew of her goings-on with Edmund, though if I know my Irish peasants you would go through a parade of being the outraged husband. Husband! Jean-Paul told me you're not married at all, that that was a *blague* invented to get the police off your back.

"I can see Jeanne's point of view. I'm all for saving one's skin. People who submit to their misfortunes deserve all they get. No more of that for me – it took me a long time to come to my senses. It was pretty clever of Jeanne to crawl into your bed, once she knew her constitution was tough enough to stand it. You would be a good deal too unsavoury for me.

"But she has a mind like a sewer. She actually thinks that I sleep with Colman. She can't imagine how we could travel together without doing that too. The idea of a woman named French, however poor, sleeping with that peasant – I'd as soon sleep with a horse. I wish I were as tough as Jeanne, as well able to tolerate the hell of living. It gets no less with time – none of your business what I'm talking about."

Had he answered? The door was locked. She was alone in the pleasant spacious room on the second floor, with three windows looking out on the park and the gardens. Jeanne gave her that room the first evening, when she arrived exhausted with Edmund and Colman. It was a replica of the room at the far end of the corridor that Jeanne shared with Burke. In between were two rooms that Edmund and Colman used when they came back from their travels. Colman was away a great deal but lately Edmund was spending far more time here, up to no good when Burke was out. Rose laughed aloud.

"They go off to the orchard and lie in the grass beyond the trees. If it rains they just use Edmund's room. It's your own fault for keeping such regular hours. By the time you come roaring in for your dinner they're sitting like a couple of pussy-cats full of milk. You seem quite unaware of what's going on between them, though I noticed it at once. It was as if birds flew from one of them to the other, little red birds with orange-coloured beaks. I don't see how you can miss it. You just sit like the clod you are, shifting your big doggy eyes from your book to the fire, as if you didn't hear a word of the conversation, or as if you had talked yourself out over dinner. It's very innocent conversation, about Edmund's half-brother Robert and his wife and children in Saintes, and when Colman will be back from Paris, like the talk of strangers but all with a double meaning. Now Edmund pairs me off with Colman too, smirking at me every time his name is mentioned. The only time you lift

113

your fat head is if there is talk of farming, cattle or horse breeding, chickens or ducks or pheasants. Then you look up and you have something to say, which proves you're keeping one ear open all the time.

"Oh, I can talk to you about those things! I know so much more about them than those two, and I know how important they are, not just to you but to the whole world. Your horses, that you collect for the army – there could be no war without them. When you told us about coming home, leaving the College and everything you had fought for so hard, Edmund and Jeanne looked at each other and gave that odious smirk. I could see that you were torn in two. When I found the diary it was all much clearer. I know exactly how you feel about Ireland too. Now in the spring the days are lengthening and there is a cold, clear light over the fields and on the bare trees. Clouds blow across and the wind sings in the tops of the pine-trees and sends the jackdaws wild while they try to build their nests. They caw and shriek and flop about and drop pieces of clean branches on the grass, beech and ash with tiny black buds at their tips. The daffodils are just beginning to bud and the primroses are mixed with the wild violets at the edge of the stream by the avenue gate. There are long threads of watercress on the stream. The bees are beginning to wake up – "

Rose stood up quickly and went to the wardrobe that filled the end wall of the room, fumbling in her pocket for the key. She watched herself approach, in the long glass, noticing that even in her hurry she kept her back straight and her head high. Five o'clock – the stable clock was striking. It was legitimate by her own rules to have a glass of wine now, before Burke got home. It gave her courage – it gave her life – it gave her energy to go down and face that fat old bitch of a henwife in the kitchen – Anna – and force her to cook the things that Burke liked. It gave her strength to smooth away every sign of life from her face when she encountered Jeanne, to give her monosyllabic answers to questions about dinner, assuring her that all was in order.

114

Rose had moved deliberately into the position of house-keeper, since Jeanne had no taste for it, and since there was no stigma attached to caring for the kitchen, in France. On the contrary, Rose found that it gave her prestige, established her with rights over cupboards and keys that would other-wise have been cut off from her. In October, when the wine was brought in, she made sure to get hold of a key to the cellar. It had been a dangerous operation, the only time she had ever penetrated Burke's bedroom. Having searched everywhere else without success, she had become convinced that the keys could only be there, and there they were, labelled in Irish: '*Fíon.*' She almost laughed aloud at that. There were two, and she abstracted one and had the journey-man blacksmith copy it, not the one in the village. The hours when the key was missing from Burke's room were dangerous but she picked a day when a foal was dying, and he was not home until seven o'clock. Edmund and Jeanne were disporting themselves in the garden until six, by which time the man had come back with the key and gone off about his business. She always wore her outdoor cloak when she went to the cellar, so that she had a ready hiding-place if she ran into anyone on her way back upstairs.

She poured the wine carefully, not to disturb the sediment. The last of the sunlight caught the glass so that a paler jewel glowed inside the ruby darkness. She let it sit for a moment. She loved wine but she had more sense than to become a slave to it. She had seen enough of that at Mount Brien, Sir Maurice in a stupor every evening, weeping maudlin tears over all kinds of half-explained misfortunes that he had brought on himself. It had taken Rose a long time to work out the details of them. She needed to know, since her life was enclosed by the Briens and their doings. In the end it was her knowledge that led to her escape.

# _7_

ROSE SIPPED THE WINE SLOWLY. IT WAS PERFECT, LIKE A MEAL, not too heavy, with a perfume of summer. She said:

"I wish you could see me now, Madame Sophie, sitting in my own room, the best room at the Château Rochechouart, with a glass of the finest Médoc, nothing to do except what I want and wish. My room is a great deal bigger than yours, that room above the front door of Mount Brien from which you could look down your nose at the comings and goings of everyone. I wish I could have seen you, when you found out that I was gone. I wonder if you were embarrassed. You had thought I might run off with Hubert, or worse still stay at home with him, and now I was gone with Edmund instead.

"I enjoyed the idea that you might think I had run off with your pet grandson Edmund. You would have shed no tears over Hubert, the great hulking lout as you call him. Poor old Hubert – no one has any respect for him but he is a good-hearted boy. Not a boy at all. Twenty-six years old. How little you know about people, after all, Madame Sophie. I and Hubert – it's ridiculous. He could be my son, not my lover. I don't suppose I'll ever have a child now. But if I had one, he would have a good life. I would respect him, I'd ask his opinion, I'd consult him as a man, I'd make him independent as early as possible, I'd teach him how to protect himself from the stinking curs and bitches of this world – "

She realised that she was shouting angrily. She paused to take a longer drink. Burke drank very little, though it was obvious he enjoyed his wine and knew the different vintages, year by year. He avoided those strong liqueurs that everyone

116

around Saint Jacques knew how to make – he had an old-fashioned expression concerning them, that there was a devil in every bottle. When Jean-Paul brought him some plum brandy as a present from his mother, Burke actually poured it away. Rose fumed over the waste but no doubt he was right. Burke mentioned devils quite often, as if he believed in them. If Sophie believed in them, one would never guess it. Rose said:

"My son would have been fair and tall like me, not short and black-haired like Rabbit. Two-thirds of the breeding is in the dam. You have the idea that all the Irish are ugly and ignorant, all French people are handsome and aristocratic. You should see the Garonne peasants. Sometimes I felt quite sorry for you, so far from home and so full of hatred for everything around you. It's not easy to know the Irish. My family has lived there for a thousand years and we're still foreigners. There was no hope of your ever being one of them, even if you had wished for it. And there is protection in that isolation. Foreigners are not to be judged in the same way as the natives. If a farmer had seduced his son's fiancée and fathered her child, as Sir Maurice did, the people would have burned down his house, perhaps with him inside it. The fact that he had a French mother probably saved him.

"For a while after Rabbit went away, until I was certain that I was not going to have his child, I had moments almost of amusement while I thought of how you would take the news. I was terrified, of course, but I could almost have laughed too.

"Hubert. Hubert was sorry for me. That was why he used to stay and talk to me in the evenings when everyone else had left the drawing-room. He had plenty of troubles of his own but he always spoke to me so kindly about mine. He said to me last year: 'Get out. I would, if I could. Why do you stay here? Can't you feel how the air is poisoned?'

"I said: 'Where can I go?'

" 'Anywhere – America – England. You might get work in England. Dublin – why don't you go to Dublin?'

" 'Why don't you go yourself?'

117

" 'I can't desert my father.'

"I couldn't tell him that I was waiting for Rabbit to come back to me. I almost did but I stopped in time. The most dangerous moment is when you see the soft, friendly light in the eye, when you tell yourself that this person would really be fit to receive your confidence. Then a darker light crosses the other one and you have your warning. I never fail to see that second light. The mouth changes very slightly at the same moment, there is a tiny swallowing motion, as if the person can't wait for the morsel of you that he – or more usually she – is going to eat up. The second light never showed in Hubert's eye but he's so stupid, I couldn't be sure that someone wouldn't worm our conversation out of him. He's past being bullied but he could always be cajoled. He never learned the lessons that I did – I haven't revealed myself to anyone since I left home at twenty, except to Rabbit.

"There was a time when you tried to cultivate me, Madame Sophie, but I didn't respond. You thought I could be your companion. When you tried Hubert you did better but even he was able to see through you. He said to me one evening:

" 'My grandmother despises me.'

"I couldn't deny it. I said: 'Does it matter?'

"For some reason that answer relieved him. He hadn't thought of despising you – perhaps he has never learned to do it. You have a great way of making people feel your superiority. You probably expect that God will make special arrangements for you in heaven. For all I know He will. Miserable people spread misery. If I had the things that you have, I would be happy all day long. I told Hubert: 'Cultivate your grandmother and try to please her. She's a disappointed woman.'

"He said: 'That's governess talk.'

" 'What, then?'

" 'I'll wait until she's dead and then I'll never have to think about her again. Why should a grown man be insulted by his grandmother?'

118

"But his revolt didn't last long. You were able to make him cringe with a look, every time he opened his mouth, so that he scarcely ever spoke if you were in the room. What a triumph that was for you, to pour out your bitterness on a young man until you had destroyed him. Even with me he became more silent, after that, though he always stopped and talked to me when we met outside. Every afternoon I went for the same walk, down the avenue and into the walled garden, where we went to pick the peach. Even when the pain hardened and grew less, I kept going back there. I was not able to leave Mount Brien. Who would I ask for a reference? How would I go about getting another place, without influence or friends? I had sworn not to go home to Rocklawn – things were as bad as ever there. And if I went anywhere else, Rabbit might never find me."

Rose put out a steady hand to pick up her glass. She was a fool to speak to Sophie. She had come a thousand miles to get away from her. Rose herself had behaved ridiculously in hanging on and on in that dreadful household, far longer than she need have done. No doubt her own motives had included an unwillingness to part with the comforts she had there. Rabbit? Of course he was the most important reason for staying, but in France surely she would be even closer to him. Get out, Hubert had said. The idea was in her mind already. His advice made her realise clearly that she was determined to go.

She watched for opportunities. She began to ask the travelling teachers about the possibilities of work somewhere else. Some were sympathetic, all agreed not to report the conversation to anyone in the family, and so far as she knew no one had ever betrayed her. All said the same thing: upper-class Catholic households were few. A woman who had spent all her life in Mayo and Galway would be unlikely to get work in a Dublin household. Her accent was good but she would be thought to have acquired bad habits. Western servants were wild and undisciplined – she would not be able to protect the children in her care from the servants, a very important part of her work. Prospective

119

employers might even be afraid that she would be so dazzled by her new surroundings that she would fall in love with a footman and disgrace the whole household.

It was Michael MacGauran who told her that last detail. He was by far the best of the teachers. He came twice a year to teach Latin and Greek to Theo, the youngest boy, and he knew a great many of the big Catholic houses in the country. He was a priest from the diocese of Meath and though the persecution seemed to be over for good he was too nervous now to settle anywhere. He had a peculiar habit, when he sat at the dinner-table, of giving a long noisy sigh, followed by a knowing nod at no one in particular, sometimes by an exclamation: 'Ah, yes,' or 'Indeed.' It seemed that he never followed general conversation, and Rose had sometimes suspected that he was not quite aware of which great house he was the guest at the moment. However when she questioned him about her prospects he showed that he knew all about her. He said:

"You have a good name but it's not easy for such a handsome woman to get into a good family. If only you were a little more plain, they would risk it. The wives would be suspicious from the start – you don't mind my saying these things to you, I hope. It's not your fault."

Burke had written in his diary that it is a kind of freedom for a woman to be ugly, especially if she is poor. It was one of the pieces of wisdom that startled her, coming from him. Men love beautiful women, to be sure, but a great many of them love money more. A beautiful woman with money is like a rabbit among foxes. Rose was a fox with no Rabbit. Even if they had married him to some heiress she would find him.

Soothed by the wine, now in a half-dream she recalled those nights when she waited for him, heard his step, as quiet as a cat, on the stairs, saw the shadow of his head on the doorpost, in the light of the candle, felt his warm presence in the room. She had been too preoccupied with other things to attend fully to his love-making – that was not her main interest at all, though she knew at once that in

120

time she would find it delightful. What she loved was the closeness, the feeling of being wrapped around by another personality, and Rabbit's kindness and goodness to her. She guessed that there were very few men like him in this respect.

She said:

"Then why did you leave me? Sometimes I think I was a fool to come here but I know I can't die without seeing you again. Perhaps you never existed. Perhaps I made you up, a crazy middle-aged spinster inventing a lover when she can't get a real one. You're no better to me than if you were an invention. What will you say when you see me? What will you tell your wife, the rich lady in Paris? Madame Sophie is never done talking about them, how witty they are, how cultivated, how well-dressed and fashionable. You could easily have the best of them, with your straight back and your fine uniform, even though you're short and ugly. Women don't mind those things.

"You'll have to laugh when I tell you how I got to France. It was Lady Sophie's doing. Colman came in from the wild country by the lake to see her. He thought Lady Fanny and her sister would have gone to Galway as they always do on the first Thursday of the month, but they were delayed and he had to hide for an hour in the wash-house until the coast was clear. I found him there, very sorry for himself, and he told me his story. He was going to America, he said, and he wanted to see the old lady before he went. Why? Because she was always good to him. Good to him! The last place at the table, a word thrown as you might throw a bone to a dog now and then, a few French lessons when he was young, dropped like a hot potato as soon as the two grand-children went off to France, working for a pittance with the sheep, shearing and lambing thrown in out of gratitude for dinner now and then and the right to walk fifteen miles there and back to get it. Colman said I was a bitter, ungrateful woman and that I should remember all the years I had lived like a lady with the family in Mount Brien. I was remembering them, I said.

121

"He spent a few hours with Lady Sophie, in the drawing-room, wine and cake brought up by his cousin Fursey, the footman, then out to the stable to pick a good horse to ride to Galway. I couldn't make out what they were at. I took a walk down the avenue as he was leaving and stopped him by the gate. I said:

"'If you don't tell me what's going on, I'll tell Lady Fanny all about your visit when she comes back.'

"'Nothing,' he said, 'nothing.'

"But I wouldn't let him go. I held on to the horse's mane and dared him to drag me with him. At last he said:

"'You'll find out anyway, I suppose, with your nose in everyone's business. I'm going to France, on my way to America. She gave me the money for my ticket. She asked me to go to her grandson Robert and tell him to come home, that he's needed here, and he can bring his wife.'

"I said: 'Did she mention that the scheming governess was after Hubert and would marry him to get her hands on the estate?'

"I could see by his face that she had said something of the kind but Colman wouldn't repeat it. I sometimes think he's more of a gentleman than many that have some claim to the name. I said: 'If you go to France, take me with you.'

"He said he would not, and we argued for a full minute, until I said: 'If you don't take me with you, I'll say that you stole the horse. There will be ructions when Fanny finds out that it's gone. I'll make you a laughing-stock and a disgrace. Lady Sophie will pretend to be innocent – am I right?'

"Again I could see that they had talked about that. Colman is transparent. He had to agree. I made him swear by the holy mother of God that he would come to the wash-house again in the evening, on his way home from Galway, and I would have the money for my ticket then. He said there was no need for money, that she had given him too much but I said I would pay for my own ticket so that they couldn't have me arrested as a thief after they found I was gone.

"He went off then and I went to Edmund to get the

money from him because I had none of my own. I hadn't had wages for eight years, since I stopped teaching Theo, only a new dress now and then to make me fit to be seen. Edmund gave me the money but of course he asked what I wanted it for. I told him, foolishly, and he said he would come with us. At first I was angry but then I saw that with Edmund in the company there would be no fear that Colman would get ideas about me. I knew I was in no danger from Edmund, a cold-hearted boy and a cold-hearted man now, twenty-four years old and never chased a girl in his life, until he saw Burke's Jeanne.

"There was blue murder about the horse and I sat tight. Old Sophie was on pins but she never opened her mouth. She looked so innocent, I began to wonder if she was a pastmaster of this kind of thing. Lady Fanny shouted and abused everyone and finally called on her husband to defend his property from the bunch of thieves and knaves that hang around his house. She went too far there. Sir Maurice thumped the table and said he would listen to no more brawling, and the whole thing died down. Colman knew nothing about that. He sneaked into the wash-house late in the evening and gave me my ticket, and I handed over the money. I knew I could trust him. There is not a dishonest bone in him. Then he took the horse home and hid him, to ride to Galway when he would have word of the ship to take us to France. He left him at Daly's stables in the end, and I suppose they sent him back to Mount Brien.

"I rode down with Edmund and we boarded the ship by night. It was a terrible journey, a filthy little ship full of rats, five days of sickness and misery though the captain said it was an easy crossing. Then we walked through Bordeaux, like gypsies, covered with mud and salt and rain, until we got a carriage and came here to the Château to find Mr. Burke up to some lunatic affair in Bordeaux, locked into the Irish College, saying he'd stay there until he died. Well, that finished and I thought I would be on my way to you long ago, but Jeanne was pregnant, if you please, and they asked me to stay with them. So life goes on – how do people always know I'll be foolish enough to do what they tell me? It must be written on my face – she's a servant – let her serve.

"I had to stay. I had no idea until I came here of how everything had changed in France, hardly any servants, doctors, nurses – I couldn't leave the poor creature alone with no one of her own class to take care of her, her father and mother gone, her sister too, all taken away and guillotined.

"I didn't know much about babies but I know it all now. He was born on the first day of November, the feast of All Saints, as Burke told us several dozen times. Jeanne didn't make a fuss, to give her her due, and she was glad to have me there. Was that why I stayed? Because she thanked me and said she would have been much worse off without me? That's enough to make me lick anyone's foot.

"There is another reason. Ignorant lump as he is, Burke is in with the highest in the land. They stopped the sale of the Irish College because they needed him, to get the farmers to send in horses and fodder for the army. He has all the farmers for miles around eating out of his hand. He works like a slave. In Bordeaux when he goes down with his list of figures and his account of what the area can supply, they put down the red carpet for him. I saw it – it was amazing, the mayor coming out himself to shake his hand and pat him on the shoulder, old Burke shrugging him off as much as to say that he was too busy for that kind of nonsense.

"I won't be in rags when you see me, Rabbit, my Rabbit. Burke took me to Bordeaux with him once. He looked at me from under his hairy eyebrows and said: 'You need an outing, child. You need a few new dresses too. You can come with me for the day. Jeanne can mind the house for once.'

"He got out the old *berline* – it was like something out of the ark – and off we went. He bought me three dresses and turned his back while I bought drawers and chemises. It would make a cat laugh to see him. Then he went to the Town Hall and he introduced me as an Irish lady, very much interested in the Revolution. My French is good now – that's one thing I've really gained."

So Burke's power in Bordeaux was the reason why she stayed. If anyone could help her, surely it would be he. He talked familiarly to the officials there about transport, and fodder for the horses, and who the agent should see in Paris so that the right number of animals arrived at the depots. Notes and certificates were to be handed from one agent to the next, to ensure that the horses were not stolen and sold back to the government later. It was Burke who gave all the orders, in his vile French, and the officials listened respectfully and said: "Yes, citizen. Certainly, citizen. We'll see to it, citizen." Burke loved every minute of it and was very excited all the way back to Saint Jacques, moving restlessly about in the carriage as if he would have been much happier galloping his horse.

Alone with him on that journey, Rose might have spoken to him of Rabbit. She was on the brink of it more than once, but each time she drew back at the last moment. If she had not read the journal it might have been possible. She might have taken him at his face value, a gross, ignorant country-man with no interest beyond farming. She remembered his description of himself, a dirty, foolish, wandering, lost sheep but good mutton for all that, and his remarks about being so much healthier now than when he was professor of Latin at the College. These comments revealed a far more complex person than the one he allowed the world to see. Still she might have told him her grisly little secret and hoped for understanding and help, if she had not read the story of Louise.

Rose found that she could not understand that side of Burke. It was a mystery, and she hated mysteries. This was the reason, as Colman had said, why she had her nose in everyone's affairs. A locked box, a secret drawer, a sealed letter were challenges to her. Burke's journal was a pure joy until she came to what he called his sin of Louise. First there was the slip of paper with her name on it in careful script, as if it were a reminder, then all those cryptic statements about her, and about his obsession for her. How could this great earthy lout have restrained himself with such refinement and delicacy? Until she understood that, Rose could not bring herself to tell him her own secrets. The thought of being in his power repelled her. But in fact the boot was on the other foot – he was in her power, if she wished it. She might use that power some day, if she were driven to it.

Living in his house had affected her in many ways. In Ireland, after her one humiliating attempt to bring some comfort into the housekeeping, she had realised that even to be interested in such mechanical affairs was taken as a sign of an inferior mind. Here, on the contrary, Burke often commended her for specially tasty meals which he knew she had ordered in detail, forcing old Anna to dig back into her childhood for lore that she had inherited from her mother, who was a renowned cook in her day. Even if she had worked in the kitchen with Anna, no one would have thought less of her except Edmund. So long as he was in the house she was careful to keep her standards pure. And Burke was lonely for intelligent company. Once he found out that Rose understood his various projects, his goats and his poultry and his horse-breeding, he took to addressing his dinner-table remarks on these subjects directly to her, ignoring the disgusted looks of the other two. Rose would have looked disgusted too, if she had not long ago schooled herself to present a blank face. She tried to imagine herself taking him aside and telling him that he was not behaving like a gentleman. She would never do it. He was the father of the family, the head of the house. He had them all under his thumb. Even Edmund was in awe of him, though he had known him from his childhood, when Burke was the priest who tutored his half-brother and sister in Mount Brien.

When Burke talked of his voluntary imprisonment in the Irish College, as he often did, Rose sat terrified lest she might reveal by some remark that she knew more about that episode than she should.

It was time to go downstairs. Soon the baby would be brought to the salon for half an hour before dinner. Rose had found a nurse for him, a girl named Bernadette who was engaged to be married to that strange little peasant, Jean-Paul, who was Burke's confidant and right-hand man. She was a good girl, absolutely obedient to Jean-Paul, and therefore to Rose as his deputy. There was very little fluttering and fussing over the baby, though he was the only child in the house. Bernadette kept him with her own nephew, whose mother was his wet-nurse, bringing him to be shown to his parents every evening just as was done in Ireland. This was Rose's idea. Jeanne made no objection, and it was hard to tell how much she cared about the child. Burke gave her very little encouragement, almost as if he welcomed her lack of interest. He had deliberately excluded her when he baptised his son in a secret ceremony in the kitchen one night, after everyone had gone to bed. He had no witness but Rose. He came home a little early, when the baby was a month old, and went to look for Rose, saying:

"Keep that child with you tonight."

"Why?"

"Never mind. I'll explain later. You can say he has a cold – anything you like."

He tapped on her door at eleven o'clock and said:

"You can come now. Wrap him up well."

"Where are we going?"

Was he going to send the child away and Rose with it? Burke laughed softly as if he read her thoughts.

"I'm only going to christen him. Do you want him to grow up a pagan?"

"What's the mystery?"

"This country is full of mysteries, woman. Come along before someone pokes their nose in."

He held the lamp high and she followed him down the stairs, through the draughty corridors and down the short stone stairs that led to the kitchen. He had prepared everything, oil and water and a fine china jug and basin, all laid out on the long scrubbed table.

He turned to her suddenly, saying: "What are you afraid of? I thought you had more spirit in you."

"Where is Jeanne? Isn't it her business to be here, not me?"

"Do you think I would ask her? Don't you know well that she wouldn't come? She'd think it was not decent, a priest baptising his own child."

This same thought had occurred to Rose. Again he seemed to read her thoughts.

He said: "And who else do you think I could get to do it? Most of the priests are shivering in their breeches for fear someone will come and chop their heads off, and the rest of them are not too sure about the morality of baptising a priest's baby at all. But I say, let's do it anyway and the Lord God can decide whether we did right or wrong."

He pulled a purple stole and a small, black-covered book out of his pocket, slipped the stole around his neck and went through the short ceremony while Rose held the baby. As he rolled up the stole and put it away again he said:

"His name is René. When he grows up you can tell him he's named after René Descartes, a prudent gentleman who always kept out of trouble except when he went to teach philosophy to a queen. He should have known it couldn't be done. You're his godmother. It will be your business to make sure that he grows up a Christian."

"And how am I to do that, if you please?"

"You can do anything in the world that you want."

"That's news to me. It seems that I've never done much but what everyone else wants."

"What about coming here? Don't tell me the others invited you."

"No."

"I thought not. And what are you going to do next?"

"I haven't decided."

"Stay here, if you like, and teach that child. We'll need to have someone."

"Thank you."

Did he really imagine that Jeanne and he would move into old age together, sharing the growth of their son, perhaps have other children? There was no telling. Burke said:

128

"I can't see you staying forever. You'll light out for a more exciting life after a while."

Now was the moment when she could have asked him about Rabaut. He was another crack-pot, like herself. He might understand perfectly. But he was thinking again about the child.

He said: "I'll leave a letter in my desk, to say that you're to have the care of him, especially in matters of religion."

"What do you mean? Are you going away?"

"We're all going away sooner or later. I'm not likely to see him grow up. He looks healthy. God knows what will become of him."

Then he picked up the jug and basin, seized the lamp and plunged out of the kitchen, leaving Rose to catch up with him as best she could. She noticed, however, that he walked very quietly once they were back in the main part of the house.

Burke never referred to that strange episode in the kitchen, not so much as by a knowing glance. His eyes were often opaque, preoccupied, as if the people around him were trees or plants among which he was making his way to some important destination. A bit mad, Rose thought, but he was too efficient to be dismissed in that way. He wrote the letter that he had mentioned. He never showed it to her but she found it in the drawer of his desk, at the very back, on one of her searchings when everyone was busy elsewhere. If only he would take up his journal again – it would be splendid to find that he was writing about her. If he did, some day she might write something there too. Perhaps in this way they would begin to communicate with deadly honesty. The notion amused her. Each could write a paragraph or two now and then and hide it behind the desk, the other would find it and reply.

But he would never write in the journal again. She was sure of that. And for her it would be the maddest act of her mad life to make even the smallest mark on it, to reveal that she had seen it.

Once or twice she regretted that she had missed her

chance in the dark kitchen, in the tense moment when she was holding his child and he was going through a ritual which he believed essential to its survival. He had made her a part of it because he needed her, and in return she might well have asked him to help her. The moment was gone. It sometimes seemed as if he was taking care that it did not recur.

Approaching the salon she became aware that there was an extra voice. Colman. Instantly she felt calmer. The painful force of her concentration seemed to melt and flow away with the return of all the memories she shared with him. Yet they had little in common except poverty and oppression. His version was preferable to hers – his full of family love, close friendship, faith in God, belief in some better future however distant – hers deprived of all support, cut off by the family oddity as much as by the long weedy avenue from all outside friendship, God no more than a myth, no future except the likelihood of withering away in genteel starvation. Colman would probably not have believed in the similarity of their conditions. A family with the name of French must be rich and powerful, able to get help from their fine connections when they fell on hard times, free to travel the world and tackle it on equal terms. One sign that Colman might have sensed a bond was that his manner to her was never subservient as it was to the Briens, though it was not familiar either.

But Colman was becoming more and more of a stranger. He had changed beyond belief since he had come to France, returning each time to the Château more self-assured and better dressed, almost as if he had been taken up by a mistress in Paris and was being licked into shape.

The thought caused a little spurt of anger in Rose's brain as she entered the salon. What right had anyone to remove her one lifeline? Without Colman she would be left here to rot. That was a favourite expression of her mother's – Rose didn't really believe in it. One leaves oneself to rot, she knew, but nothing would be easy. What then was she planning? All at once she realised that she was going to turn

130

again to Colman for help. She had waited long enough, probably too long, as usual.

He sprang to his feet the moment she came into the salon. Not so Edmund, who was lounging on a sofa near the window, close to Jeanne, who seemed preoccupied with her embroidery, picking up tiny stitches and drawing thread through the linen with her head bent in total concentration. The idiocy of this occupation never failed to infuriate Rose. Jeanne was very skilled. It occurred to Rose that women use embroidery to hide their vacant or scheming eyes in company – now there was a good reason for it.

Edmund was watching her hands avidly but he could not see her face. Then, as Rose came in, Jeanne lifted her head and gave him a long look, as if she were taking leave of him until they could be alone again. Burke had not yet arrived, but before Colman could speak they heard him crash the door of his study shut and march heavily across the hall. A moment later Edmund was upright, Jeanne's head was down again, Colman had time for only one short, friendly glance at Rose before transferring his attention to Burke, who came plunging forward, calling out as if he were summoning one of his shepherds down from the mountains.

"Colman, my boy, there you are, home from your wanderings. Let me look at you – did anyone put a drink in your hand after your journey? When did you get here? Where have you been? Sit here beside me. Rose will get you a glass of wine. Rose takes care of us all."

With a hearty thump on the shoulder he pushed Colman down on to the chair in which he had been sitting when Rose came. She poured the wine and brought it to him – Rose French bringing a glass of wine to Colman Folan who had to hide in the wash-house at Mount Brien only a year ago – it was a mad world indeed. Colman looked up into her face with an amused, conspiratorial expression as she handed him the glass. Burke watched with obvious pleasure. Behind her, Jeanne and Edmund were probably enjoying the spectacle in their own way. But she no longer cared a rap for any of them. Soon it would all be over.

# _8_

It seemed to Rose now that Burke was determined to prevent her from being alone with Colman. He stayed at home the next day, something he had never done in all the months she had been in his house. She found him rambling about like an aged bull, in the kitchen and the cellars and around the hall, as if he could not decide where to settle, until at last he took Colman into his study and shut the door. Sitting in her room with a glass of wine at noon, Rose said:

"What the hell do you mean by taking him away when I need him? Why are you not out with your cows and your chickens? That's your proper company, you great lout, you boor. You drive me to this. Am I always to be shut up, put away, never have what I want, at everyone's beck and call –"

She stood up, finishing the glass in one long swallow. It calmed her, made her see more clearly. Better to keep quiet, with so many people in the house. Wine to cheer the heart of man – it did that for her. There was time. Colman had not said he was leaving today. But he might need a great deal of persuasion. He was not to be bullied as easily now as he had been when he was a greenhorn in the wilds of Ireland.

Extraordinary what one glass of wine could do. She felt courage gradually take hold of her. She had another method at her disposal now, perhaps a more effective one than the threats she had used on Colman before. She said:

"I can draw you to me. You're watching me. I think you know more about the world now than you did when you left Ireland. So do I. You'll get nothing from me, of course. There could be no question of that. I'll tell you nothing about Rabbit. But if it had not been for Rabbit I would never recognise the look on your face now."

She sang softly, moving in a kind of slow dance around the room:

> " 'But when freedom I'm pursuing,
> Though resolved I cannot run.
> Fonder still of my undoing,
> I embrace the death I shun.

You will never lay a hand on me.'

"Money. I'll need money. Burke has plenty, hidden under the floor-boards of his room. I've counted it but I won't tell you how much there is. The trouble is that he might miss it. I bet he takes it out and counts it, and fingers it, and *misses* it, every now and then. I wonder now if I could have – "

It was the best plan of all, perhaps, but she should have thought of it months ago. As she plunged after this idea, quickly filling in details of how she might have removed the gold a little at a time, it was as if another self sat watching her and listening to her plans. For the first time in her life she addressed that self:

"So you're a thief now, as well. What is so dreadful about that? Why should that clod have a stack of gold under his bedroom floor while you haven't a brass farthing? Besides, you can give it back when you find Rabbit."

A blank wall seemed to rise up before her, a nothingness. She need never think beyond finding him. Once she was with him again, everything would fall into place.

Was she going to steal from Burke, then? It seemed that some new element had come into his life. After today, his movements were no longer predictable, Edmund and Jeanne would have to change too. They must be at least as uneasy as Rose.

She almost laughed when she saw them. They sat at luncheon like a couple of mice when the cat is around. Burke said heartily as he finished his meal:

"That was a great deal better than I get out at the farms. This is all Rose's doing, Colman. Anna would never cook

133

for Jeanne but Rose manages to get her to do great things. Was that chicken or veal?"

"Chicken," Rose said.

"See, she's blushing. We don't compliment her often enough."

Everyone was smiling graciously at her, taking Burke's lead. It was hatred that had made her blush but none of them seemed to know. Rose could see into them quite clearly. Sometimes it seemed to her that the whole world was arranged and ruled by fools and rogues. Power and wealth seemed to fall from the air on to the heads of whoever happened to be beneath. Gifts and intelligence like hers were not needed – they were not missed by people who could not even imagine their existence.

To her very finger-tips she felt now that there was a mystery about, something that the two men were conspiring over in the study. They went back there immediately after luncheon. There was no possibility of eavesdropping. Burke's study was directly under his bedroom, at the other end of the Château from Rose. It ran the full depth of the house, built high over the cellars, a good eight feet from the ground.

Back in her room, Rose walked up and down, up and down, pausing now and then to look out at the damp landscape where the warm rain was flying over the fields and vineyards. It was another kind of spring here, not the sharp cold of Ireland, where the light hardened and changed and was somehow almost as threatening as winter. Here the shades of light were softer, the air was full of scents, full of promises of stirring life. Although it was only March, the swallows were shrieking and squeaking in and out of their nests under the eaves. Those that intended going on to Ireland would give it another month to warm up. Last year, when she came here at this very time, she was so tired and frightened that she had barely noticed all these differences. This year she was part of it herself, as if sap were rising in her body, as if she might at any moment run like the animals in the fields, to find a mate. It was disgusting, at her age and with her breeding. This must be how the country girls felt in the spring, free and easy with their sex, waiting and giggling for the boys to come by.

Thinking of such things at all was a mistake. She crossed to the wardrobe and poured herself a glass of wine, drank it quickly and then seized the long black cloak that she had worn on the ship from Ireland. She had heavy shoes too, of the kind that no one but the peasants wore here. With the hood up, she went quietly downstairs and out by the garden door on to the long roofless terrace that ran across the back of the Château. Up and down, forty steps each way, three for the turn – battering her wings against the bars of the cage, exactly as she had done at Rocklawn and at Mount Brien. In spite of the hood, she felt the soft rain on her face. At least she would be tired at the end of it. If she were a man, she would go to the stables now and take out a horse and gallop through the fields and pastures. No one would think it odd, in a man. In a woman it would be taken as a sign of derangement.

At dinner-time she dressed carefully, having in mind her new plan of captivating Colman. She would be a mixture of grandeur and seduction. Burke commented on it immediately.

"Doesn't she look gorgeous, a real Rose? I declare she gets handsomer every day. She goes out in the fresh air, that's why. She had a good walk on the terrace this afternoon." Of course they had seen her from the study windows. "Now why don't you do that, Jeanne? You look quite peaked these days."

It was true. Her weaselly face was thin, so that her small chin jutted unbecomingly. Burke went on: "Too much embroidery – we'll have enough for two lifetimes, at the rate you're going. A long walk every day would set you up, a tour of the farms with me."

"No, thanks. I had enough of that when you were in the College."

"Edmund would take you for a walk on the avenue – wouldn't you Edmund?"

135

"Certainly."

His expression gave no sign of anything more than a wish to be obliging. He turned to look at Jeanne brightly, as if she were a stranger. He was a far better actor than she was. Watching them, Rose saw Jeanne's expression soften and change. So she really is in love with him, Rose thought. How marvellous and pleasant that is. Until now Rose had almost believed that Jeanne was incapable of anything but a kind of petulant revenge on Burke. It was a far more natural alliance, between her and Edmund, both the same age and from the same class. Jeanne was lucky – but Edmund would never be able to rescue her from Burke. What he had, he held. His great countryman's paws were a symbol of his grasping nature. He was smiling benignly now, his glance shifting from Edmund to Jeanne and back again, as if they were his children. Could anyone be so thick-skinned? Even Edmund was not quite proof against this. He gave an embarrassed twitch of his shoulders and said rather too loudly to Colman: "So you have been at brother Robert's place – how are they all over there?"

"All very well." Colman turned back to Burke. "The children are beautiful. The second little girl is a replica of Louise."

"She will be a beauty, then."

Burke's round brown eyes seemed to widen a little, proving that her name could still affect him.

Edmund asked: "Did he say when he's going to Ireland?"

This was news. Rose had not heard that a decision had been made.

Colman said: "He can't leave his family defenceless. He asked again if you can go to Saintes soon, and stay with them while he is in Ireland. It would be at least three months, probably longer. He must go alone first, then decide if he will take his family there for good."

"Yes, I'll do that. He should go soon."

Now Jeanne looked as if all belonging to her had died. Her face shrivelled up, as if she were old and sick, and her thin lips pressed together as if she had to keep them closed

136

by force. Edmund glanced at her and away again. Rose got a strong impression that this conversation had been planned by him to take place in company. He could easily have had it alone with Colman before now. Surely he was not trying to manoeuvre Burke in some way – no, it was done for Jeanne's benefit. That was it. Edmund, hard as nails, was making sure that Jeanne could not make a scene when she learned that he would have to go to Saintes for three months. No wonder Hubert and his little brother Theo disliked him so much.

Jeanne said in a rasping tone, quite unlike her usual one: "Couldn't you stay with them, Colman? Surely all the dangers are over now."

Colman said: "I'm not free to stay long enough. They would need a protector. There will be new purges. They may not be as thorough as last time but there will be more arrests and especially around Saintes."

She said venomously: "You know a lot."

"Yes."

Looking at Colman now, one would never suspect that he had been brought up in a leaky cabin on a mountainside above Lough Corrib. He wore his good clothes easily, his cropped hair showed the almost elegant lines of his face, confident and intelligent in a way that Rose had never observed in Ireland.

Burke said: "It's true. Sometimes I think it will all break out again. That's when we'll need our friends. Don't look so frightened, Jeanne. Don't you know that you can never get the same fright twice? We'll all look after you. You'll never be abandoned again."

She glared at him contemptuously but he seemed quite unaware of it. Soon afterwards he stood up, seeming to tower over everyone else in the room, saying: "Well Colman, back to work. Can you come with us, Rose?"

What now? Burke was going on: "I want you to tell me how Jacques Fournier is doing. You know, Colman, we've found a perfect footman just when we thought the breed had died out. They need the money and those that don't want to go to the army might as well be servants. I've got my eye on another one too – "

With his hand on Colman's shoulder, Burke left the room and Rose could do nothing but follow. As she was approaching the door, the same Jacques appeared to take away the dishes. Jeanne and Edmund went towards the salon, where a good fire of chestnut logs was blazing.

At the study door Rose heard Burke say cheerfully: "Every second man hereabouts is named Jacques, after our patron. Either their mothers or their grandmothers decided that they needed the best possible protection, and they couldn't go higher."

"What about the new babies? Are they being named Égalité and Fraternité?"

"Not yet. Jacques' grandmother says they'll wait a while to see if those ideas stick, but the saints go on forever. Not much humour in our neighbours until they get old. Then they bring out what was in their minds all the time. There you are, Rose. Come and sit down."

In spite of its size the room was warm, the heat spreading from the wide fireplace on the far wall. When the Château was looted after Jeanne's father's arrest and execution, the huge iron fire-dogs must have been too heavy and awkward to be conveniently moved. For the same reason, various pieces of furniture, including the big desk that stood beside the fireplace, had been left in position. Rose glanced at it the moment she entered the room. Everything was as usual, the desk pushed as close as possible against the wall, its top littered with papers and account books. In her first searchings she had quickly noticed that the top projected at the back as well as on the other three sides, so that the desk could be placed in the middle of a room. This created the narrow space between it and the wall, where she had found the diary.

Burke placed a chair for her, not too close to the fire, arranging it precisely. No point in looking nervous – with someone as peculiar as Burke this would be sure to bring on the wrong reaction, as they said happens with biting dogs.

Colman looked decidedly uncomfortable, as if he knew there was something unpleasant afoot. Burke threw himself into the big chair that he kept by the fireside, with the books he was reading on a small table beside him. There were usually four or five of these, and he seemed to read them simultaneously, keeping them all lying open one on top of the other. Colman picked up a chair and brought it between the other two, forming a half-circle.

Rose said: "Jacques is doing very well – he worked here as a boy."

"Never mind Jacques," Burke said impatiently. "I know all about him. We just wanted an excuse to talk to you alone."

That damned diary – or the wine – what was on his mind? But he was barely looking at either of them. Was he going to ask them to leave? He was perfectly entitled to do this, since he had given them hospitality for a year. It was true that Rose kept house and had made herself useful in a thousand ways, including acting as midwife to Jeanne, and lately Edmund had begun to help with the farming, especially with the horses. He had a real gift with them, diagnosing their illnesses and treating them with remarkable success, as Burke had pointed out on several occasions.

Burke said, in a low tone quite unlike his usual one: "There are so many things to tell, I hardly know where to begin. We'll begin with politics."

"I know nothing about politics," Rose said.

"You know more than you pretend, more than you think. Well, you surely know that another attempt is going to be made in Ireland, against English rule?"

"I heard a lot of talk about that but it has nothing to do with me."

"Perhaps not. But it will have, if we succeed."

While he talked, Rose fell into a dream of how it would be to own such a room, with its fire-dogs and its desk and gold-painted chairs and wall tapestries of deer-hunts – not to be a perpetual servant but really to have it for her own. If she owned a house like this, every morning she would come slowly into each room in turn, and look around to see that everything was in order. Then, according to her mood, she would choose which room to sit in that day. She would have a special chair in each of the rooms, which would be hers alone. Everyone else could take what was left. At Mount Brien she was always the last to be seated. She had developed a habit of slowing down as she entered a room, as if she were preoccupied with something else, then taking her place deliberately as if she were not in the least interested in its position. Thus she was always in a draught, or in the darkest place, or on the smallest chair, and she had learned to make it seem a choice. She had continued the custom here but if Burke was present he never allowed it. To give him his due, he made no difference between her and Jeanne in this respect, always making sure that she was comfortably placed. He was talking about pikes and guns now, getting more and more excited as he spoke:

"The whole country will rise. The people are well armed, for the first time in a hundred years. When they hear that the French have landed they'll flock to the United Irishmen. With the war on in Europe there is hardly any English force in Ireland. The army will march on Dublin and set up a provisional government there. Lord Edward Fitzgerald and Mr. Tone and Mr. Arthur O'Connor will organise national guards to keep order in the towns and villages all over the country."

Rose was listening now, all right. She said: "What about the landlords? What about the people with the big estates – they'll fight on the English side, you may be sure."

"You see?" Burke said to Colman. "I told you she has a head on her. Any of them who fight against their own country or who remain in the English army will have their estates confiscated. The French will insist on all Church property becoming the property of the state. That will give two sources of revenue to help to set up the new state. The arms that were bought for the Volunteers are all in good condition and they'll be available to the governors of the different provinces."

"What about the northern Protestants?"

"They're all republicans. Most of them are in the United Irishmen. They know the French will come to help us get our independence. After that the French will go about their business and leave us to ours, as they did in America under General Rochambeau. There is plenty of support in the north, and as many good leaders as we have in the south. Henry Grattan will come out on our side – "

"*Our* side?"

"Of course I'll be in it up to my neck. All we have to do in return is to promise that our new government will recognise the French Republic and let the French people make their own arrangements at home, without interference. Then Ireland will be free, from the centre to the sea, and England will be better pleased in the end."

"I doubt that."

"I'm talking about twenty years from now. You'll see, it will come. The first thing is to get our army in the field. We have the help of General Hoche for that. If he had been at the head of the troops last year in Bantry Bay, instead of that ditherer Grouchy, he would have landed them immediately and we'd be a free country by now. Next time it will be different."

"So they're coming again?"

He would go to Mount Brien to find her and she would not be there.

"They will come. Colman has been with the leaders in Paris. But General Hoche is sick. We must hurry. It would be much more difficult without him."

"Why are you telling me all this? Are you putting women into your army too?"

Colman said: "You will be in no danger, Rose. We need your help – or rather, Mr. Burke does, so that he can be free to help us in Paris. He has powerful friends there."

Burke laughed, a deep gurgling sound that seemed to shake him throughout his whole body. It was such a rare sound that Rose found herself affected by it. One could almost like him, at times.

141

He said: "I know no one else who can help me. All my old Irish friends in Bordeaux have lost faith in me, though I've saved their skins for them several times. Not much charity in the Irish, Rose, as we all know. They think I've done too well for myself." And he quoted softly:

"'To all my foes, dear Fortune, send
Thy gifts, but never to my friend:
I tamely can endure the first,
But this with envy makes me burst.'

"'Twas ever thus, Rose. We must make our friends among people without envy, if this is possible. That was why I thought of you."

"You have been very good to me."

"It was nothing. Now I need something from you."

Would he never get down to it? He seemed almost embarrassed at what he had to say. It was like seeing a dog embarrassed, as they sometimes are for some failure in achievement, twisting and turning their heads, wriggling their bodies ingratiatingly.

Burke said: "You're laughing at me, I can see. You're saying to yourself: 'Why doesn't he come straight out with it?' Well, here it is, then. I need to be free of family life. I know a great many people in Paris since the bad days here in Bordeaux. I can get to some of them in a way that no one else can. I want to devote my whole time now to that project."

"You're going back to live in Ireland?"

"I didn't say that. I may still want to be a Frenchman at the end of it. I've made my home here. No wonder you look bewildered. Damn it all, Rose, I want to get rid of Jeanne."

"I can understand that."

"I see that I've explained it well, that side of it at least. The next part is not so easy. Your pupil – Edmund – what do you think of him?"

"I didn't teach him much. He taught himself mostly. He read all day, your friend Swift, *Gulliver's Travels*. It used to drive his mother wild. She tried to burn the book, once."

"That was strange reading in a Catholic household."

142

"Not in that one."

"Have you read Swift yourself?"

"Enough to recognise your quotations. One must read something."

"You haven't said what you think of Edmund."

"Is that what you want from me?"

"Partly."

"Edmund is very clever. He is hard-hearted because of the way he was brought up but there is a possibility of improvement."

"How was he brought up?"

"His mother used to whip him every day, until one day he told her that if she attempted to do it again he would kill her. She believed him, and she stopped."

"God above, what a child!"

"He meant it. I was there, and saw it happen. His mother is not a lady."

"I remember her very well. How old was he when this happened?"

"Twelve."

His head was back and his eyes seemed almost shut. When he opened them there was a new sharpness about him. He asked: "Would you say Edmund is a cruel man?"

"The reverse. He hates violent behaviour. He would do anything to avoid it."

"You know a great deal about him."

"Mr. Burke, I am not enjoying this conversation. You asked me about Edmund. I've known him since he was a child. Now if you don't mind, I think I'll go to my room."

"No, no. Please don't go. I haven't finished yet."

Rose leaned back, watching him. He was positively writhing, pawing his jaws, twitching his huge shoulders, shifting himself in his chair so that it creaked. At last he said: "You may not know that Jeanne and I were never married."

She made no answer. After a moment he went on: "Perhaps you don't know either that Edmund and Jeanne fornicate with each other when I'm out on the farms."

She bent her head. If he was aware of that, God alone

143

knew what else he had discovered. Almost apologetically he said: "It's only natural. They're the same age. You must have noticed how they look at each other."

She nodded, but still said nothing. Burke said impatiently: "God help us, I'm not blaming you. You weren't supposed to be their chaperone. Just tell me honestly – did you know this was going on?"

"Yes."

He sounded almost relieved as he said: "In that case I know what to do. They can be married soon."

"Have you asked them?"

"She won't make any objection."

"Perhaps not. What about him?"

"When he hears my proposal I think he will agree to it. I'm going to give the Château Rochechouart back to Jeanne. Edmund will make a success of it. He knows a lot about horses and I'll teach him more."

There was a long pause. This time Rose was determined that she would make no move. It was his turn to ask her to leave. Colman was still sitting there, watching him, as if he knew there was more to come.

At last Burke said: "It's a great favour I'm going to ask of you, Rose. My trouble is that it will take a few weeks or maybe months to make all the arrangements for handing the Château back to Jeanne. Down in Bordeaux they don't like to see the aristocrats crawling back into their great houses again. I'll have to make sure that they understand about Edmund, that he's an Irishman and that the place will be his rather than hers. In the meantime I'll have to get her away from him for a while. Lord God, what would I do if she gets pregnant? There she would be, trying to make a good story of it for my benefit. I'd rather avoid that, if I can. Rose, will you take her to Paris for me?"

Rose leaped to her feet, her fists clenched. Colman and Burke both stood up quickly also and Colman said: "Rose, what's the matter? It's not such a terrifying place."

Burke said: "Sit down, girl. There, now. Put your head back on the cushion. I didn't think you would be frightened

144

so easily. Paris is quite safe now. Everything is back to normal. We were talking at dinner about the bad times coming back but you would be quite safe. And it wouldn't be for long, only a couple of months. Jeanne likes you. She won't be bad company, especially when I give her the money to buy some dresses."

She let him rattle on. He would explain his plan to Jeanne and Edmund at once, then separate them as soon as possible until he had made all the legal arrangements. Colman would accompany Rose and Jeanne to Paris and see them into suitable lodgings. He would escort them back to Saint Jacques when the time came. It was a four-day journey but they would be protected all the way, and they would stop at decent inns every night.

At last Rose said: "Mr. Burke, I don't know why you think I'm afraid to go to Paris. Of course I'll do this for you. Why not?"

He was gazing at her with eyes more like a fox than a dog now. This sharpness of his was shocking – how could she have been so mistaken? Country craft and cunning were what he had, covered over with an appearance of dullness, a perfect disguise. To have observed Jeanne and Edmund so accurately – but Colman could have been Burke's informant. However, she knew he would not have done that, first of all because he expected no better of the gentry, and secondly because his class allowed the gentry to sink or swim as they pleased.

Burke was saying: "You approve of my plan, then? You think I'm doing the right thing?"

"It's as you please. If that is what you want, it's a good solution."

"You think Edmund will accept?"

"I'm not sure if he cares enough for Jeanne."

"You think that would affect him?"

"Perhaps not. Who can see into the mind of a young man? I think it would be a good thing for him."

"May I tell him you said so?"

"I doubt if he would be influenced by me."

145

"You haven't asked what will become of you."

"Time enough for that." She spoke too quickly.

Burke said: "You are very unselfish. Of course you will be provided for. I'll see to it myself."

Heaven alone knew what he was thinking of. She would be disposed of, as one might dispose of an old basket, too good to throw out, not fit for public show. Put it in the linen-room or the kitchen where it can be useful for a while.

Burke heaved himself to his feet and began to pace up and down the room excitedly, his tread as heavy as if he were out in a ploughed field. He rubbed his great meaty paws together and said: "This rising will change the whole face of Ireland. Perhaps I'll see it in my lifetime, our own government in Dublin, Catholic and Protestant gentlemen side by side, making laws that will be fair to all and sundry, tax-money spent in our own country – Rose, you must think I'm mad."

Suddenly the fox's eyes were on her again. She said: "I can see what interests you most. I told you, I know nothing about politics."

"Well, why should you? I'll arrange everything and I'll tell you as soon as possible when you should get ready to go to Paris. The change will be good for you. Life is too quiet for you here."

"I'm quite happy here."

"Well, perhaps you are."

So she was free to go. Colman made a move to accompany her but Burke called him back saying: "Wait a while, Colman, wait a while. I want to hear more."

Get rid of all the women and leave the men to plot the world – that was Burke's idea. She walked demurely to the door and waited for Colman to close it behind her. Then she fled up the stairs to her room, running lightly, taking them two at a time, able to run all the way to Paris, all the way into Rabbit's arms.

She fetched her candles and lit them with a steady hand from the lamp that stood on a table outside her bedroom door. She carried them inside and set them evenly on the dressing-table and on the table by the bed, four candles in all. Then she closed the door and went to stand in front of the long wardrobe glass, breathing in and out, in and out, six times, each time with a deeper breath. When she was ready, she began to sing, letting her voice out so that it filled the room. It didn't matter now whether they heard her or not. They needed her. They could no longer put her in the lowest place. She was one of them, as good as anyone in the house. Soon she would be better. Better than who? Than Burke, or Colman? What a slough she had fallen into, to wish to excel those peasants.

# _9_

Rose said:

"So you have taken to questioning me now, Mr. Burke.
Some day I may wring your fat neck when you ask me how
it feels to be a miserable, ignorant Irish spinster without a
penny to her name. That's what your questions amount to
though you seem to think I shouldn't mind. Did my father
never try to find me a husband? Did the Briens take me into
society? You know as well as I do that there is no society out
there in the wilds. Did I ever consider transporting myself
to Dublin where the rich young men would be lined up
waiting for a beautiful wife even if she hadn't a stitch on her
back? You blunder about among these questions like a cow
stumbling through a potato field. For a while I wondered if
you were considering me as a replacement for your Jeanne
but now I don't believe that. God alone knows what you're
at. Did none of my sisters marry? Could I be a maiden aunt
to some of their children? I might have answered that
I'm not a maiden but that's the last thing you'll hear from
me.

"And my singing – it was a sorry day that I let myself go,
and sang loud and clear, so that you heard and told the
whole world about me. That was mine, mine, mine. You
should know about private things, with your journal that
you hide so carefully. One look at my face when you asked
me to sing in the drawing-room should have told you to
shut your stupid mouth and let me alone. Not at all. 'A fine,
strong voice,' you said, making it sound like an insult. So I
sang, and made it an insult that you could understand. It's
your own fault. I thought that we would be off at once,
within a couple of days at least. It didn't matter what I said

148

or did, since I would soon be finished with the whole boiling of you. But days and days go by and we seem no nearer to leaving."

Her revenge had been to sing glorious Handel:

"'He was despised, rejected and deserted, a man of sorrows, acquainted with grief.'"

Burke asked sharply: "What's that? Where did you learn that?"

"My mother taught me. It's Handel, the *Messiah*."

"Not a drawing-room song."

"What is a drawing-room song?"

Jeanne said: "I don't like that music. It sounds like music for a church."

Edmund avoided sitting near Jeanne now. Burke had taken to inviting him on his tours of the farms. When they were not at that they were in the stables, always together, as if Burke were keeping an eye on him, as indeed he probably was. After a whole day in the stables they both smelt of horse-dung, but Edmund cleaned himself up before entering the dining-room. When Jeanne objected to the smell of Burke's clothes he said heartily: "You should be used to it by now. I'm not going to eat with Jean-Paul in the kitchen, if that's what's in your mind."

Jeanne said: "I wish that little man wouldn't eat here at all. Why doesn't he go home?"

"He has eaten here for years," Burke said. "He's being entertained by Bernadette. Don't forget that I have dinner with him and his mother most days, at Saint André. I asked him if he would eat with us here in the dining-room these evenings, while we're working with the horses, but he said he prefers not to."

"You asked him! What were you thinking of?"

"Our skins. Things have changed and we must never forget it."

"I think he spies on us."

"What matter if he does? Isn't our life an open book?" Burke said blandly.

Poor Jeanne looked like a frightened fieldmouse. Edmund

149

put on the blank face that Rose remembered well from Mount Brien and that usually meant he was about to leave the scene of possible conflict. Sure enough, a moment later he said: "I think I'll be off to bed. I'm not used to all this hard work."

And he smiled at Burke as if they were the best of friends. Rose saw Burke's neck muscles tighten with fury and his lower lip pull in, showing his teeth, giving him the look of a savage dog.

At once she stood up saying: "I think I'll go too."

Burke said: "Do that. Yes. You can go. But the rest of you can sit here and listen to what I have to say."

"Are you sure you want me?" Colman asked.

"Of course I do. Don't I need someone to my back?"

Rose fled upstairs. That was one battle-field that she was glad to avoid. Jeanne's remark had put a new idea into her head. She had never given much thought to Jean-Paul, thinking of him as a sort of superior animal, a horse perhaps. That was it – a good pony. Her mother sometimes said this of a good servant, though they didn't occur very often in Rocklawn. Most servants were perfidious and Jean-Paul was no exception. Rose knew that the Lallys had been hidden by him for a while, until he became frightened for his skin and put them out. That was the end of them. With no place to go, they were soon arrested and guillotined, the whole family. Bernadette told her that, not Burke.

Rose could see that Bernadette held this betrayal against Jean-Paul. Difficult times, she said, and it was hard for a person to know what was the right thing to do. Now Colman said the bad times were coming back. Burke never talked of the horrors he had seen in Bordeaux but she knew some of them from his journal.

Still she trusted Burke, though she was afraid of him and his constant changes were hard to understand. He seemed to have developed new scruples lately. He never slept in Jeanne's bed now, the huge bed with red velvet curtains, appropriately embroidered with Judith in the act of killing Holofernes. What wit had ordered such a subject for the

150

main bed in the house? Perhaps that was what had put the fear of God into Burke.

Amused and pleased at this thought, Rose poured a glass of wine and began to make ready for bed. Not far from her window, a hunting owl burst into its fearful, savage cry. Tomorrow there would be feathers and blood on the ground beneath. No wonder the country people were afraid of owls, in spite of their pussy-cat faces and soft, bumbling flight.

She came downstairs in the morning with a sense of something splendid and exciting about to happen. The house seemed deserted. The spring flowers that she had brought into the salon yesterday, braving the wet grass to reach them, were dead in their vase, the petals falling in wrinkled heaps and the spidery stalks bare. Spring flowers were always gone in a night. The hearth was covered with ash from last night's fire. Though Burke had praised him, Rose knew that Jacques could never take indoor work seriously. It was for women. He preferred feeding the chickens or bringing in vegetables from the garden or even working the laundry pole for Anna – anything rather than dust and sweep. She drew in her breath with a hissing sound, the only sign of irritation she ever allowed herself in a public place even when she was alone, and went to open the windows. Fresh air – the French hated and feared it. Even in winter they seemed to expect clouds of mosquitoes to swarm in at every opportunity. A year ago the frames had all been immovable but Rose had loosened them one by one, in the downstairs rooms. She pushed up the heavy sash and breathed the cold air which had a tang of the distant sea in it.

As she turned back she found that Colman had come into the room behind her. She said: "Well?"

No need to beat about the bush with Colman. He always understood immediately. He closed the door carefully. She motioned to him to sit with her in the window embrasure, then said: "Tell me everything, from the beginning."

Colman said: "I was sorry for them. Madame looked as if

151

she would faint. A cornered rat, poor thing. Our Master
Edmund was a bit more brave, looking up at the ceiling,
twitching his lips as if he was going to whistle, stretching his
arm along the back of the sofa trying to look quite at ease.
That made Mr. Burke so mad that he shouted at him in
English: 'Young man, don't pretend you haven't a notion in
the world why I'm here talking to you.' Edmund stuttered a
bit and said: 'Yes – no – indeed – of course – ' and Madame
began to cry but she stopped at once when Mr. Burke said:
'You have nothing to cry about. You should be laughing.
Edmund, my boy, you can have her.' At that Edmund
looked as if he would make for the door, until Mr. Burke
said: 'And the house and land too. I'm fixing it all. Take it or
leave it.' Then Edmund looked as crafty as a man that meets
a leprechaun walking along with a pot of gold under his
arm. Mr. Burke saw that too – he sees everything. But he
didn't laugh, though I think he was near to it. He was very
gentle with Madame, as if he was talking to a child. He said:
'Will you take him? I know you have got fond of him and
why wouldn't you? He's young and strong, and I'm getting
old. I don't blame you for anything. But you can say no if
you like.' She said: 'No, no. I mean yes, I will – Yes – no – '
and Mr. Burke said: 'It's all right. I know what you mean.
What about you, Edmund? I could send you out of the
house with a kick in the arse, after what you've been at, but
it suits me better to do the opposite.' Madame put her hands
over her face and gave a sort of moan, and I wondered if she
was afraid that he would refuse her after all those insults.
But there was no fear of that. He said: 'If you've fixed it all,
I'm willing. I'm not complaining.' And Mr. Burke said:
'You haven't anything to complain about, that I can see.
The land and the house will be made over to you and you
can go in for breeding horses, what you're good at. I'll keep
an eye on you and I'll buy your stock if it's up to standard.'
Madame peeked out from behind her fingers and gave him a
look that would turn new milk sour. She said: 'What about
René? What about the child?' Mr. Burke said: 'You can have
him. It wouldn't be decent for me.' Then he turned back to

152

Edmund and said: 'So there you are with a wife and family all ready-made. Aren't you the lucky man?' God forgive me, I think he was trying to see if anything in the wide earthly world would provoke Edmund into doing what he should have done, call him a swine and a lout and tell him he could keep his house and his woman and do whatever he liked with them. Edmund didn't budge. God and the devil are the only two that know what goes on in that man's head.

"When Mr. Burke saw that Edmund was not going to give away a word he told him to get off to bed and to be up and ready for work early in the morning. I thought this was my chance to escape but he wouldn't allow it. There was something indecent in being there between the two of them. She didn't like it either. She said: 'Can't Colman go too?' But he said he wanted me there as a witness. Her hackles rose at that and she said, very snibby: 'We don't need a witness, especially not that one.' Mr. Burke said: 'Don't forget, it was he who brought them all from Ireland.' When Edmund had gone he spoke French, because Madame's English is nothing great, as you know. He said that Edmund must go at once to his brother at Saintes, as he was asked to do, and she should go to Paris with us until the legal formalities were finished and the marriage could take place. I think this was where I was really needed. He said that the marriage would have to be kept secret for a while because she was supposed to be his own wife. If the troubles started up again, people might say he was still hankering after being a priest and that he was not a true citizen of the new world at all. She looked as if nothing would please her more than to have him hauled off to the gallows but she knows better than anyone that he's her only hope."

"When? When do we go to Paris?"

"That was what Madame asked too. He said in a few days, as soon as she can get ready. Lord God, she looked as if candles had been lit all around her. For Edmund! That cold-hearted fish is able to change her whole nature. What kind of power is that?"

"The power of love. It moves mountains."

"I can believe it, after what I saw last night. They're two of a kind but after I went to bed I prayed for them. I said to myself that I had seen a miracle."

"It was all on her side, by the sound of it."

"Yes."

"Was that the end? It looks as if they're going to have a *ménage à trois*."

"*À quatre*. You're in it too."

"What do you mean?"

"What's the matter? Miss French, you said you're quite happy here. I heard you myself. Mr. Burke said you would stay on and take care of the housekeeping and help her with the child, as you have been doing."

"I would rather die."

So this was his idea, to make her into a permanent servant, to live out her days in loneliness and boredom, to be a cat, a dog, someone to be pitied, like a half-idiot who can do a few useful things but is without rights, on sufferance. The world was full of them, women who had failed to get a husband and were morally if not legally dead. He certainly was not a Frenchman of the new age. A dyed-in-the-wool Irishman.

Colman was saying reasonably: "You can always refuse. You're not at his mercy."

"Of course."

But she had revealed her agitation. The smallest sign of weakness was dangerous, an invitation to confidences. That was something she had not indulged in for years, neither to give nor to receive them. But it was not so easy to avoid it, now that she had given an opening.

Colman said: "What will you do, then?"

"I don't know."

"Do you mean to refuse?"

"No. Not at once. For God's sake don't tell Mr. Burke that I don't like his plan."

"I won't say a word."

Even with Colman she felt that such an appeal put her in his power but he had been an underdog long enough to develop a respect for the breed. She believed what he said,

154

and the look he gave her showed that he did not think less of her for having had to ask this favour.

When they all assembled in the dining-room at noon, it was true that Jeanne was glowing. Her thin, pale lips were softly parted, the peevish expression was gone, her close-set eyes were wide open, fixed in adoration on Edmund, who however seemed to be waiting for a cue from Burke. It was not long in coming. Before Jacques brought the dishes he said heartily: "So now, Rose, it's all arranged. Congratulate them."

"I do," she said after a second's hesitation, uncertain whether or not she was supposed to be in the secret, but Burke said to the others: "I consulted her, of course, in advance. She has great wisdom."

And she's an old maid, an honorary aunt, a member of the senior council. At their age, that was how a woman in her thirties looked. Burke had gone on to other things, incidentally covering Edmund's moment of embarrassment. It had been no more than a moment, with his practice in two-faced trickery. Rose had learned a great deal from him, in the last year. While the meal was being served Burke said genially: "So you're off to Paris in two days' time, if the ladies will be ready. What do you think, Rose?"

"It should be possible."

"Do you all hear how calmly she says that? Anyone would think she had been in Paris a thousand times. Let me tell you, it's not a place to be taken lightly. There is no city in the whole world like it. Jeanne has never been there either."

"Yes, I have. I went with my parents when I was ten years old," she said. "We stayed in the house of friends of theirs, in the rue du Bac. It belonged to Madame Dillon. Her husband was in the army so I never saw him."

Burke gave a heavy sigh.

"Ah, yes – all dead and gone now of course."

Speaking up like that was new for Jeanne. Usually she confined herself to sharp little comments on things that displeased her but overnight she seemed to have changed. Edmund still had a long way to go. He was watching her

155

with an anxious expression, as if he were not sure that the prize he had gained was going to be worth the trouble. Good enough for him, Rose thought. He has manipulated the world to suit himself for a long time now. The day had to come when life would catch up with him.

During the two days of preparations Rose saw very little of Edmund. Burke was keeping him out of the way, perhaps still uneasy about the possible reaction by the neighbours to his taking over the property. Jeanne however seemed unconcerned about this. She ordered Rose to help her, usually omitting the formality of politeness. At first Rose thought it was excitement, anxiety, the fever of love, but soon she concluded that it was a version of her own mother's deliberate rudeness to new servants. Her mother would say: "Begin as you mean to go on." No protests on Rose's part had ever diverted her from this principle. Jeanne was at the same game of breaking Rose in to her new position in the household. "Fetch my linen skirt – no, you idiot, the newer one. Do you think I want to look a fool with my country clothes in Paris?" Rose obeyed silently, thinking that Jeanne might relent when the packing was finished, or even that she might apologise. Nothing of the sort – on the morning of their departure, she took the best place in the coach, with her back to the horses, leaving Rose to pack in the hand-baggage, then said languidly: "Rose, you can sit in the opposite corner, I may need to stretch my legs."

Burke overheard that. He had been supervising the packing of the heavy baggage into the second coach but he had left this to help Rose climb into the first one. Holding her hand in his huge paw, he stuck his head right inside the coach and roared:

"What do you think you're at, madame? It didn't take you long to go back to your old ways. Oh, don't cry, for the love and honour of God. You're better when you're snarling."

She wailed: "You frightened me."

"Better a fright now than the one you might get later if you don't give up those la-di-da manners. You're a citizeness, don't forget. You're not a damned countess any more. Lord God, you make me think it's a mistake to turn you loose at all."

"No, no, I'll remember."

"Move your feet then and make room for Citizeness French."

She did, but after that her mouth was turned down once more and she sniffed back her tears for miles and miles of the road. Not even Edmund's farewell, which was noticeably tender, put her into a better mood. Rose found her stupidity pitiful. It was as if a toy had been given to a child and immediately taken away again. She deserved some sympathy for having lived for years with that noisy bully – how had she tolerated it? But she must have invited it. She had certainly encouraged Edmund. Burke had a certain delicacy in spite of his rough ways. He would never have forced himself on her. Rose let her mind run for an amazed minute or two on the vision of Burke, in his nightshirt, climbing into that great bed with the embroidered curtains. Forget them – soon she would see the last of them.

The long, slow journey kept her unpleasantly close to her companion. The shared meals and flea-ridden rooms at the inns where they stopped for a few hours while the horses were changed, the inevitable hours of dozing with their heads on each other's shoulders, the common boredom and pain and fatigue forced them into unwelcome intimacy. Four nights and five days of this were endured before they entered Paris, flat green cornfields suddenly giving way to a warren of crooked streets and rickety houses festooned with ragged washing. In a neighbourhood of somewhat wider streets, Burke had rented a small apartment for them, its windows tightly shut of course, worn damask draperies suffocating the one wide bed, creaking floors and uneven-legged chairs, but even Jeanne was in no condition to complain. After Colman had escorted them upstairs to this and had ordered a meal for them from the landlady, he went off to his own lodgings in a nearby street, promising to return in the morning.

157

In spite of her fatigue, for a long time Rose could not sleep. It seemed that her brain would not take orders from her, so that she felt smothered by a cloud of vague anticipation and fear. He was here, somewhere in this city, accessible through the Irish patriots. The truth was not far away. Years and years – she could scarcely remember how many. He had sworn forever. If he had forgotten, it meant that the whole world was a deception. If Rabbit was a liar, one could never believe anyone, not even God. He was not. Then what had prevented him? She knew, of course. Others had stopped his messages from going to her. He believed that it was she who was false. Her letters had been intercepted by the same people who had destroyed his letters to her. It would all come out. In a few days the waiting would be proved worthwhile. Nothing else was possible – she knew it would be so. Then all the pain would be over and she would only remember it to point up her new, constant happiness.

Burke did not come for four days, and during that time they stayed indoors most of the time, taking a short walk in the late afternoon when the streets began to quiet down. Jeanne was rather frightened, as well she might be since most of the people she had met as a child had gone to the guillotine. At night she lay perfectly still in the huge bed, whether asleep or awake Rose had no idea. Rose lay still also, in fear of disturbing her. What would he think of her when he saw her? She would know instantly. Perhaps he would find her old and unattractive. She would find him aged too – but that would mean nothing. He would know, he would revere this holy love, he would know her life and his were part and parcel of each other, he would enter that paradise as if he had never been forced to leave it. If she had been alone she would have talked to him, but now, until at last she fell asleep from exhaustion, there was no comfort.

When Burke arrived he said at once: "Rose, my girl, you look like an old hag. What have you been doing to yourself? Running around Paris, trying to see it all at once, I suppose. That's how it is with everyone. Jeanne looks better than you do. I suppose you have been taking care of her. Always too good-hearted."

He was full of energetic plans, including as usual all kinds of domestic ones. He had moved into Colman's lodgings, where the daughter of the house was a dressmaker, and she had agreed to make some dresses for Jeanne. Burke had arranged this through Colman, as a special surprise, which was not to be revealed until he himself arrived in Paris. They would go around there with him next morning and get started. Their meals were to be sent in by a pastry-cook since he had no faith in the landlady. They were to walk every day, then come home to rest and have some entertainment in the evenings. He fussed over Jeanne's comfort as if she were still his wife. Enjoy it while you can, my lady, Rose thought: you won't get too much of that from Edmund.

While he chatted about the various ways in which they could occupy themselves, she had been wondering if they were to be introduced to the company he had come to meet. If not, she would have to work long and laboriously on Colman, to get the information she wanted without giving away the reason. A delay was desirable now. Burke's first words had shocked her, and she realised that she must rest and recover systematically from the recent hardships before – she recoiled from naming him now, even to herself.

That very evening, however, just as they were finishing supper, Burke came charging in, his huge bulk seeming to fill the little sitting-room to suffocation. He sat heavily on a tiny sofa, so that it creaked dangerously, wrapping his heavy black cloak tightly around him as if he knew it might knock over the gimcrack tables and chairs, saying: "Finish up there quickly. You're coming out with me. I've heard you've hardly been outside the door since you came. Fresh air and a bit of exercise is what you need. It's a short walk, just around the corner."

"Where are we going?"

"To pay a visit to some Irish friends of mine, good friends of Ireland too."

159

Jeanne said viciously: "I know who you mean – those people who are always plotting."

"That's right. Plotting is exactly what we're doing. But you needn't be afraid. I would never take you into dangerous company. We have the blessing of the highest in the land for our plots, in this country. It's only in Ireland that there is any danger."

Rose's idea of Irish conspirators was that they would be dirty and ignorant and vulgar. The truth was very different. Their host was a middle-aged doctor named Maurice FitzGerald, who lived with his wife and children in a tall house overlooking a park. The salon was crowded when they arrived, and even without his cloak, which he had left in the hall, Burke seemed to fill more than his rightful share of space. He had obviously told his friends something less than the truth about Jeanne. She was his protegée, just engaged to be married to Edmund Brien of Mount Brien in Galway. They were going to live in the Château Rochechouart which had belonged to her father. Not a word about René nor about his and Jeanne's past association, though some word of his doings must have been known in Paris. And Rose French, of Rocklawn in County Mayo, was a cousin of the Frenches of Frenchpark, who were of course connected with the Frenches of Wexford.

It was a pleasant change to be treated with such respect by all these well-bred, well-dressed, soft-spoken, elegant people. The attention so closely fixed on them was embarrassing but Rose saw that Jeanne accepted it easily, as her right. Everyone spoke in French, perhaps for the benefit of the few French people who were present, but also because most of the Irish had been at least students in France. Some had been born there, the children of emigrés from the Irish penal laws. Burke seemed to know everyone – Stack, Barry, MacSheehy, Donovan, Curry, Hickey, Mandeville – these were the names he mentioned to her as he moved through the long room, one hand on Rose's shoulder as he introduced her to them, the other guiding Jeanne by the elbow. At last this progress came to an end and Rose found herself sitting on a sofa with a young man named Jules Dorval. Someone was handing around coffee and the eyes were turned away from her at last. She had heard admiring murmurs and was gratified by them, but she needed to be relieved, to take her bearings.

The young man beside her said: "All these strangers – it's quite an ordeal."

For the first time she looked at him directly. He was broad-shouldered but not tall, with a big head of black, curly hair, very dark eyes which sparkled cheerfully and a large nose and mouth. He reminded her of Rabbit.

He asked: "What is Rocklawn?"

A hint of irony in the tone of his voice affected her answer.

"Nothing great. It's my father's house."

"And Mount Brien I know, of course."

She felt a tightness in her throat, almost a sensation of choking, but she sipped her coffee and then asked: "How?"

"I've never been there, though I may go some day. A good house for a French visitor to stay in, they say, because Lady Sophie Brien is French."

"Yes. I lived there with the family, for a number of years."

He said: "I've noticed that the Irish always introduce each other with as much family history as one can decently get into a few words, and very often with the name of their estate included. For a country which is such a strong supporter of our Revolution, don't you think that is peculiar?"

Rose answered quickly, barely attending to what she was saying: "They want their own aristocracy back instead of the foreign one that they have had for the last hundred years. They want to be sure to identify them when the time comes."

"An aristocracy! Why do they want one at all? Will it not be democratic rule, when Ireland is free?"

"They know you must start somewhere. They always depended on their great families as leaders. They want to go back to an older way of life altogether."

161

"Do you think that is possible?"

"I don't see why not. For ordinary people, things don't change much. They need to feel safe, and have enough to eat, and be able to educate their children and die in peace in their own beds. They don't mind which master's saddle they wear, so long as they have control over their own affairs."

"I see you have read your Rousseau. What a wise lady you are."

"Wise, indeed, and learned too."

She had not noticed that Burke had moved in beside her and was standing there, as tall as a chimney, his coffee-cup clutched incongruously in his huge hand. Her fingers were tingling, her head pounding with a painfully fast pulse, her whole body hot with fever from her excited brain. Nothing would stop her now, not even that malign presence at her elbow. The sound of her own voice amazed her, it was so detached and calm. Taking no notice of Burke, she spoke directly to Jules Dorval.

"Since you know the people who visit at Mount Brien, perhaps you know Rabaut de Saint Etienne?"

She lifted her chin slightly as she said his name, the first time she had ever said it to anyone. Dorval looked blank, then seemed to recollect something. Before he could speak, however, Burke's voice boomed out: "Rabaut de Saint Etienne? I remember him well. He's dead and gone. That poor devil was guillotined four years ago, in '93, in the month of August – "

She half-rose to her feet, intending to batter out his brains with her fists. Before she could lift her arms, a black wave seemed to break over her, and with humiliating slowness she slid gently downwards into unconsciousness.

162

# _10_

ROSE LAY VERY QUIETLY IN THE SMALL BEDROOM WHERE they had taken her. She remembered being helped in there, fighting down the nausea that threatened to disgrace her still further. The ladies were very kind. They wondered anxiously why she had fainted – the journey, the over-crowded room, the excitement of visiting Paris for the first time were all blamed. Burke, with his usual astuteness, was the only one who had the right idea. As she leaned on Madame FitzGerald and Madame Barry, dragging herself painfully along the corridor, he stood in the doorway watching, and she heard him say to Dorval: "That was the stupidest thing I've ever done in my life. I had no notion that she would care about him. Sure, she can only have seen him once in her life, when he was in Ireland."

Once she had heard that, there was no possibility of getting up and going back to the lodgings with Jeanne, listening every day to his heavy-handed chatter, waiting in terror for his ferocious questions. There was safety in this quiet room at the back of the house, where the door could remain unlocked since no one entered without knocking, where Madame FitzGerald's maid Lucie brought her de-licious meals and sat doing her embroidery by the window until they were eaten up, where the lady of the house came twice a day to see her and talk to her for a while and tell her she was welcome to stay as long as she liked. A doctor came too, and said she was exhausted and needed a long rest. She glared at him when he first came in, thinking that he had come to tell her she could get up and go home, but what he said was the exact opposite. She was to be protected from all stress, both physical and mental, drink plenty of good red wine and sleep as much as possible. Madame FitzGerald said they would see his instructions were carried out and they would call him again if they needed him.

Rose knew they would not need him so long as she was allowed to stay where she was. When she tried to get up, her whole body shook while ghastly visions of Rabbit's last days crossed and recrossed before her – Rabbit condemned to death, Rabbit in the wretched cart on the way to the guillotine, Rabbit in the hands of the executioner – these horrors sprang into her mind again and again, no matter how she tried to eliminate them.

What was she doing on that day in August, four years ago? She should have known what was happening. Deep inside her, an idea had taken hold, that she had never cared for Rabbit at all, that she had only been in love with love. If this were so, he was nothing more than the instrument of her release, the key that was to let her out into the wide world where she would be free to follow all the good things she knew existed, but that were completely absent from her life in Ireland. Then that marvellous vision of hope that had sustained her last few years was a complete deception. She was a fool, living in a fool's world of imagination and fantasy, like someone who calls up spirits from the lower world, to keep him company in his search for excitement and mystery.

She revolted against this idea. It could not be true, with her. When he had held her in his arms and promised to come back to her, everything about him was honest and good. That was why she had waited and hoped for him long after reason should have told her that he would never come again. Reason had told her the opposite, that it would be a crime to doubt him. Throughout all that time, when she had felt abandoned by the whole world, she had been quite sure that he was the one who would be with her always. It was true that even if he had never come to give her this hope, she would not have been able to resign herself to a lifetime in the cage where she was imprisoned. Her whole nature was too fiery to accept the vulgarity, the dirt, the

164

bullying, the petty pride and deceit and especially the deliberate destructiveness of the people around her. Lying there in the half-darkness she began to understand Lady Sophie Brien at last. Everything at Mount Brien that was clean and orderly was her doing. Now and then, when Rose had visited the neighbouring landlords, the contrast was overwhelming – dogs and cats roaming free in all the rooms, children gone wild, swarms of idle unpaid servants, tea served from battered tea-pots in chipped cups without apology – in all of this Rose had seen laziness and bitterness and inefficiency. Now she realised that the real cause was despair. These people were paradoxically proud of their family names – O'Flaherty and Burke and D'Arcy and Daly – honourable names in Ireland. Once they had fought for their rights but that was a different generation which remembered the days of their glory. This generation was beaten into the ground, never to rise again.

Rose would rise. She would never lie down to order, like a dog. This made her ridiculous, as it did Madame Sophie, with her silk dresses and her lace tablecloths and her fine china that she had brought from France as a bride. The envy of these poverty-stricken neighbours was only partly relieved by the family disgrace of the Briens, and by the obvious vulgarities of Lady Fanny.

Jeanne came to see her after several days. Madame FitzGerald brought her straight to the bedroom without asking Rose's leave, but in fact it would have been impossible to get out of the meeting. She kept her shaking hands under the covers.

Jeanne came close to peer at her, saying: "I must say you don't look too bad. Mr. Burke said I was only to stay ten minutes but there is so much to talk about. When are you getting up?"

"Not yet, I believe."

"You're missing everything."

"Yes."

"What happened to you? Mr. Burke said he told you something that made you fall in a faint. What was it?"

"Mr. Burke told you that?"

"Yes. Then he wouldn't tell me what it was. I was looking for the young man who was sitting with you – what was his name? – to ask him, but I haven't been able to find him. What was all the fuss about?"

"It was nothing – it was not that – the room was very hot – I could hardly breathe – "

Jeanne said: "So there was something. I can tell by the way you deny it. Mr. Burke said he would never have spoken if he had known you knew the man. Who was the man?"

Damn Burke and his open mouth. Rose said: "Someone I met long ago."

Rose closed her eyes to get away from Jeanne, who said pettishly: "Oh, very well, if you don't want to tell. I wish you would come home. I can't go out unless someone comes to fetch me and Mr. Burke is always busy. You could rest at home just as well as here."

Rose said carefully: "The doctor said I can't go for a while. He said I'm suffering from shock and stress."

"And what about me?"

"Yes, Jeanne, I know it's been bad for you too, but the man – that man – is the first I actually knew who died in that horrible way – "

"I did my crying long ago," Jeanne said contemptuously, watching dispassionately as the tears flowed down Rose's cheeks. "You'll get over it." She pinched in her mouth so that tiny wrinkles formed along her upper lip. "We're alive and they're dead. We can do nothing for them. Every day that goes by, we grow older. What good does it do, to spend our time going over and over what's past? I made up my mind long ago that I wouldn't do that."

She paused, staring at Rose doubtfully, as if she could find no more to say to her. Perhaps she would go soon, Rose thought frantically. Her ten minutes were almost up. But instead she was drawing her little feet together and squeezing her hands in their tight gloves. There was more to come, whatever it was. Rose found her handkerchief and

166

dried her eyes – what idiotic weakness, to weep in the presence of this little viper. Now Jeanne was looking frightened. Perhaps she was afraid that someone would come in and blame her for Rose's distress. Her voice actually shook as she began again: "Rose, I have something very embarrassing to say to you."

Her eyes darted to the door, as if she would like to run from the room. In spite of everything, Rose almost felt like laughing. She said: "Well, say it, whatever it is, and be done with it."

"You're always so strong."

This was said without irony, almost with envy. Rose said: "For heaven's sake, Jeanne, say what you want to say."

Her fright was possibly caused by a memory of Burke's warning, but then she seemed to realise that she could not put off the moment any longer. She said: "It's Edmund – yes, Edmund. You were his governess. He says that when he's married he doesn't want to have you to live with us. It's natural, he says. Mr. Burke – " She stopped again, as if she were making an effort to remember what she had been told to say: "Edmund will have help with the horses and with the land. We will be quite rich. He wants you to have an income from our estate, to live somewhere else – he should have come and told you himself!" she finished with a wail.

Rose said: "But by now he is in Saintes. It would be very far to come."

"Then you're not insulted?"

"Why should I be? It will cost a lot of money. Can he afford it?"

"He says that he can. I don't know much about money. He says you are to live well, find an apartment, anywhere you like."

"Does Mr. Burke know about this offer?"

"Yes."

"And he approves? He thinks Edmund can afford it?"

"Yes."

"It was I who brought Edmund to France. He would never have left home, but for me."

"I know. He told me."

"How does he get my answer? Through Mr. Burke?"

Again that frightened look. Jeanne said: "Yes."

"You can tell him that I am not insulted, and that I accept. And you can say that I said: 'Many persons have done a just, many a generous, but few a grateful act.' Will you remember that, in those words?"

"Yes, if I write them down."

There were pens and paper on the table by the window; and Jeanne laboriously wrote what Rose dictated. Then she folded the paper and put it in her pocket, saying: "Where will you live?"

"In Paris, I think."

"Alone?"

"Of course not. Madame FitzGerald will find me a maid."

"I don't know how I'll manage without you. I know nothing about housekeeping."

"Didn't you discuss all this with Edmund?"

"No. He makes all the arrangements, for everyone."As she stood up to go she said: "I'm sure I've said all the wrong things. I was not supposed to say I'll miss your help."

"Edmund will help you, since he's so practical."

"Yes, Edmund."

For a moment she had the look of total happiness that Rose had seen once or twice before, when she was with Edmund. This time it flashed and was gone, and her mouth tightened up again. In her governess mood, which had given rise to the Swift quotation, Rose felt inclined to say: "Don't do that to your mouth, dear. It looks ugly." Impossible, of course. Would she never go? She did, dropping on one knee to kiss Rose on the forehead, unexpectedly. They had never been on kissing terms.

Blessedly alone again, Rose rolled over and over in her mind the extraordinary turn that events had taken. She was to live alone, independently. It could scarcely be believed but there was no question about it. Anything that came through Burke had to be believed. Now she was amazed that it had never occurred to her that she might not be welcome to live, forever, that ghastly life at the Château Rochechouart. Accustomed to the Irish mode, where there was always room for another slave in the various categories, she had never doubted that she would be received for her usefulness. Jeanne would make dreadful mistakes, day after day, never learning to avoid them and always adding new ones. That was no longer the concern of Rose.

How Edmund must hate her, to be willing to pay so much to be rid of her. Rose had never realised it. She had rather imagined the reverse, in fact, since she had often defended him against his mother, especially against her raids on his books. Lady Fanny referred to *Gulliver's Travels* as "that bloody book", hating it with a personal feeling that summed up her main feelings for her son.

Why with her own hatred of the life she had led in Mount Brien should Rose now feel a pang for the smell of scythed grass, the sound of swallows, the bark of dogs, the intense night-time quiet that was like no other silence on earth? It was monstrously unjust that all these things should be so little enjoyed by the very people who inhabited that world. They seemed to have an infinite capacity to destroy and embitter what was in fact reasonable behaviour. Nothing was reasonable there, no one behaved logically, she thought wildly. But she knew already that she would dream of Ireland now and then, and smell those damp, insinuating smells, even in her sleep.

In the following days she became accustomed to the new idea. Burke called but she refused to see him. Madame FitzGerald was disappointed – Burke was such a fine man, such anxiety about Rose, always calling to find out how she was doing. Rose said she would see him soon, not today, never today.

When he came, at last, there was no escape. She was sitting by the window, fully dressed for the first time, her hands and her mind idle, when the door opened abruptly and there he was. She made no move. He closed the door behind him and came forward saying: "I thought I would never get in to see you. They always said you were resting, or asleep, or not well enough. I must say you look well enough to me."

"That is what Jeanne said when she came."

"Jeanne! That woman! Rose, I came to apologise for her."

"It was not necessary."

"Don't play the grande dame with me, for God's sake. She's a little bitch and it's I that knows it. She overheard me say something that evening you fainted, and ever since then she has been trying to get it out of me, who the person was whose death meant so much to you."

"How did you get in now?"

"Madame is out. One of the maids showed me up. Don't get anxious, girl. I won't upset you. I'm leaving Paris. I couldn't go without seeing you, after all the time you lived in my house."

"Thank you for your hospitality."

"You did more for me than I ever did for you."

"You know I'm not going back there? Jeanne said she told you of Edmund's offer."

She had not invited him to sit down but he looked around for a chair, found one that seemed strong enough and sat on it with great care. Then he said: "Yes, she told me that you've accepted the offer. I think it's a good thing."

"Can he afford it?"

"Of course. The farm alone is worth a fortune, and he'll have the horse-breeding as well. I'll keep an eye on him."

"He has fallen on his feet. I suppose he feels that it would never have happened but for me."

"Yes. That's the reason he gave. You need have no scruples about taking it."

"I can't afford scruples."

"Rose, I must tell you – no one heard that name except Jules Dorval and he has sworn never to mention it to anyone."

"Have you been discussing me with him, Mr. Burke?"

"No! Look, I'm trying to bring you comfort. Don't be so

170

suspicious. When I saw what the mention of that name did to you, I told Dorval that if he ever spoke of that man in connection with you, I'd have the hide off him. That was the most elementary good sense."

"Did it occur to you he might never have thought of such a connection, if you had not mentioned it?"

"Lord God, girl, you looked as if you wanted to kill me. You'd have gone for my throat, if you hadn't fallen to the floor."

And she would have, indeed. Watching her, Burke said: "Thank God you can still laugh."

"I was not laughing."

"Not exactly. Women have a great deal to put up with."

"Including Jeanne?"

"She gives as good as she gets. Rose, she knows nothing, nothing at all. I guessed you didn't want to see me after what happened, but I couldn't go without being sure you understand that Jeanne knows nothing."

"There is nothing to know."

"All the better."

But those round, doggy eyes seemed to bore right through her, picking up things here and there like someone going through a not-very-interesting antique-shop. After a moment he said: "Then I won't see you again?"

"No."

"Madame FitzGerald will help you to find an apartment where you can live safely. At your age it's respectable for a woman to live alone. She will introduce you to her friends too – she has been singing your praises to everyone, so you won't be lonely."

"That's all right. I'm accustomed to being alone."

Unexpectedly he said: "So am I. I envy you, living in Paris. There is no city in the world like it."

"Could you not live here yourself?"

"No. I'm a farmer. In any case I must go to Ireland now, before I decide anything else."

"You haven't been there for a long time."

"Not since my father died – not since I took Robert and

Louise Brien here to Paris, to finish their education, God help us."

"Will you go to Mount Brien?"

"I'm not sure of my welcome. What do you think?"

"Lady Sophie is always glad to see anyone from France."

"Even me? Perhaps you're right. I'll certainly be in the neighbourhood, with Colman. You haven't asked about him."

"Should I have?"

"He was one of your party."

"Yes, I suppose he was, in a way."

"He wants to come to see you, before we leave."

"When is that?"

"In a few days. When we get a passage from Brest."

"I'm not sure that I want to see Colman. I'm not feeling well enough to be sociable."

"You don't have to be sociable with him. It would be a great kindness to see him, if only for a few minutes."

"Oh, very well. I haven't been downstairs yet but I'll make the effort if you think I should."

"Can't you receive him here?"

"Mr. Burke, what can you be thinking of? How could I possibly do such a thing?"

"Oh – well – I'm not too well versed in that kind of manners. Do what you think best. But you will see him?"

"I suppose it would be hard to refuse."

"May I tell him to come, then?"

"I suppose so. He can make an appointment with Madame FitzGerald."

"You don't seem pleased at the idea of seeing him."

"Why should I be? I barely knew him, as a shepherd who came sometimes to Mount Brien and was brought into the dining-room to the great annoyance of some members of the family."

"Colman is not just a shepherd. He's quite well educated."

"Yes, that is true. It has been good for him to be in France."

"France is good for everyone. When I come back,

Madame FitzGerald will tell me where to find you, I hope."

"No doubt."

There was no point in telling him that she hoped she had seen the last of him. He did not break the chair but stood up slowly and carefully, letting out one of those long windy sighs that were sometimes accompanied by a sound like the moan of a cow in the evening. This time he confined himself to breathing heavily. She stood up also, so that he could not hang over her, and took his offered hand in hers for a second, letting it drop at once, then moving towards the door. He could do nothing but follow, though she could have sworn that he had more to say.

On the threshold she said, holding the door open: "Good-bye, Mr. Burke. I hope you have a safe journey."

"I don't enjoy sailing but there's no other way to get to Ireland. Good-bye, Miss French." He had not called her this for a long time. "I wish you luck in your new life. You may be able to move quite soon."

"I'll probably begin to make arrangements at once."

Before he had taken two steps away from the door, she had shut it behind him, not sharply but firmly enough for him to understand that she was glad the interview had ended.

Back in her chair by the window, she found herself suddenly impatient with her life as an invalid. Burke's visit had stimulated her. Until now, perhaps she had not quite believed in her good fortune, or had even been afraid to make a move towards it. There was a coarse truth about everything he said and did, which was possibly the reason for his easy friendships with all classes of people. Madame FitzGerald had called him a good man, the last adjective that Rose would have applied to him. Jean-Paul adored him unquestioningly. So did his dogs. She had never seen him ill-treat one of them, nor fail to respond to their sudden need for affectionate handling. Sitting by the fire with his book held towards the lamp, his hand would stretch to fondle the ears of that red setter bitch Banba, without once looking down at her. How did he know she had edged in beside

173

him? It seemed to be the same instinct that led him to friendship with Colman, and with Jean-Paul and his mother and the other peasants who constantly consulted him about their affairs, though he was no longer their priest.

Rose's most urgent need now was to avoid going back to live with Jeanne. Burke's remark about her improved appearance warned her that she should not delay in finding an apartment of her own. She found that some money had been lodged by Burke with Madame FitzGerald, who said: "Mr. Burke thought you would like to begin at once to take a place. He asked me to help you and of course I will, though I would have liked you to stay longer with us."

"Did he suggest a place?"

If he had, it would be the first to be rejected, but he had not. He was still in Paris, she said, but very busy, and had said that he would probably not be able to see Rose again. She felt quite safe in dressing early every day, then walking out with Madame FitzGerald to look at rooms, coming back to rest and consider what she had seen. Thus she was alone in the salon a few days later when Lucie announced that there was a gentleman to see her.

There was no escape. Colman was in the room before she could stand up, and Lucie had disappeared, shutting the door. With his trimmed hair and neat clothes he looked well. Hard to believe that he was in his late thirties, as she was. That lean, tall, healthy figure was deceptive. He had an air of confidence now, which was a development of something that had always been there. France had indeed been good for him, as Burke had said.

His manners had always been perfect. He waited until she invited him to sit down, and made a few pleasant remarks on her improved appearance.

Rose said: "Mr. Burke said you're going back to Ireland soon."

"Yes. We have done everything we can here. We're going to Rouen next week. We'll sail the week after, if the weather holds."

"April is a good time, they say."

174

"Yes."

"You'll see your mother. Do you plan to go to Mount Brien?"

"Of course."

"You don't think you'll be blamed for taking Edmund and me away with you?"

"That's water under the bridge by now. Besides, I did what I was asked to do. Robert is probably there already."

She had almost forgotten how important this mission had seemed to Colman, at the time of their departure.

"Has Robert left for Ireland, then?"

"Did Mr. Burke not tell you? Edmund is in charge at Saintes, until Robert comes back. Even Lady Fanny should be grateful to me, for taking Edmund to the place where he found his fortune."

"Poor Edmund will pay dearly for it, I'm afraid."

"He seems content. He can look after himself, as he always did. Mr. Burke has told me about you, that you're going to live alone in Paris now."

"Yes. It seems that Edmund finds it worth while paying me to go, and it suits me very well, so everyone is happy."

She spoke quickly, angrily. Burke seemed to have told her business to everyone.

Colman said: "I'm afraid you're not as pleased at this turn of affairs as Mr. Burke thinks you are."

"I am pleased. It's what I've always wanted, to be independent of everyone. I've been at the beck and call of the whole world for most of my life."

"I scarcely knew what freedom was either, until I came to France. In Ireland we're so used to the bad life that most of us put up with it, though we talk about freedom all the time."

"Do you mean to stay in Ireland then?"

"I meant to go to America. That was always my plan. Now I'm not so sure. You know we're going to have a rising in Ireland, with the help of the French."

"I heard them talking about it, the first evening we came here."

175

"Mr. Burke has done wonders for our plans. He knows so many people, he smoothed a lot of paths for us. It's certain now that an army will be sent to Ireland very soon. Our business is to go back with that news and help to organise the country to rise when the time comes."

"Can that be done?"

"It has been done already. The only thing that is not certain is the date."

"All that seems very far away to me."

"Naturally. You have been ill." He paused then said: "If the rising is successful I'll probably stay in Ireland for a while at least, though we want to model a great many new things on the American plan. Perhaps I will go to America eventually. Miss French, there is one thing I must say to you before I go."

Suddenly his manner had changed from the easy, familiar one that suited him so well. Watching him strain with his tongue, Rose reflected that it would take several generations to make gentlemen of these revolutionaries. Here was one who had had every advantage, who should be quite at home in every company, yet he was apparently in dreadful agony at the prospect of expressing his thanks, or at making his farewell speech, or whatever it was that was on his mind.

He looked up suddenly and caught her gazing at him. Her face evidently showed something of her thoughts. He said abruptly: "I'm afraid you're laughing at me."

"Well, you do look so miserable. What do you want to say? Why don't you get it out, and be done with it?"

"You always say that – I've heard it so often."

"I can't bear it when people beat around the bush."

"Very well, then. I want to ask you to marry me."

Rose gazed at him in astonishment. No warning had been given of this. She had had absolutely no premonition of what was about to happen. Colman went on after a moment, in which he gazed at her with an expression which she had seen only once in all her life before:

"Miss French, Rose, of course you are surprised. A few

years ago such an idea would have been quite impossible, but now things have changed. The whole world is different. I've loved you for years and years, all the time I knew you in Mount Brien. When I walked those weary miles once a month, I kept up my courage with the thought of seeing you at the end of it. When we sat together in the dining-room, I was in heaven, just to be near you. Ever since we came to France I've been dreaming about this day when I would tell you my thoughts." His voice had softened, almost as if he were talking to himself, and he murmured a few words in Irish which she barely understood, something about a little bright rose. Then he went on: "So I couldn't go away without asking you this question. There is no need to answer at once, unless you want to. I'll come back in a few months and then you can tell me what you have decided. All I ask now is that you promise to think it over."

By the time he had come to the end of this final, stilted speech, which he had obviously rehearsed, she had recovered. Very carefully, speaking with measured breath, she said: "I have a question of my own. Did Mr. Burke know you were going to ask me this?"

"Yes. I spoke to him about it because he has always been my friend."

"And did he give you reason to think that I would agree?"

"This has nothing to do with Mr. Burke. He said I had a perfect right to ask."

"You have not answered my question."

"Yes, he thought you might agree."

"I see. I'm sorry to have to tell you, Colman, that I can't imagine any circumstances under which I would consent to be your wife. I don't blame you for asking. Mr. Burke should have told you it is out of the question."

"How should he have known?"

"He knows my family background as well as I know it myself."

For a moment she thought that he would try to continue the conversation. He gave her a long, sad look, like a disappointed child. He stood up, drawing himself to his full

177

height as if he had difficulty in controlling his body, at last saying slowly and painfully: "I had no idea that you would feel like this. Your family came to Galway in the twelfth century as traders and merchants. Mine were kings in Ireland before Christ was born."

After he had gone she sat alone for a long time, going over and over what had happened. At last she decided that no one but Burke could possibly have any knowledge of it. She had every hope that she would never see either of them again.

# PART THREE

## _1798_

# _11_

"CHRISTMAS DAY, DECEMBER 25, 1798. PATRICK MARTIN'S House, Cashel, County Tipperary.

"Dear Dr. Everard:

"I find that I must leave you a letter in case they catch me. I feel no restraint in expressing my most intimate thoughts to you and I am sure I may rely on you to destroy this after you have read it. You will need to keep the first page to show as my last will and testament, which is one of the purposes of the letter.

"I hereby give and bequeath all my property whatsoever, in France or in any other country, to the Collège des Irlandais at Bordeaux, the money to be used for the re-establishment of the College as a seminary for Irish boys and as a school of medicine for such Irish or French boys as may wish to come. I direct that a Requiem Mass be said for the repose of my soul on one day a week forever, the stipend to be paid out of the income from my property, and I further direct that the students of the said Irish College be obliged to pray for me in their common prayers on the feasts of Saint Patrick, Saint Bridget, Saint Colmcille, Saint Columbanus, Saint Killian, Saint Brendan, Saint Fiacre, and Saint Gall."

As he wrote the last name, Burke stabbed the pen so hard that he almost broke the carefully cut nib. He read what he had written. There was room at the end of the sheet for his signature. Mrs. Martin and her husband could witness it and he would impress on them that they must remember the occasion. He trusted that the document would be considered legally sound. Pity not to be there when Dr. Everard would read it. That bit about property in France or in any other country would drive them all wild. He had no property in any other country, unless by chance he were to inherit from some unexpected source. Who in their right mind would leave him anything in a will? He would certainly never own anything in Ireland.

He took a fresh sheet of paper and went on:

"I have a strong notion that God is not going to ask the advice of the Bishops of Ireland before disposing of me for all eternity. If He did, I am not in much doubt as to what that advice would be. It is not to improve their Lordships' opinion of me that I write this letter, since I know very well that this would be impossible. I don't want to claim indulgence for anything I have ever done, since I intend to confine explanations in such matters to God. But it seems to me that of all the prelates who have seen fit to condemn me, you are the one most likely to understand the motives that drove me and the difficulty that everyone experienced in making right decisions in these terrible times. You and I remember the cursed executions in the Place Dauphine. Was anyone the same again, after having witnessed the horrors of that period? On that account I partly excuse the bishops and the professors of Maynooth for their present attitude to all of us who took part in this year's attempted revolution in Ireland. As we know well, many of them only escaped with their shirt-tails on fire from that same Terror and it's natural that they should want to avoid walking into the same things, or worse, at home. I'm not suggesting that holy men of God would have anything but the highest reasons for their statements and actions. I'm speaking only of the human or natural side of mankind."

Poor Dr. Everard. It was a shame to tease him like this. On the other hand, an Archbishop should develop a thick hide, if he has not got one already.

Burke was never clear about Dr. Everard's sympathy or lack of it in relation to the attempted revolution in Ireland. The bishops in general condemned it and at Maynooth College any student who was found to have had anything to do with it was expelled forthwith. That part was fair enough, since it was a hard-won seminary for the education of priests, something that would have been unthinkable as lately as ten years ago. But there must surely be limits. From their recent behaviour it seemed likely that the Irish bishops would be pulling their forelocks to the British government for the next hundred years, in thanksgiving for being allowed to live in their own country without fear for their skins. They detested the United Irishmen, though any man worth his salt throughout the whole country, both Protestant and Catholic, was a member by the spring of this year. In the name of the good God, how could you possibly take care of a man's soul unless you took heed of his body also? Ordering him to bow the knee in the face of oppression was a crime in the name of Christianity. How could you tell a man who sees his wife and children starving that his first duty is to the landlord? His first duty, as anyone could see, was to his family. God protect me from ever being a bishop.

Fuming and raging, Burke heaved himself to his feet. Though he was grateful to Dr. Everard for the refuge he had found him, there was no denying that his quarters were very narrow. It was an attic room in the gardener's lodge of a big house some miles from Cashel. Burke had no idea who lived in the big house, nor whether its inhabitants were aware of his presence. Since his arrival three days ago he had not been outside the door and had seen no one but Mrs. Martin. Her husband never came near him after the first evening. Burke would have enjoyed a chat with Mrs. Martin when she brought his meals on a tray but she barely replied to his civilities and then scuttled off downstairs again. Troubled times made everyone nervous. Who could blame her for being afraid of harbouring a monstrous man, in French clothes, after what had happened in Ireland in the last few months? She was obviously doing it out of friendship for Dr. Everard but she would not even pause to speak of him, or of when he was likely to call.

The room covered the whole area of the tiny house but Burke could only stand erect in a small square in the middle of it, the roof sloped so sharply. It was a nuisance to be so big, to occupy so much space in the world. Burke had never really minded it until he found himself on the run in Ireland. Even in Wexford, where the men were big and strong, never having been starved, he stood out like a sore thumb. They apologised for the size of the horse they found him there, though it must have been sixteen hands. The Wexford men and the Carlow men were good to him, risking their own lives to get him safely away, several of them saying the same thing as they passed him on to the next refuge: "We'll meet soon in Paris."

How many of them were still alive? Poor Father Michael Murphy – he could scarcely bear to think of that. And Colman, who had come so far with him, to be killed at the battle of Arklow. At least he had imagined before he died that the rising was a success and that the rebels would march on and capture Dublin.

Burke walked four steps towards the hearth, four steps back, clenching and unclenching his huge fists as if this would somehow relieve his pain. In a way it did. Any activity of the body was better than none. On the first morning, when Mrs. Martin silently took away his slops, he stopped her, embarrassed, saying: "You needn't do that for me, woman. I'm well able to take it down myself if you'll show me where to go."

"Dr. Everard said you are not to leave this room on any account," she said, keeping her eyes down, as if even that contact with him was forbidden. "I'm quite used to it. My father spent the last six years of his life here."

"Poor man. What was the matter with him?"

"Paralysed."

That was the end of the conversation. Off she went with her bucket. At least when he was holed up in the Irish College in Bordeaux he was able to make his own arrangements. He got more exercise too. That was a queer time of his life - who would have thought he would be locked in again so soon? It was his own doing. The only time he was ever shut in against his will was when he was arrested in Bordeaux. Anyone looking at his life from the outside

184

would say that he had a liking for the hen-coop. Hens again. Like them, he made for the coop every now and then.

He took a chair and placed it near the one window, then stooped his back and went in under the low ceiling to sit on it. From this position he could see out over the huge sloping park on whose summit the great house was perched. Men would kill and starve and hang their neighbours to own and keep a house like that. Once Burke thought he would have done the same but he had given away his lovely Château without a pang. It was at least as handsome as this one but more economically laid out as to the grounds. You would never find a Frenchman of any class keeping such an enormous spread of grass just to look at. In France that space would have been covered with vines, beautiful in all seasons, bare as your fingers at this time of the year but with a promise of wonders to come, if you knew the secrets of good pruning. The whole shooting match was well gone, to get rid of Jeanne. That was one plot of his that had turned out well, both parties quite satisfied. Burke's gift for organisation trapped him into gross mistakes from time to time. The affair of Rose French was one of them.

The afternoon was darkening. A yellowish tinge in the heavy clouds suggested that there might be snow. This morning he had been awakened by the sound of sleet beating against the window-panes but later the sun came out. Yes, snow was possible. A huge basket of dry turf stood beside the fire, which he kept alight both day and night. The first evening, as Mrs. Martin led him into the room, he was seized with primitive terror of the dark. It was ridiculous, of course. This was not in the least like the Irish College. There was a tall brass oil-lamp, which he could light whenever he wished with a spill of paper from the fire. Throughout the night a little soft flame from the hearth kept the devils away. His meals were hot and comforting, soups and roasts and plenty of good Irish potatoes. Tipperary was so different from the hungry west that it might as well be another

185

country. Here the poor people were better fed and had knuckled under. What else would they do? In general people don't plan revolution on a full belly. But Martin, the gardener at the great house, was putting himself in danger by hiding Burke. The landlord was away in England at this season of the year and no doubt this was why he felt safe in sheltering him.

It was chilly by the window. In the last few minutes the light had changed and the whole landscape had darkened. Lamps were lit in the distant big house and one was being carried from room to room, probably by a servant on his rounds. A little glow, like a rising and setting sun, grew and faded behind each window of the long drawing-room. Burke heard the sound of someone coming in, downstairs. He would have liked to be able to see the road outside, to watch who passed by and who came and went, but no doubt this house had been selected for him precisely because the window of his room did not give on the road.

Dr. Everard had warned him not to show a light. The window was provided with shutters as well as thick curtains, and he closed these carefully before lighting the lamp. His letter lay on the table. It was foolish to believe that anyone would take care of his problems once he was dead. That meant that he should take all precautions to stay alive and this he intended to do. Still he must make some attempt to pass on responsibility for Rose, though she would not thank him for it. He could imagine the reception she would give her would-be rescuer. Probably bite him in the leg. Well, that was a bishop's business, to be bitten from time to time.

His head came up suddenly, like a gun-dog's, at the sound of horses trampling and more people arriving – were the Martins having a party for Christmas? It seemed most unlikely. She would have said it. Perhaps her sister was coming to celebrate Christmas. She had mentioned a sister. Surely if it was someone to arrest him there would be shouts and a louder noise. He would die here in a rage, like a poisoned rat in a hole, as friend Swift said. His hands felt hot. In the College at least there were two doors. And there was the attic. He might have been able to get out on to the roof there, though he had never worked it out. The journal, the worn bundle of papers in his pocket – no time to burn it now. It would have to stay in his pocket until he found a moment to destroy it. This letter that he was writing – he picked it up as a timid tap on the door sounded like a pistol-shot in his ears. He plunged forward to open the door, then stood like a monument in the opening, facing Mrs. Martin as if she were about to sabre him to death on the spot.

The darkness of the landing concealed his expression. She said: "Dr. Everard is downstairs, asking if he may come up to see you."

All that, just for Dr. Everard. It should be a lesson to him. He said quietly: "Of course. I heard the sounds of people coming in. I wondered who they were."

"First my husband, then Dr. Everard and his man. I'll tell him."

She slipped past him into the room and knelt to repair the fire, then went to straighten the quilt on the narrow bed. When she had gone he tidied the papers on the table, placing the blotter on top of his letter. Then Dr. Everard was in the room, embracing him, raising his hand in a blessing. No harm in that. It was God's blessing, not his, and as it went through him it might do him some good. Burke gazed at him without expression, hoping his thoughts did not show, then said: "Thank you. Come and sit down."

It was a good sign. You don't give your blessing to someone that you suspect will have no use for it. Dr. Everard looked tired, and every minute of his age, which must be the early seventies. Burke was fifty-nine and he remembered Everard, already thin as a cabbage-stalk and scholarly pale, when he went to Bordeaux as a student. Everard had worn rather well, in fact, considering the excitements of the last few years. Burke drew the better chair up to the fire for him and insisted on his taking it, then placed the one he had been using at the table for himself.

187

Everard said: "I see you have been writing. I didn't leave you pens and paper. Do be careful – nothing political."

"It's all right. I asked Mrs. Martin for them. The time passes slowly enough."

"Yes. I remember that from Bordeaux. Of course I went out very often to say Mass when I was in hiding there."

And Burke, the sinner, was not to say Mass. He was not ready for that yet. Seeing Everard's embarrassment he said kindly: "That was very brave of you."

"It never occurred to me not to do it. It was foolhardy, as I think of it now. Are you comfortable here?"

"Perfectly. I'm only worried for the people of the house."

"They're prepared to take the risk. You're safer here than you would be in my own house."

Burke had spent one night there and had no wish to return. Too many prayers. The decision to write a letter was the right one. No one could speak freely to this cold fish, except another cold fish, accustomed to formality. If Burke were to try it he would be quite certain to put his foot in it after a minute or two. "Writing maketh an exact man," said Bacon. That was the only way for Burke. Still he was glad to see Everard or anyone else who would break the monotony of his prison life. He sat back in his chair and asked: "Well, how are things in the outside world? Is there any news?"

Everard said tightly: "You should forget about politics now. You have been lucky to get away alive."

"Is it as bad as that?"

"Or as good, depending on how you look at it. There is a feeling of peace in the country, quite different from what we have had for the last year. The people have realised that it's all over. They are tired."

"Tired or terrified or dead, it's all the same. Or in despair."

"I see you are incorrigible. Would you like to see the massacre continue?"

"You know I would not. But I know mankind well enough to be able to tell that a consequence will follow from the brutalities of the landed gentry in the last few months. I

188

heard General Hoche say it in Paris, the last time I saw him: 'For every man we guillotine, while we get rid of the individual we create a hundred new enemies of our system.' If they had come to Ireland there would have been no slaughter. The landlords would have been brought to places of safety or let out of the country. That was his plan. It's God's pity that he died so soon."

"You think we would have been better with ten thousand French troops rampaging all over the country?"

"Fifty thousand was what he promised."

Dr. Everard clasped his hands together, then turned around in his chair to gaze directly at Burke. After a pause he said: "Dr. Glynn always said you should never have been a priest."

"He was wrong," Burke said angrily. "In my father's house there are many mansions and no doubt many tenants in them. I'm not interested in politics but in people. My record shows it, every time."

"I shouldn't have said that. You're right – no one but God can track a soul. But I believe that priests must keep out of wars and revolutions. That's the policy of the bishops."

"Policy? Is that why they condemned the actions of John Murphy, and Michael Murphy?"

"They had cast themselves out, by taking up arms."

"Greater love than this no man hath, that a man lay down his life for his friends."

"They led the people into battle. That's a different thing."

"God help them. The people were like sheep without a shepherd."

"A good shepherd leads his sheep into safety, not into battle."

"Does he stand by, holding the sheep quiet, while the wolf goes methodically through the flock and slaughters them one by one? That was what would have happened if John Murphy had done nothing. He was a good priest – he told the people they should give up their arms and live peacefully and have no more talk of revolution and he

189

promised that the government would protect every home and family in the country in return. He even put an advertisement in the paper, promising loyalty to the Crown. The people brought their weapons – pikes and guns of all descriptions to his church in Boulavogue. He handed them on to Lord Mountmorris's deputy and they were all stored in the big house at Camolin Park. Then on Whit Saturday, May 26, the yeoman cavalry set out burning and destroying all before them, knowing they couldn't be stopped. John Murphy's chapel in Boulavogue, and his house, and a great many houses in the parish were burned to the ground, some with the people inside, doors locked so that they couldn't escape. Any man that got away and was discovered on the road or in hiding was murdered, or else they were gathered in a little group and slaughtered together. They took out the prisoners and executed them in Dunlavin and Carnew. They called men to the doors of their houses and shot them down without ceremony. And the torture, the caps of hot pitch, and the floggings, and the lingering deaths that those devils devised – could anyone stand by and see it happen, and do nothing?

"The evening of that day, Father John's neighbours, his *sheep*, his parishioners were gathered around him in a wood, not one of them with a roof to shelter him for the night. He laid the plan, and he carried it out, that they would get what weapons they could, pitchforks and spades and farm tools, and ambush those limbs of Satan in the darkness on their way back from their outing. They blocked the road near Camolin Park and fell on them without warning and killed most of them and got their guns and their horses and sabres and swords. By the next day John Murphy had five thousand men, armed with pitchforks and the few captured weapons, all depending on him. After that there was nothing they could do but fight for their lives. What would those men have said to him if he had told them to go quietly home and wait for the butchers to come again and slaughter them? Even as a priest he had a duty to save the people's lives. The next day, and that was Whit Sunday, they fought a pitched battle on Oulart Hill, and killed majors and captains and lieutenants and privates by the hundred. That was where I joined him, with Michael Murphy of Monageer. His chapel was burned too, and his house. I remembered him well from Bordeaux, a quiet, pious boy, as innocent as a baby, no capacity for fighting – you remember him too. He rode into the battle of Arklow carrying a green flag with a cross on it, wherever he got it, and he was shot dead at that battle."

Burke's voice had gone lower and lower as he went on speaking. God alone knew what Everard was thinking but Burke no longer cared. Poor Michael – all he had wanted was to get back to his little church and say Mass for his people. Policies! After that tirade, Everard would probably throw Burke to the wolves with the greatest of pleasure.

There was a long pause, then Everard said: "If all the priests had acted as those two Murphys did, and Philip Roche, it would have been said that it was an uprising of Catholics against Protestants."

"They're saying that anyway," Burke growled. "But it's not true. There were plenty of Protestants on our side. The reason they failed was that they had no leaders. If all the priests had led the people as those Wexford priests did, Ireland would be a free country at this moment."

"Or if the French had landed?"

"Once Hoche was dead there was no hope of that. General Bonaparte hated him – he always did the opposite of anything Hoche recommended."

"You know a great deal about it."

"I was in their councils."

"In Wexford too?"

"Yes."

"Is that how you know so much about what happened there?"

"Yes."

"Have you ever carried arms?"

"Never."

"That makes it easier, though I may not be able to get anyone to believe it."

The plans for his escape, whatever they were. It almost sounded as if Everard was hoping to get him a passport. Downstairs there was a murmur of voices, the Martins entertaining the bishop's servant and perhaps talking about the dangerous guest they were harbouring. It was hard to believe that they had any sympathy with him or with the mission that brought him to Ireland. No point in talking to Everard about this. Burke had sailed pretty close to the wind in suggesting that the priests of Ireland would have been the right military leaders of the people. He knew well that according to the bishops the reason they had not taken on that leadership was that they were good priests. The awful warning given was Talleyrand the bishop of Autun, who had abandoned his bishopric, they said, for the more exciting prospects of Paris. It would be a waste of his breath to try to explain that French people did not see it like that at all. Neither did the general run of the Irish, so far as Burke knew, but then the Irish never saw what they were supposed to see. There was not even much sympathy in Ireland for the Pope, fleeing for his life before the French army. Better to keep his mouth shut. A shut mouth catches no flies, his mother used to say. He should never have tried to convert Everard away from his policy, as he called it.

A sod of turf fell forward, sending a little jet of ash on to the hearth. Burke leaned in to replace it with the tongs, and to add two more sods, one at either side. He said: "A great thing about Ireland, they would never leave you without a good fire. In the College, when I was there alone, I nearly froze to death."

"I remember the cold of French houses too," Everard said. "They don't seem to feel it, or they think one can keep some of the summer heat in store until it's needed." There might almost be a chuckle behind the dry, light voice. Then he said: "We have been through bad times, James. I know your conscience directs you differently from mine. The Irish bishops are in a desperate state at this moment."

Wondering whose arse should they lick next. Shut your mouth. You have your orders, my boy. Keep mum. Burke said: "I can see that. They were expected to control the people and they couldn't do it."

"That's only part of the truth. If you're caught now, you will be hanged, as surely as I'm sitting here. That would stir up the people again. They would be furiously angry at the execution of a priest, since John Murphy's death."

Now if it were a bishop, it would be different. The people wouldn't mind at all – can he possibly mean that? Burke said politely: "I can see the bishops' difficulty. They don't want any more national heroes."

"Exactly. I'm glad you appreciate the position."

No trouble. It was as clear as daylight. Their lordships wanted him safely out of the country, not for love of him but for reasons of policy. He could imagine how they would squirm when they gave the directions to the scholars and students of Bordeaux to pray to the Irish saints for his soul. Nothing to stop them from adding a footnote to say that he needed praying for. He wouldn't put it past them. It might be possible to circumvent them by adding a piece to his will saying that he particularly wished no details of his life and works to be supplied. But did he really wish that? It would be good for future generations to know that there were some steadfast Irishmen in France who fought for the right, without fear or favour, no whispering behind doors, no cuffuffling in corners, everything out in the open and above board. Well, almost everything.

He said: "I'm a very plain, straightforward man, Dr. Everard. I've been so all my life. It's too late to change. I don't think their Lordships will find that I have injured the Church. On the contrary. We have instructions to love God and love our neighbours but the proportion is not specified. I've always been strong on the love of my neighbours. That can hardly be counted against me."

Everard gave his dry smile, then said: "I'll put it to them like that, if it crops up. But I don't think you need to apologise for yourself. There are fifty young priests in Ireland at this moment who might not be alive if you hadn't intervened to save them five years ago."

"Is it only five years? It feels like a lifetime. When I saw them last they didn't seem too grateful."

"Perhaps they were not quite sure then that you were their rescuer."

"You told them, very plainly. They called me Judas, the brats. I hope they were seasick on the way home."

"They were. The young are very single-minded."

"So in fact the bishops would like me to get out of the country alive, because I'll give less trouble all round that way. Well, I can tell you that I'm quite anxious to escape too, though for other reasons. They're bad at hanging big men. Remember how they worked on Father Ledwitche's brother. It must have taken them half an hour."

Everard looked pained. He said: "Of course the bishops would help you in any case, as far as they're able. Don't be such an *enfant terrible*. I don't know how you can joke about such things."

"Neither do I. It's not a matter for jokes. 'How cold is your bath, O king,' as Jugurtha said the day long ago. I always thought that was in bad taste. What are your plans?"

"We hope to get you a passport under an assumed name, as a businessman."

"Dr. Everard, I'm surprised at you."

"Don't tease me, James. It's about the best way. If you were younger and less remarkable we would arrange to have you ship as a sailor. That's one of the best ways we have found."

"So I'm not the only one?"

"No. Almost all of them got away safely. The most dangerous part will be getting you to some Irish port. Dublin would be the best. It's too big for them to keep a close watch. Waterford is nearer but it's almost impossible to get out of there without being noticed, and there may be people there who would recognise you, since you landed there. Cork is not so bad but we're making every effort to get you a ship from Dublin."

"Where would it take me?"

"France, we would hope, perhaps even to Bordeaux.

Some people have got to Hamburg. It's not too difficult to go back to France from there."

"When do you think it will happen?"

"It might be quite soon or it might be several weeks. We're not going to take any risks with you."

James Burke was not going to be allowed to embarrass the bishops any further. They had had enough of him. He said: "If they do catch me, I'll have no hard feelings, remember. I wouldn't like anyone to blame themselves on my account. Please tell them that I'm really grateful for their trouble."

"I will. And of course I'll come the moment I have news."

"Thank you."

Everard stood up saying: "Have you enough books?"

They were piled on the table, the collection he had brought the last time.

Burke said: "I'd like Jonathan Swift's poems, if you have them."

That was a mistake. Everard's mouth always gave him away. He said: "I'll see what I can find. I know it's terrible to be shut in all the time. It's not even safe for you to take a walk at night. Martin has told me he thinks someone is watching the house. He wouldn't give any details. It would be dangerous for you to appear at all."

"That's all right. Don't worry about me."

"I do worry about you. After all, you're one of my oldest friends."

He said this in a tone almost of surprise, for which Burke could not blame him. At the door he paused and said: "I pray for you every day."

"Thank you."

After he had gone the little room felt much more comfortable. Perhaps he was unjust to Everard. No wonder he and Glynn were such friends. Though he had kindly described Burke as a friend too, there could never be any real *rapport* between them, no more than there could be between a couple of herons and a farmyard duck.

Poultry – was Anna taking proper care of them? She

195

swore she would follow all his rules as strictly as if he were watching her but she could easily get careless once he was out of sight. She never really believed that grown hens need fresh water every day, though she knew the little chickens died of dirty water. He had meant to stay in Ireland for a month or at most for six weeks. Now it was almost a year and no guarantee that he would ever get home. If he were hanged Anna would abandon the poultry, that was certain. She had lost patience with them in recent years, after her spell as cook at the Château Rochechouart under Rose's direction. She had become a splendid cook and yet that little fool Jeanne sacked her. Said she was spying on her. Burke doubted it. Besides what was there to spy on, now that Edmund and Jeanne were married? Jeanne had a secretive streak in her but she was not very good at keeping secrets.

Delectable smells began to seep upward from the kitchen. Mrs. Martin was a good cook too though she had no French ideas. Still she did the best possible with Irish materials and customs. In spite of his restricted life Burke's appetite had not diminished. He began to salivate. Better get on with that letter to take his mind off dinner. As it was Christmas Day she might well have planned something special, which would inevitably take longer. There was plenty of paper. His little homily on the attitudes of the bishops led up naturally to what he wanted to say next. If he began with Rose he might get on to other things later. though there might be no need to tell all, now or ever.

He wrote: "These being my views, and with my past history as you know it, you will readily understand that my actions often depart from the conventional and prudent, especially if it seems to me that convention and prudence will not serve the purpose. I must stress that in the case I am going to describe I had no personal involvement whatever. Unless you believe this you will be able to do nothing for the unfortunate woman concerned."

Unfortunate? Perhaps she was delighted with herself. He had not seen her, and he would accept no other evidence than that of his own eyes as to her condition.

196

"Her name is Rose French. She came from Ireland to Bordeaux with Edmund Brien of Mount Brien Court and a patriotic Irishman named Colman Folan, now dead. All three stayed in my house for a year. As Edmund Brien's marriage to a local lady approached, I escorted Rose French and the lady to Paris. Finding that she would have no home once the marriage took place, as she was not welcome to live with the young couple, I thought to make some provision for her and to leave her independent. The result of my scheme was not what I expected. Instead of freeing her from the attentions of unworthy men – she is a beautiful woman – all unwittingly I set her up as a high-class whore."

# _12_

HE SHOULD HAVE KNOWN BETTER. HE WAS PROBABLY THE only person who realised what an oddity Rose had become, if she was not always so. Still with his passionate belief in the human intelligence and its capacity to search out the truth, he had imagined that Rose would save herself if she were once given peace. Descartes would have agreed with him. In all her life she had never before been independent. He had been experimenting with her but if the experiment had worked out well he would have preened himself, instead of cursing his stupidity in interfering with her.

What sort of life would she have had if he had let her alone? Perpetual housekeeping, probably. She was very good at it, too good, a treasure to be kept locked up and out of sight lest someone might make off with her. That was how Jeanne saw her. She put up quite a fight to keep her, wailing that no one else would be able to take care of the house and the child, and even the farmyard as Rose did.

"Nonsense," Burke said. "Any Frenchwoman could do it on her ear."

Jeanne said: "You know that's not true. They would do it as a peasant does. Rose does it like a lady. She gives the whole house style."

"All the more reason for you not to have her. She looks too aristocratic for the present climate of France."

"I'll never be able to live like a peasant."

"If you don't watch out you'll die like a lady."

Jeanne said spitefully: "I think I know why you want to take her away. You want her in your bed."

Then she cowered away from him, having seen him clench his fists in fury. But he would never lay a hand on her. He had come near it once and it was only the mercy of God that had saved him.

After a pause he said: "No. I've had enough of that."

Perhaps. But Rose was too spiny for him. He had been quite unprepared for what happened. He had known for some months that he would have to get her away. Her mind might crack at any moment, with those peculiar habits she had. Talking loudly, all alone in her room – he came back one day without warning and went looking for her. Hearing a voice in her room he stopped and listened at the door. What he heard raised the hair on his scalp. Cracked already, she was. Talking to Lady Sophie Brien as if she were present in the room. For a moment he thought she was drunk. He knew she had got a key to the wine-cellar somehow and was able to keep herself supplied. She didn't take much, however, and always the best. This must have been natural good taste since she could not have had access to such good wine in Ireland. Jeanne or even Edmund might stumble on her thieving by accident when he was gone, and put her out of the house. It would not end with the wine. As sure as eggs she would develop some other light-fingered habits.

Where that glorious voice fitted in was still a mystery to him. He had thought to free her from some of her restraints by asking her to sing in the drawing-room one evening. The look she gave him should have dropped him dead like a grouse. And she had chosen to sing a sort of hymn, instead of the heavenly song that he had heard one day. There was nothing he could do. If he had asked her to sing 'Love's a dear deceitful jewel' she would have guessed at once that in order to have heard the words he must have been right by her door. She knew well that this kind of knowledge was not part of him. A pity Jeanne was so surly with her. Another woman might have helped her to soften up.

It was Jeanne's behaviour towards Rose that had finally forced Burke to make up his mind about her. No sooner had she accepted the marriage with Edmund than she had begun to treat Rose like a lady's maid, ordering her around, putting her in charge of the clothes and the packing, demanding to have Rose brush and arrange her hair. Rose acquiesced quietly, perhaps thinking she had no choice.

Burke marvelled at the way women knuckled under to other women, the highest in the land willing to serve the body of the queen, God rest her, then all the way down to the farmer's wife yelling obscenities at her maid-of-all-work in the kitchen. Somehow it seemed to him more reasonable for men to be in this kind of bondage.

Having converted her into a servant, in her own mind, Jeanne was all the more angry when Burke informed her that he would not allow this. After Rose's collapse at the FitzGeralds' house, Burke had seen the look of hatred that she gave him. Back at the rooms he had taken for the two women, he said to Jeanne: "That settles it. Rose is not going to live at Bordeaux with you."

"She'll be happy enough. Why don't you let her alone?"

"Someone must protect her."

"And how is she going to live? Are you going to get her work here in Paris as a housekeeper? It's all she's fit for."

"Nothing of the sort. She must get a pension."

"And where is that to come from? It would cost a lot to keep her in Paris."

"I'll take care of it." Inspiration struck him. "You must tell her that it comes from you. Three thousand francs a year."

"I will not. That's a fortune."

"From Edmund, then."

"Why Edmund?"

"She's a protegée of his family. It would be quite proper. She's very far from home. That's what will be done and you will do as I say. Don't forget, Madame, that I'm setting you up with a château and a husband to your liking. You had better co-operate."

If any more women glared at him this evening he would be burned to a crisp.

She said through her teeth: "Very well, Mr. Burke. You must have your way."

He schooled her well in what she was to say, going over and over it until he had her in tears. God help her, she had

200

the brains of a hen. But she got it in the end, and then there was a long spell when she was not allowed in to see Rose, still languishing at Madame FitzGerald's house. When the interview took place at last, he questioned Jeanne closely about it.

"Did you mention my name?"

"She mentioned it. When I told her about the pension, she asked at once if you knew of it."

"Was she angry when she found that I did?"

"No. She wouldn't have believed that it would work, unless you approved. She thinks nothing of Edmund."

"Teachers often feel like that about their pupils."

"I told her that Edmund doesn't want her in the house. It was very embarrassing. I hope you'll be able to explain it to him."

"I'll take care of all that. So long as her pension doesn't come out of his pocket he won't object, if I know Master Edmund."

Watch out or she'll say she won't marry a mean man. But she's more likely to think that's an asset in him. There's a pair of them there. As God made them he matched them, Burke's mother used to say.

Jeanne said: "And she made me write something down, to give to Edmund." She was pulling a piece of paper out of her pocket as if it were a snake, her forehead wrinkled with irritation.

He took it from her, read it and laughed.

"Swift – she has him at her fingers' ends."

"I don't understand. Who is Swift?"

"An Irish writer, long dead. This is for Edmund, not for me?"

"Why should it be for you? She thinks her good fortune is due to Edmund."

"Did she mention Colman?"

"I don't think so. I certainly didn't."

That was one of his greatest stupidities, encouraging Colman to ask her to marry him. Afterwards he could scarcely believe that he had done it. He had thought of every

201

reason for her peculiarities – poverty, isolation, lack of family affection – he guessed at all of these from the way she spoke of her time at Mount Brien. He never dreamed that the root of her trouble was pride, natural pride, slighted pride, injured pride, concealed pride, growing day by day as she herself realised her capacities more and more. God help her, with no one else to talk to, why should she not talk to herself? What a wife she would have made – she was not his kind but for someone else she was indeed a very attractive woman.

He would have thought that Colman was an equally attractive man, tall, muscular, well-built, extremely clever, as even Rose must know, the sort of man who makes a fortune in America. Colman himself had had doubts. Two days after the night that Rose fainted, he said: "If only I could take care of her – this kind of thing should never happen."

It was a new idea to Burke. He began to examine it at once.

"Have you asked her?"

"Of course not. How could I?"

"You're a fine, upstanding young man. Why shouldn't you?"

"Why, indeed? God knows I've wanted her for long enough."

"How long?"

"Seven years." Colman laughed. "It sounds like one of the old stories. There was a girl in my village who would have married me but after I saw Rose I could never look at her again."

"Does Rose know how much you care for her?"

"Of course not. I've never said anything to her."

"Women often sense these things. For all you know, she may be waiting to be asked."

But Colman had more wits than that. He said: "I think she would be shocked. After all, she is Miss French."

"That's not a great title these days. The whole world has changed."

"Some things will never change. I know she trusts me. She has always been friendly to me, since we sat in the lowest places at Mount Brien."

"It would be worth a chance."

Damned meddler. Poor Colman took heart and began to think of his possibilities. So did Burke. Rose would still need her pension, until Colman was free to earn a living for her, either in France or in Ireland if the projected rising were successful, as it looked like being. The pension would then make a nice little dowry for Rose. He was full of plans. She was not too old to have children – he had got as far as that when Colman asked if he would find out whether or not Rose would receive him. When he visited her himself, Burke almost gave her a hint of what was to come. By the mercy of God he saw in time that it was better not to mention it, except to say that Colman would like to pay her a visit before they left France.

Colman came back from that interview with his tail between his legs, about as chopfallen as a man could be, but to give him his due he never blamed Burke for his humiliation.

"You were right. It was worth a chance," he said, and that was all.

Burke waited, but Colman was more of a gentleman than he was. He would not discuss a lady with anyone. All through their campaign together, only once he had mentioned her, to say bitterly: "Rose had good sense, after all, not to tie herself to a wandering hero like me."

That was before they left Paris, when they were kicking their heels week after week, waiting for news that the great army was ready to set out for Ireland. Jeanne was back in Bordeaux, safely married to Edmund. Burke was free as air. He loved the opera, and he introduced Colman to it. When they went together in the evening, there was Rose, always with a group of young men, always beautifully dressed, looking as if she had never known another life. She was made for it. She was born to decorate the world. It was a crime that she was only getting her chance now. It should have been hers when she was twenty, with a mother hovering behind her to make sure that she got the best advantage out of it. No society existed in Ireland, fit for a young beauty to show herself in. The landlords and the gentry preferred to be ignored in London rather than to shine at home, as her friend Swift said.

The whole débâcle of Rose was Burke's fault. He had given her too much money. Three thousand francs a year – a third of that would have kept her in decency, in a lodging house with a motherly landlady. He had not wanted that. He wanted her to be able to drive in the Bois de Boulogne and go to the Opéra and attract rich young men, one of whom would marry her. Rose carried out the first part of that plan but she ruined the second part by grabbing everything at once. Burke knew her reputation. Madame FitzGerald told him of it sadly, her big innocent eyes full of pain and reproach.

"I thought she knew how to behave. I found her a good maid who would have acted as a chaperone but she soon got rid of her and brought in a flighty little brat who has taught her all kinds of tricks. Everyone knows that she has at least three lovers. I can't invite her to the house any more. She comes wearing such extraordinary clothes, and even her voice has changed. She uses a loud, sharp tone that sounds like a trumpet-call in our kind of company."

Nothing surprising in that – those worthy brown Irish hens would never take to his gorgeous peacock. How could a woman be a peacock? That one was. No other word for her, a lovely, delicate peacock, flourishing best in her uselessness.

The Frenchwomen of Paris would kill him for that idea. Since he had been in Ireland he missed them constantly, their scathing tongues, their fascination with philosophy, their love of food and men and their talk, talk, talk. If he got his heels out of Ireland safely now, he would never come back.

The decision surprised him, coming at him like that without warning when he was weak and frightened. Yes, he was frightened of the violent death that was in store for him if he chanced to be caught, though he could pretend to face it like a man, or a saint. He would never be able to take matters into his own hands as Mr. Tone had done. This courageous lively little man had always said he would not wait for the executioner. When death was certain, he said in Burke's presence one evening at dinner, in Paris, a man had a right to choose the moment of it. The other Irishmen at the table put up all kinds of defences of the Church's position and one of them added a ludicrous reason for submitting to being hanged and beheaded and disembowelled, that in future times the tyrants would be disgraced over the bodies of their martyrs. Mr. Tone laughed heartily at this idea and was delighted when Burke quoted Swift: What need of all this cookery?

Well, Mr. Tone beat them all, cutting his throat with a pocket-knife while they continued to build the gallows outside his window. The bishops were using that act now to prove to the Irish that they should never have followed such a leader, but their position was not very strong since Tone was not a member of their Church, and could not be expected to concur with all its ethics.

Bishops. It was cruel to send them after Rose but Burke could think of no one else with the mobility to attend to her. After their defence of English law in Ireland, surely they would be given some reward, in the form of freedom to travel to Europe when they needed it. A bishop would be given a safe conduct. Everard wouldn't dare to refuse the challenge of saving Rose's soul. Burke knew he had no need to emphasise that. If he failed in his duty, Burke would haunt him in his palace – a scandalous, dreadful idea – where had it come from? No wonder his mother used to fore-tell that he would land himself in hell some day, with his wicked thoughts. She had done her part, with threats and execrations and prayers. He remembered her hurling prayers after his departing ship, like the giant hurling rocks after Ulysses' boat.

Thinking of his mother always reduced Burke to a dither. He knew what she would advise at this moment: martyrdom.

He should walk out of the house now and ramble around until he was picked up by the army or the police, then suffer a hero's death with his eyes fixed on the light of heaven, shining conveniently down at a slant to catch the glint in his pious eyes. Two advantages at one blow – Burke safe in heaven, England further coated with mud for her treatment of the poor Irish. All very neat. His mother waiting for him at the other side, smiling with approval at last.

But she would not. She would have some complaint or other for all eternity. He could see her pulling at Saint Peter's sleeve to remind him that Burke should still do time in Purgatory, that his martyr's death was only a cheap ticket – what a flippant rogue he was, utterly incorrigible. Dr. Everard had been shocked at the way he could joke about such things.

Women. If he ever found himself travelling across the abominable plain that he had seen in his vision of hell, it would be on account of Rose or Louise, not Jeanne. Better finish that letter to Dr. Everard now, while the humour was on him.

What was she cooking downstairs? It smelt like chicken. There was onion somewhere there too.

The whole point in getting Dr. Everard to take charge of Rose was to see that she got her pension. As long as she had enough to live on, there was some hope that she would extricate herself. Take care of the body and the soul will take care of itself. He would never get a bishop to believe that. Perhaps he could risk a quotation from Saint Thomas: Virtue does not flower where there is great poverty. That would cause a flutter in the hen-house. They could argue, as Burke himself believed, that wealth had done her more harm than good. But that was not the whole of her story. Bishops everywhere would have to go back to school and re-learn philosophy. Burke would not be there to see the results. Keep it simple. Everard was no fool – in fact he was at least as clever as Burke. He would read between the lines. Funny thing, how he had almost apologised for being Burke's oldest friend.

Something else besides onion – it could never be tarragon in this benighted country.

Swallowing heavily, Burke wrote:

"As you know, I have valuable estates in Bordeaux which I hereby, and in the manner I have said, bequeath to the Irish College there. At one time I was also the owner of the Château Rochechouart, which is now occupied by Edmund Brien and his wife Jeanne, formerly the Countess de Rochechouart. On their marriage I made over this part of my property to them but I now request that the said Edmund Brien continue to pay Rose French a pension of three thousand francs a year."

Why was he using that legal jargon? His request had no legal value whatever. The best he could hope for was that Edmund would soften his heart enough to keep Rose going for old times' sake, and on pressure from Dr. Everard. Jeanne would be hopping mad, that was certain, unless her new baby had improved her. Burke hoped that it was a girl. The news had revived all kinds of nasty memories for him.

There was a trap here, if he were not careful. Everard might go to the Château Rochechouart and see René walking about, the image of Burke if the devil had done his work properly. No good purpose would be served by that – what Everard didn't know wouldn't trouble him. He wrote quickly:

"There should be no need for you to go to visit these people. You can send a messenger and Edmund Brien will come to see you in Bordeaux, or even in Paris." Yes, Paris would be better. "You will find him pleasant and intelligent. He will be happy to spare you the long, tiresome journey out to his Château." Don't protest too much or he'll smell a rat. "Rose French has always believed that Edmund Brien is her patron. There will be no need to inform her that in fact it was myself."

He felt as weary as if he had spent the day on horseback. Thinking about Rose reminded him painfully of Paris. Those silly young men, who fluttered around her and her like, had ruined the great Revolution between them. They seemed to have no understanding of the need to keep up the pressure, to fight all day and every day so as not to lose what had been gained over the last agonising years. Burke knew this from his hens and ducks and from his farming but city men thought that what was built remains forever. They moved on to the next stage – individual ambition – much too quickly.

Dr. Glynn had a favourite quotation from Saint Augustine, that he had aimed more than once at Burke in his younger days: Thou hast made us for thyself, O God, and our hearts will not rest until they rest in thee. Poor Glynn – he must be turning in his grave at the things that Burke had done in the last couple of years. In many ways he had done better than the revolutionaries, with more single-minded fortitude and more certainty of right and wrong. Or was it lack of imagination that destroyed them? Burke would never understand why they were letting everything slip away. Going after foreign loot would cost them dearly in the end.

Dinner – it was here at last. He knew by the slow steps on the stairs that she was carrying the tray. When he judged that she was almost there, he opened the door and stood aside to let her in. Three dishes, all with battered silver covers, probably gifts of cast-offs from the kitchen of the big house. She would be shocked if he were to plunge forward and lift those covers. He did nothing of the kind. He waited politely while she laid the tray on the table, then set a place for him with a napkin and with the cutlery in the right places. She must have been a servant at the big house once. The concentration on her face suggested that she was recalling an almost lost skill. She placed the dishes at last and removed the covers.

She had outdone herself – a whole roast chicken with potatoes and carrots and parsnips, a baked apple with a crust of golden sugar, a slice of cake, some walnuts and raisins.

She said: "Dr. Everard brought the nuts and raisins, and there's a bottle of wine too. It's hard to be spending Christmas like a bird in a cage."

"You treat me so well, it's not such a hardship."

"My husband would like to come up and smoke a pipe with you when you're finished, to take some of the lonesome off you."

"Thank you, I'd like that."

She had the bottle ready, uncorked. When she was gone with her tray, he stood behind his chair and blessed himself, then said aloud: "*Benedic,Domine,nos,et haec tua dona, quae de tua largitate sumus sumpturi. Per Christum Dominum nostrum.*"

He sat down quickly and unfolded the clean white napkin. Funny that she had not stayed to serve him on this special occasion – he felt sure it was in her mind. That Latin Grace had brought back Bordeaux, the cook standing by with his knife at the ready, the boys with downcast eyes speculating on what was for dinner, their hungry young stomachs tortured by the wait while their elders, with little or no appetite, moved ceremoniously through a long ritual which included a *Gloria Patri* and a *Pater Noster* and various trimmings. He was glad she had not stayed. She would have remained silent, probably just out of sight, watching him chew and swallow, handing him things as he needed them. He had had enough of that at Mount Brien – it always seemed a ludicrous way for an able-bodied man to eat his dinner. Jeanne had tried very hard to reimpose the discipline on him, when they got Jacques Fournier as a servant at last. Burke would not stir. God help her, she probably had it all set up again by now. He would see when he went back there, if he ever went back.

It was a splendid meal. There was no tarragon but she had put mint and sage and a little onion in the stuffing. Burke was as happy as a baby at the breast, replete. The wine went down smoothly, Bordeaux wine of course, wherever Everard had got it. Not enough to raise a devil – Burke had seen enough devils to last him a lifetime. That little grey devil had been real, no question about it. They came a lot faster with the encouragement of strong drink. It was thirsty work, being a devil. For God's sake don't joke about those lads. Asking for trouble, as usual.

He left one quarter of the chicken, out of decency, poured the last of the wine and turned his chair around towards the fire. He found himself relaxing automatically, his heavy flesh and strong muscles responding to the charm of the fire's glow and to the glow in his stomach. Let the day be time enough to mourn. The shipwreck of my ill-adventured youth – what a rag-bag his mind had become – what was the beginning? It came after a moment:

> Care-charmer, Sleep, son of the sable night,
> Brother to Death, in silent darkness born,
> Relieve my languish and restore the light,
> With dark forgetting of my care return,
> And let the day be time enough –

A discreet knock at the door. What else? Let waking eyes suffice to wail their –

Another knock. He called out: "Come in – the door is open."

Then he remembered – Patrick Martin. *Je vis de bonne soupe et non de beau langage.* No tottering – his head was getting soft, in spite of hard training. Perfectly steadily he stood up and went to the door to let in the good man who was standing there with an apologetic smile.

Burke said: "Come along in. It's good of you to spend a little time with me. I do appreciate it."

"Christmas times can be lonesome," Martin said, sidling into the room, taking a chair and placing it beside Burke's in front of the fire. "I hope you enjoyed your dinner."

"As you see, I did. Scarcely a bite left."

"She will be pleased. She's a good cook, when she has the stuff to cook."

"I'm putting you to a lot of trouble."

"It's a privilege. Dr. Everard says you'll be leaving soon."

"He has plans. He didn't tell me too much about them."

"When you go back to France, you won't forget old Ireland."

The remark was so unexpected that Burke turned to look at him. Earnest brown eyes, a wrinkled, harrowed face, far too wrinkled for his age – his hair was hardly beginning to grey. Big, competent hands – Burke would have given him a job at once, on the strength of those hands. But Martin had not seemed to have the look of a rebel, with his safe trade and his little house and his air of being beaten down and past all such thoughts.

Burke said: "I won't forget. You're a Tipperary man?"

"Yes, from the Galtees. I've been working in the gardens here since I was ten years old – since I was old enough to walk down from the mountain every morning and home at night without dropping dead on the way."

"It was a hard life for a child."

"Yes, but I love the gardens. I wish I could show them to you, though they don't look much in the depths of winter."

"There's nothing I'd like better than a walk at this moment. Could we do it? Christmas night, there should be no one out and about."

"You'd be risking your life. They're still combing the country for people, names given out and money paid to informers. If you were caught, I'd never again look the Bishop in the face."

"He said you think there is someone watching the house."

"We have some bad neighbours. It's not just that they were frightened by the rising – they were always given to spying and watching, even when there was no need for it. Some people – you'd think the devil is on them from the beginning, God forgive me for saying it."

"What do you grow in the garden?"

"Everything – peas and carrots and beans and artichokes and asparagus and leeks and cauliflowers – it's a grand big garden with high walls all around. I have room for flowers too, and greenhouses, and fruit. I have four men and a boy under me. When my lady comes in the summertime she asks for all those things and she knows the good stuff when she sees it. But sure they didn't come at all this year, on account of the fighting, and the stuff was wasted. It would break your heart to see the lovely vegetables going to rot. We sold some of them, but the people that have need of them couldn't buy a jacket for a gooseberry and the rest of

211

them have gardens of their own. That's how it will be in Ireland now, for evermore. We'll be worse off than ever we were."

"Were you in the United Irishmen?"

"I was, of course. But we're always let down in the end. We gave up our pikes to make it easy for them to slaughter whoever they liked. If we hadn't the hope of Heaven we'd have nothing at all to pray for. We hear on all sides that there's a great life now in France and America. Those are the places to be, if we were young and strong enough to go. There's nothing more for anyone now, in Ireland."

"The good times might come some day."

"You and I will never see it."

This was the man who had come to cheer his Christmas evening. Burke had felt a lot better before his arrival. He seemed to become aware of this now, saying: "I shouldn't be talking to you like that, and you with plenty of troubles of your own. You did what you could, you and all the others that came over to help us. Tell me now, why in the name of God didn't the French come, after promising for so long and getting up our courage? If we hadn't had that promise, we'd have known it was useless, though we might have chanced it anyway. What came over them, in the end?"

Would he have to go through it all again? Burke had given dozens of discourses on that subject, finding it more depressing each time. He said: "We must remember that Ireland is a very small country to the French."

"Small but important," Martin said eagerly. "They knew very well that if they had control of Ireland they could stop the English ships from raiding the high seas and preventing trade with every country but their own. That's what we were told by our own leaders and anyone can see that it's true."

"The man who saw it most clearly was General Hoche. He was the one that pressed it day and night on the Council. They agreed – they would have given him anything he wanted, they trusted his judgment, he was their favourite, the one they knew would lead them to victory. His men would have fought like tigers for him. And he was as clever as the bees – he knew how to handle people, how to get the best out of them."

"Did you really know him?" Martin asked in awe.

"I met him several times and he had that good thing about him, that he always knew me again. Some great men are so great that they have to be introduced to the same people over and over. General Bonaparte is one of those, full of himself, full of pride and with big ideas. His family are strong people in Corsica and now he wants to be a strong man in France. That's why he hated General Hoche. So whatever General Hoche wanted, General Bonaparte will not do, though poor Hoche is dead and gone and need never trouble him again."

This was what he had told Dr. Everard. Burke knew that what he said was the exact truth. He had told it everywhere he went in Ireland. Bonaparte was a deceiver, as well as being jealous. He could have told what he was planning, or at least enough of it so that the poor gullible Irish wouldn't walk into a battle waving sticks, with no one to their back. Keeping them waiting at Brest for months was a crime, and so was appointing old General Kilmaine there, instead of some lively lad that would have done something useful.

They sat in silence for a few minutes while Martin got his pipe out of his pocket and lit it carefully with a tiny piece of burning turf, which he held expertly with the strip-metal tongs.

At last he said: "This was a terrible year in Ireland. May we never have another like it. What got into the gentry and the yeomen and the big-wigs in Dublin that should have been protecting the people? You're a priest, and can you tell me the answer to that?"

"When people get leave to hate," Burke said slowly, "they go slightly mad. I saw it in France, and I saw it with the North Cork Militia in Wexford – "

"Wexford! God help us, we heard stories from there that you would deny but that the people who told them were

213

there and saw it happening. I didn't know men could do such things to each other, and laughing and enjoying it at the time. Did you see that?"

"Yes, in Wexford and in France." Lacombe was one, gloating over the prisoners with the look of a mad dog in his eye. "People go mad with killing because it's unnatural, it's too exciting, it draws a part of them out into the open that they usually keep well under control. Some were hardened to it. The Wexford people had a name for the gentry that treated them the worst – the foxhunters. They had learned it in the hunting-field, and it was all one to them what the quarry was, men or deer or foxes. The beating and the burnings – they were used to that too, with their servants and their tenants. They said in Wexford that the kindly landlords, the good ones that cared for their tenants, didn't go out killing and burning like the rest of them."

"Those things will never be forgotten. They're making the ballads and the songs about them already."

"We must forgive our enemies."

"That's God's business. If we forget those things, or forgive them, we deserve no better in the times to come."

# _13_

Martin stayed a few minutes longer, until his pipe was finished. When he had closed the door courteously behind him, thanking him for his visit, Burke blew out the lamp. He waited for a moment until he had adjusted to the dim light of the fire. Then he crossed to the window and drew back the heavy curtains, opened the window and stood there for a long time, breathing in the cold night air. A high, white, full moon flooded the landscape with light, picking out the elegantly-placed trees on the lawn and outlining the roof and the chimneys of the big house. Nothing moved, not even a hunting fox. He surveyed it in all directions, with the eyes of a hunted man. A cottage light showed here and there in the foothills of the Galtee mountains. There would be no snow after all. Probably that was a good thing. Horsemen move too quietly in the snow – Martin and his talk of Wexford had aroused horrible memories. Burke put up both hands and stroked his cheeks and temples, as if he hoped to press those memories out of his brain.

Why had God picked him out of the huge rubbish-heap at his disposal and again and again given him the job of. leading his fellow man? The world was full of sleek, efficient, clever, conscientious people who were qualified to do the things that had been presented to Burke. Men like Hoche – yet God slew him with consumption and left Burke. Wolfe Tone was dead and Burke was hiding out in comparative safety. A football, fit for nothing else, always rescued in time to be kicked off in another crazy direction.

Perhaps it was the devil – he turned quickly but there was no one there. Whatever about devils, he had no wish to see God yet. He had a strong feeling that God was not ready to

215

see him either. But so had felt the men who were slaughtered this very year, fathers of families, loved husbands and sons.

The silly thing was that no one cared a curse for Burke. Why should they? But he cared for them. He had none of the 'priestly independence' that Dr. Glynn was always talking about. Burke always had to love something or someone – if it was not a woman, it was his dogs and his chickens and ducks, and his horses. When Glynn walked up the ladder to his execution in Bordeaux, he left behind nothing that he cared for. He walked straight into the arms of God, as a true martyr should. Burke would have been thinking of chicken-feed and pups and brood mares. The cruelty was in creating him like this and them leading him by the nose into so many impossible positions.

Free will was a trap, he thought in anguish. In every case where he had assumed leadership, a wise man would have let well alone. Did God need the Irish College in Bordeaux? He had it now, whether he wanted it or not. Did God need the Countess Jeanne de Rochechouart alive, alone of all her family, to nag Edmund Brien and perpetuate her stupidity and snobbery? He had her too. Did God need another whore in Paris, the beautiful Rose French? Or did he need Burke in Ireland, leading a gaggle of hunted peasants about like a shepherd, until the wolves caught up with them?

Perhaps the idea was that Burke would provide each of these people with a last chance of survival – when everyone else had the wits to back away, Burke could be trusted to come bumbling in and have another try. What would God do with Burke himself, then, in the end? That was to be a surprise, perhaps the biggest surprise of all. Better put it out of his head – but that was impossible. He would never be rid of a scene containing terrified old men and women and children and cows, all backed into a remote valley with no exit, the old and sick sleeping in a cave, the rest out in the open, in the marvellous warm summer of this year.

Anyone but Burke would have seen that it was hopeless to try to lead them to safety. No one but Burke would have

216

been so conveniently there with them in the first place. He had not dared to give Everard any details of his campaign. Everard had probably avoided asking, in fear of what he would be told. He had only asked if Burke had borne arms, and Burke could honestly say that he had not. The vision of himself carrying a pike or a sabre was so funny that he could almost laugh.

It had begun early in March while Burke was in Paris. The papers there had reported that the Committee of United Irishmen for the province of Leinster had been arrested. The list included Emmet, MacNeven, Dr. Sweetman, Oliver Bond, Jackson and his son – names with which Burke was familiar from his Irish associates. Warrants had also been issued for the arrest of Lord Edward FitzGerald and some others but they had not yet been found. Obviously a spy had given the list of names, it was so accurate. The arrests amounted to a declaration of war, and by the end of March it was clear that the Government in Ireland was not going to wait for an armed rising to erupt.

In April the Directory at Paris conferred the command of both the army and the fleet on General Bonaparte, with orders to proceed to Brest where the Armée d'Angleterre had been preparing for months past. Huge transport barges were being built on the river at Rouen, and the army was instructed daily in the geography and conditions of the south of England, where some of the landings were to take place. The rest were to be in Ireland. Talleyrand assured Tone and his colleagues that France would never grant a peace to England on any terms short of the independence of Ireland, but even Talleyrand seemed uncertain of what General Bonaparte was planning in the long term. It was common talk that the great French army was on its way to the Mediterranean, some said to Egypt – certainly not to Ireland.

Burke and Colman were summoned to Rouen to receive their instructions. They found the Irishmen there puzzled and dismayed, scarcely able to believe that the plans were to be changed at this late date. To avoid a massacre, they said, the rising should be postponed still further. Burke and Colman had been chosen as reputable messengers. They were to say that the United Irishmen must wait for the Directory's next decision.

Burke blurted out before he could stop himself: "A bunch of muddlers, that Directory. No better than the Garonne peasants – why don't they make a good plan and stick to it?"

But the messengers were instructed not to destroy all hope in Ireland. There would be a better opportunity. Burke bit his tongue. When would that be? When General Bonaparte had conquered the world.

Waiting in Rouen for the ship that took him and Colman to Waterford, he had no idea whatever of becoming any sort of warrior. Colman was different. He was full of plans for striking a blow with his own hand – he was young and strong, and these were proper sentiments in him. For himself, Burke knew he was a necessary messenger to Ireland but he had no wish to get any nearer to the action than he had been obliged to do in Bordeaux. He was too old. He was too large and noticeable. The terrain was not familiar. He had been so long out of Ireland that his natural language was French, or English with French words shoved in anywhere and everywhere. He had no fighting skills but in the event he found that neither had most of the men who were his comrades in that war.

They reached Waterford in the second week of May. It was already much too late. Before they left France, the Paris papers had been printing news that the insurrection had already begun. These were contradicted later but alarming news began to come in of the Government's plans to terrify the population. An ominous sign was that some of the gentry, including Sir Lawrence Parsons of Birr, had resigned command of their local militia rather than carry out the grisly campaign that had been outlined to them. Walking off the ship at Waterford, Burke was not surprised to find himself being closely questioned about his passport. Everything was in order – Citizen Burke of Paris on a visit to his Irish relations – there was no reason to hold him but for a few nasty minutes it seemed as if they were going to arrest him on suspicion anyway. Colman, the firebrand, was not stopped at all.

The farther they penetrated into the country, the more often they heard the same story repeated. A great many of the rank and file of the United Irishmen were handing in their pikes so fast that their storage became a problem. At the same time the militia was running wild through the villages and farms, sure of the support of the magistrates and the gentry in general, who had suddenly taken to wearing orange symbols to prove their loyalty. There were ghastly stories of tortures – half hangings, men and women flogged to death, lingering deaths perpetrated on anyone and everyone, in a mad frenzy which seemed to have little to do with keeping law and order. In their terror men even bought pikes and handed them in, so as to be on record for having done so, but this was not a guarantee of safety. The climax came for Burke, as he had told Everard, when he found himself with his old pupil, Michael Murphy, a fugitive from the tiny village where he was the curate and suddenly transformed into the general of an army.

A sod of turf flared suddenly on the hearth, lighting up the whole room. Burke quickly twitched the curtains across, then felt behind them for the shutters, closing them too. The chances were all against the light having been seen – he had observed the empty landscape for half an hour at least. Still he felt a spasm of sheer terror at the notion that he might be betrayed. Ever since the Bordeaux terror he had dreaded violent death above all things, especially death deliberately imposed by ritualistic outside forces. Fire, earthquake, a bolting horse – anything was endurable compared with this. Suicide was an impossibility for him, though it had occurred to him several times that a prudent man would make sure to be prepared for it, as Tone was. For all his fighting spirit in intellectual matters he knew that he would be quite incapable of fighting for his life, which was the other way to lose it quickly. He would go as quietly as a cow, with about as much wit to save himself.

He doused the fire with fresh turf, crushing down the temptation then to slip behind the curtains, open the shutters a crack and have one peek out over the fields. If he began that, there would be no end to it. Instead he opened the room door very quietly and listened. The soft, gentle voices of the Martins reassured him. He closed the door without a sound and went to the table where he tore off a strip of his writing paper to make a spill.

He enjoyed the business of blowing the fire to flame, pushing in the spill and carrying it quickly to set it to the wick, as if these actions gave him a stronger hold on life. He collected the ashes of the paper in his palm and stood for a moment admiring the light he had created. The trouble it had been to get the candle alight in the College – he was astonished now at the endurance he had summoned up there. The mice, the cold, the dirt, the hunger, the loneliness – but he had not been in fear of his life in Bordeaux, except once in the early days.

The first delightful drowsiness induced by the wine had worn off. If he had another bottle handy he would open it now. Everard had probably thought the one he brought would do for several days. Burke felt alert as a fox. Without exercise he needed very little sleep. He picked up the pages of his letter, three of them, not very large. He could imagine Everard's face when they would be delivered to him, even before he began to read. More trouble, he would think. Nothing but trouble ever, from that quarter. The will might soften him but the piece about Rose French would give him a pain in the belly for a week. Well, Burke could do something about that. He placed the last sheet squarely on the table and wrote: "Every word of the story of my relationship with Rose French is true, as I prepare to meet my God."

Everard would be obliged to believe him, in the circumstances. He would never see this letter unless Burke was caught. The moment he had his tail out of Ireland, it would be destroyed and he would make a new will with the same provisions, later. There would be no need of letters then. First he would go to Bordeaux, to Saint Jacques d'Ambes.

He could imagine Jean-Paul's mother looking up from her pot of soup perpetually simmering over the fire, saying: "So you're back. You took long enough about it."

Then Banba would come waggling to him, and he would ask about the horses and the sheep, and Jean-Paul might even have some new pups for him. The cows would be all right – they always were. He might give warning of his coming, though it was tempting not to. No point in catching them red-handed, disobeying his instructions. One look at the animals would tell him enough.

He had not thought much about where he would live now that he had given away the Château Rochechouart. He had always liked it, and for Jeanne it was home. She had it now, and there was no more need for him to live her kind of life. The drawbacks of a big house were endless, unless you had a horde of servants as they did in Ireland. You were never close enough to the fire, there were always too many steps, up and downstairs, a bed like a room, an army of rats and mice ready to move into the cellars at the first loss of vigilance. The farmhouse was the place he had loved first, pigeons under the eaves, flowers by the door, creepers on the walls, only a solid stone wall between him and the silent fields, no avenues, no high front steps, no ceremony, the kitchen table for his accounts late at night after a hard day's work. It would not be a great misfortune to go back there.

Just one thing troubled that peaceful picture. He had not forgotten his oath taken in the desolate library in Bordeaux. He had sworn then that he would repent and go back to his ministry, if they would let him. There were a few small signs that religion would be re-established in France some day, perhaps not too distant. Then, it seemed, he might be sent back to his little house by the church, where he had kept chickens in the tiny garden and where his first lust for farming had taken root. He could imagine how some of his neighbours would scrabble and grab to get his land, if he put it up for sale. From watching him they should know that a small farm is not worth the work put into it, yet they all longed passionately to own even a tiny patch. If he never got back alive, their greed would increase the price of his land to the benefit of the College. He added a paragraph:

"Referring back to my Will, it should be realised that my land in and around Saint Jacques and Saint André de Cubzac will fetch a good price. Edmund Brien knows my agents and he will guide you. Do not take advice from my servant Jean-Paul nor from any of his family as they would have an interest in keeping the price low."

Edmund would have to help, though he would be disappointed at not being the legatee. Burke had never promised him anything more than the Château but he could well be angry at having no provision made for René.

With his pen in the ink, ready to add a piece about his son, Burke paused in time. That would be a disaster indeed. The child was his mother's responsibility. She would take care of him. Better not to mention René at all.

In the short time that he had been able to enjoy him, Burke had developed an intense love for his son. Once he had decided never to take his place as René's father, he knew that he should keep his distance but this had become more painful every day. Rose was the one who should be in charge of him, as she was supposed to be in charge of his soul.

She would have made a splendid mother, with her air of calm wisdom, and her singing, and her perpetual readiness to be of service to everyone who needed her. She was part of nature's wastefulness, like the frozen birds he sometimes found in the fields. And she would be a delightful lover, he was certain. She seemed to have retained a passion for that Count de Saint Etienne over several years, after no more than one meeting. Burke suspected that Saint Etienne had primed the pump while he was in Ireland. Poor devil, perhaps he would have married her if he had not had his head cut off. An honorary eunuch, as Burke now intended to be, had no business with thoughts like that. No wonder the Archbishop was so distrustful of him.

Several times before she left Bordeaux, it had occurred to Burke that Rose with her nosiness might have discovered and read his precious journal. It was impossible, of course. It never moved from its hiding-place behind the big desk in his study. She would not have had the nerve to take it up to her room where she could read it in peace. If she had read it, her comments would have been priceless, he was sure. She might have had the courage to make some, if he gave her any encouragement. There was always a strong flavour of disapproval, even of dislike, in her attitude towards him, though it was not the bitchy kind that Jeanne had.

Was he really in love with her, then? He marshalled the evidence. They had a secret life, a special understanding which needed no words. When either of them came into a room, the other looked up and established instant communion. Each knew when the other was about to speak and waited with interest, sometimes with obvious impatience, for the words. Obsession – hatred – it could be any one of a number of relationships. Oh, to be young again! But the young Burke would have got no more notice from Rose French than a yard dog would. Finished with all that. It was a relief, a liberation.

The will – it was time to get it signed. At any moment now they might come for him. If Everard came, Burke had no intention of giving him the letter at once. No dithering – he had never dithered in his life but with the onset of old age anything might happen. A memory shot into his mind, of the old people around his home, saying that one of the pleasures of old age was in going over and over one's life and estimating one's achievements. That would not do for Burke. He would have to create a new past. Never too soon to begin.

He took the first page of the letter and opened the door. They were quiet now but he sensed that they had not yet gone to bed. The kitchen lamp still shed light halfway up the stairs, warming the aged wood to a soft orange colour. At the foot of the stairs, a little to the left, he could see a part of the house door. With his eye on that danger point, he crept down a few steps, until he could look into the kitchen. They were there, all right. They had each turned a chair with its back to the fire, and they were kneeling on the floor, resting their arms on the seats, looking into the dying fire, saying their prayers. The murmur he had heard must have been the Rosary. Now they had moved on to their private prayers, individual and lengthy. For a full five minutes he stayed there, watching, until at last Mrs. Martin stood up with a groan of pain, rubbing her tired hip joints with both hands. She lifted her chair and turned it around, and sat there waiting for her husband to finish. He was not long, perhaps a minute. Then he also stood up.

Burke descended the stairs. The moment they heard him they turned sharply. Martin said: "Don't come down. What is it?"

The single window had a worn shutter and curtains which were more ornamental than useful.

Burke backed up a step saying: "Just a document for you to witness."

"We'll go up. You need both of us?"

"Yes."

With a disproportionate sense of loss, he turned back into his room. To have been allowed to sit for half an hour in the kitchen seemed at that moment the most desirable privilege in the world. Every day of theirs was like this, a long round of familiar work, then leisure in the evening to offer it up to the loving God who took care that he saw every sparrow fall with a crash to the earth. Burke, the sinner, had not prayed like that for a long time. If he had asked them to let him join in the Rosary they might have permitted it, but they might have expected him to add something of his own. Better to keep out of that until he had time to re-learn his old skills. They would be shocked out of their wits if they knew the story of his life.

They came into the room awkwardly, Martin saying: "I'm sorry to be your gaoler, Mr. Burke. I can see you're sick and tired of being a prisoner, a big, hearty man like you."

"I shouldn't have gone down. It's just this paper – I need to make my will."

It was necessary to tell them what it was, otherwise he

would not have given them the pain of realising how his thoughts were running. He laid the sheet of paper on the table, pointing to the space he had left for their names. There was no need for them to read it. Until this moment it had not occurred to him that they might be illiterate. Martin would have said so, at once. The Irish, even the poorest of them, always made a point of educating their children.

Burke dipped the pen and wrote his own name first, then said: "Now both of you can say that you saw me write it."

Each of them stooped and wrote laboriously. Her name was Hanora Abigail. It gave her a different personality. Martin never referred to her by her name. There was no way of finding out what he called her in private. Even a sparrow might have a name for his wife.

Burke folded the sheet of paper and said: "Dr. Everard will arrange for me to go but there is no certainty that I'll ever reach my destination. I want you to keep this until you hear that I have arrived somewhere safely in Europe, then burn it."

"Burn it?"

"Yes. I'll make another one then, probably make a better job of it, so there will be no more need for this."

"I see."

He was still doubtful. Burke wondered if he was afraid. That might be so. If the house were raided and this little bit of evidence found, Martin and his wife would be finished.

Burke said: "Keep it somewhere near the fire, under one of those blue china vases, or inside it. Then if the militia come you drop it quickly into the fire and burn it."

He had guessed right. Martin said: "What do I do if you're captured on the way out of Ireland? God forbid it will happen but in these times no one is safe."

"Then you give it to Dr. Everard. He will take care of it."

"I see."

He probably also saw that Burke did not want Everard to have that document a moment sooner than was necessary. And there was the rest of the letter. Burke said: "This is the will, that you have signed. There will be a letter with it, to be given to Dr. Everard at the same time. Be quite sure to burn the whole package, when you hear that I'm safely back in France. Dr. Everard himself will tell you, but in that case don't tell him that I gave you the letter and the will."

"I think I understand."

And he has decided that I'm stone mad, Burke thought. No wonder. He said: "I'll seal it up, if you have some wax. Remember, if the militia come you're quite welcome to burn the whole lot. We can't fix everything to our satis- faction in this life."

"I have some wax. I'll get it for you."

A good thing about sealing the letter was that he could not add anything to it. In his present mood he was capable of writing more and more, explaining himself and his doings on page after page of that letter. It would be a disaster. Everard would hide it away from all eyes, or burn it, so as not to disgrace Burke any further, but then he would have to carry the weight of his secrets forever.

Martin came back almost at once with a short stick of wax, saying: "That's all I have, I'm afraid. It's not a thing we use much ourselves."

Burke folded the letter carefully, then enclosed it in a fresh sheet of paper which he sealed with the wax. Martin stood by, waiting for it, until Burke said: "I can give it to you in the morning."

"The sooner the better. If they're coming, we'll hear them before you do."

"You expect them, then?"

"I expect nothing any more. I'm past it. Better to be sure than sorry."

"Very well."

At last he was gone. With the departure of the letter, there was nothing to do. Some Swift now would have been soothing – *The Battle of the Books*, or *A Tale of a Tub* – something that would make him laugh at the world even for a short time. Everard had brought him a New Testament and some lives of the saints. These last were not useful to him at his present stage, since most of the saints had solved their character defects in early life. He opened the letter of Saint Paul to the Philippians, on the readiness to live or die – very appropriate: "But I am straitened between two: having a desire to be dissolved and to be with Christ, a thing by far the better. But to abide still in the flesh is needful for you." Well, they got Paul in the end, kept him in a hole in the ground until they were ready to kill him. Pity Everard had not brought an Old Testament – there was a roll and flow to that which would have soothed his mind, though he had lost his taste for battles and fighting.

The lamp began to burn low. He lifted it and shook it gently from side to side, hearing the dry rattle that showed its tank was almost empty. Martin had given him the impression that it was only a question of time before he was found. At last he was beginning to feel drowsy, yet he had a premonition that something would happen tonight. The will, and Saint Paul, and Christmas – everything had sharpened his senses. Better to lie on the bed and rest a while. He would not sleep, just lie there in his clothes, ready for anything that might happen.

He awoke to utter darkness and crawled off the bed to revive the fire. The air was stale and rancid, and bitterly cold. He felt for the tongs and raked out the ashes, finding the still-living coals, setting them against fresh turf, waiting for a sign of life. The hot pieces of turf glowed dimly, insulated in their nest of soft brown ashes. A flame appeared and vanished. He waited for it to come again. This time it stayed, uncertain and alone, until another appeared beside it. He sat back on his heels and watched until the centre of the fire was well alight. Corners of the room began to appear, losing their mystery one by one.

He stood up stiffly, took a chair and placed it close to the fire. Not to know the time was torture. He could not bear to sit down, like a cat, and spend an undefined number of hours warming himself. Better open the shutters and take a look out, if only for a moment. He went to the window and loosened the latch, then lifted the curtain aside quickly, twitched the latch across and opened one shutter a crack.

The splendid panorama out there was intoxicating to him. It was almost daylight. A purple reflection was giving way to grey. The grass glistened with frost, with here and there jet-black trees showing the pattern of all their branches. It was so still that not even their tops moved. Its empty, unused beauty was an insult to God and man. The murder and slaughter that had been done to keep it intact for people who had no use for it in the first place! The cows you could keep on that pasture, the oats and barley you could grow! There was nothing like it in the west, where his own brother had fought all his life to keep the family's lease for himself. As Patrick Martin had said, neither he nor Burke would ever see the day when things would be different. Better forget it. He had come into this room without a single possession, except for his clothes. He could leave it at a moment's notice.

He stood there, watching, until the light was rose-red on the frost. A red sky in the morning is the shepherd's warning. But the sky was clear, not a cloud in sight. Then the sun came up and the trees made long blue shadows. He opened the window and breathed in the delicious cold air for several minutes, reckless as to whether or not that spy would notice him.

When he turned back into the room he found that the fire had also enjoyed the open window and was blazing gloriously. Breakfast might come soon. There was some kind of stir downstairs, he could not be sure what. It would hardly be the Wren Boys, with the present condition of the country. This was their day to run from house to house with a captured wren in a cage, singing old rhymes and hoping for pennies. It was a survival of some pagan rite, no doubt, always carried out on the day after Christmas, Saint Stephen's day. Saint Stephen, the first martyr, stoned to death, a young man – there was tragedy in that. Burke at his age would be no loss to anyone.

Horses. No doubt about it. Let them come – there was no more fight in him, only sadness and gloom and weariness – a child could lead him away at this moment. He was finished.

228

A quick hand on the door-knob – it didn't sound like one of the Martins. He sprang to his feet when he saw that it was Everard, as he had not looked since Burke saw him in Bordeaux before he left with the students. His clothes were always clean and neat now but he had the same frantic look as if he felt he was being hunted.

He said: "Thank God you're out of bed. They thought you might still be asleep. There's no time to lose. Have you been up all night?"

"A good deal of it. I had a feeling you might send for me. You shouldn't have come yourself."

"I had to put you safely on the road. My man will go with you. He has a horse for you."

"Where am I going?"

"Dublin. It's more than a hundred miles. Word came a few minutes ago. I have your passport. I wanted to see you myself, James. This may be the last time."

"I know."

"I want to ask you, in case anything goes wrong, if you have made your peace with God. It's my duty to ask."

I've always been at peace with God – man is my trouble. Keep quiet, you fool. Why upset this poor old man? He has enough trouble on him, from you. Burke said: "Yes, a long time ago, when I was in the College, I decided to go back to the arms of Mother Church eventually, if she'll have me."

Even that was too flippant for Everard. He turned his eyes down as he said: "Thank God. I thought you would do that. I can give you conditional absolution now. When you go to your bishop in France, there will be a ritual to observe. He'll tell you exactly what to do. I didn't want you to leave here without the consolation of absolution. I've brought along my little book." This from Everard was a joke. Burke appreciated the effort. "Now if you will kneel down, I can read the prayers for you."

No point in telling him that he might not come across a live bishop in France for years. The prayers were short. Everard read them with a French accent to his Latin, as he

229

had learned when he was a student, recalling to Burke the old days of certainty when right was right and wrong was wrong and Burke was usually in the wrong. He had never understood how they let him teach in that same College at all, since so many of them disapproved of him. He stood up when Everard had finished and suddenly, without warning, extended his arms and took the old man by the shoulders and pressed him in a long embrace.

Everard returned the pressure, trembling against Burke's chest, then said: "God bless you, James. I'll pray for you night and day until I hear that you're safe."

"And you'll let the Martins know at once, when you have news of me. They have been very good to me."

"Of course. Now we must go down."

With one last look at his latest prison, Burke threw on his heavy cloak and followed Everard downstairs. Knowing he was to go without breakfast, Mrs. Martin – Hanora Abigail – had prepared a bag with bread and eggs and meat, which she had already given to Everard's man. He was sitting on his horse, ready to go, holding the bridle of Burke's horse as well as the Archbishop's. Neither of the Martins came to the door.

Patrick said: "God speed you, Father. We'll be praying for you. Farrell will take good care of you. Maybe with the help of God we'll meet again in better times."

Even as he was thanking them, Everard was pulling at his elbow, urging him to hurry. The last he saw of the old couple, they were standing side by side, backs to the fire, watching him with a look of genuine loneliness, as if he had been a valued friend instead of a nuisance and a danger to their lives. Then the door was shut and he climbed on to the horse. It was young and lively, and danced angrily at the huge weight suddenly imposed on it. Then they were trotting down the road, leaving Everard to mount and get himself home as best he could.

# _14_

PARIS, THE MARVELLOUS CITY, HAD NOT CHANGED AT ALL
when Burke reached it at last. Throughout the whole
wretched journey he had only one fixed object in mind,
apart from saving his neck – to get to Rose as quickly as
possible. At Hamburg he had sent off a letter to Everard to
tell of his safe arrival and to describe as much of the journey
as he could without incriminating any of the people who
took part in it. There was time for this to reach Cashel
before Burke got to Paris. His will and the letter he had left
for Everard should have gone up in smoke long ago, and
still Burke felt uneasy lest Everard might be on his way
already to fulfil his commission. The thought of this gave
him the creeps now, though he had been quite sure when he
wrote that letter that it was the right thing to do.

It was a walk of several miles from the coach office in rue
Montmartre to the FitzGeralds' house but Burke enjoyed
every moment of it. He felt a free man at last, swinging
along through the filthy streets with nothing to carry except
his few essential possessions in a handbag, bought with the
last of his money in Hamburg. There had been snow, and
his Hessian boots were splashed to the ankles. He would
have to get money at once. He could borrow what he
needed. Once he got home to Saint Jacques he would have
no more trouble. He might borrow from Rose – she would
like that. Still he would not beg a bed. There is no surer way
to put oneself at the mercy of another than to accept that
particular hospitality.

Mrs. FitzGerald offered it at once. They had heard a great
deal about the débâcle in Ireland, most of it accurate, some
from eye-witnesses, yet they seemed eager to hear it all

again from him. They had no idea of its awfulness, nor of the sheer impossibility of making another attempt in their lifetime. The devastation in the country would take years to rebuild, the memories of the horrors he had seen would take lifetimes to erase, if they were ever erased at all.

He said: "The people are beaten into the ground. Men who never knew anything but a sound roof and a full stomach were living in caves on the mountainside, killing and eating sheep to stay alive. The poor people didn't know what was happening. They could no more defend themselves than a flock of sheep could. It was the abomination of desolation. Their spirit is broken. They will never rise again. When that scoundrel FitzGibbon gets his Act of Union through, Ireland will be England and England Ireland. We'll never again have a parliament of our own. It's finished, over and done with."

He stopped because he saw how they were watching him, with suspicion and a trace of pity. Several people had dropped in for a chat, perhaps because they had heard he was there. Dr. FitzGerald came upstairs from his surgery and a maid was handing around coffee and cake, just like the old times. Most of the people were the same, including the man who had been sitting with Rose when Burke dropped his brick about Saint Etienne being dead. What was his name? Burke could not remember and no one told him. A real sign of a closed society is that no one bothers to make introductions. He was a pleasant man, perhaps thirty-five years old, rather heavy-set, with strong black hair which he wore cut short, proving that he was a follower of the Revolution. In this company one hardly needed evidence for that. He was rather silent, seeming content to watch the speakers' faces rather than join in their conversation. After a while Burke went to sit near him, tucking his large boots in under his chair. Though he had scraped them well at the front door they were still coated with yellow mud. Suddenly he remembered. A widower, with one daughter.

"Dorval, of course. Monsieur Dorval. We met here once before, more than a year ago."

"I remember the occasion very well. It was the evening that Miss French fainted. I wondered where you had gone. No one seemed to know."

It was never discretion that prevented them from talking about him. Paris was a spy's paradise. It was simply that he had no importance for anyone here. If he had never come back from Ireland, in a few years' time they would have difficulty in remembering who he was unless, as Everard said, he had been hanged and disembowelled and had thus become a useful martyr. On the other hand, Burke had gone to great trouble to conceal his movements. He had nothing to complain of. He could scarcely believe now that a year ago this company had been the most important in the world to him. He had given up a great many things – his son, his house, his most valuable farm, perhaps even his soul, though that was retrievable – to be with them in their plans. No – they were not the same people, after all. The company here this afternoon was always in the second rank, sincere as they were. The leaders that he had loved and admired were all dead.

But the greatest change was in himself, and he knew it. The one secret that no one shared proved it up to the hilt. Death was at his elbow. There could be no other reason for this new dryness, where he could view the deserts of vast eternity without any of the pain that he would have felt a year ago. How did it go, that nasty little poem that summed him up?

And your quaint honour turn to dust
And into ashes all my lust.
The grave's a fine and private place,
But none I think do there embrace.

Louise was no more to him now than a clever child he had once taught. In Ireland, after his escape from Wexford, he had made no attempt to go to Mount Brien, though the prospect of seeing her there had been one of his reasons for consenting to go to Ireland at all. Instead he had accepted the refuge that had been found for him in Cashel without a word. All gone, utterly gone. He heard Dorval say: "I think you're very tired. Have you found a place to sleep?"

"Not yet. I'm going back to my old lodgings. There are sure to be rooms there. I'm not staying long in Paris."

"Oh. Where will you go?"

"To Bordeaux, to take care of my property, but first I have some things to do here."

"Will you see Miss French?"

That was the second time he had mentioned her in a couple of minutes. Burke said: "I hope so. Do you know her well?"

"No. I met her here for the first time, then I've been to her apartment with friends on several occasions."

"How was she?"

"Very well indeed." There was no mistaking the eagerness this time. "She's brilliant – everyone enjoys her salons."

Salons? That was not the story Burke had heard. He said: "A good talker, is she? She was rather quiet when I knew her. Paris is good for everyone."

Dorval said: "She never does anything extravagant. Her rooms are beautifully arranged. She perpetuates the best of the old society without any of its stupidities."

Rose could never be anything but a lady, if that was what he was trying to say.

"Does she have a special day for her salons?"

"Not really. You could drop in there on any afternoon and be sure to find company."

"When did you see her last?"

"A few days ago. I don't like to go too often." He stopped for a moment, then said in a confidential tone: "To tell you the truth, I don't like some of the company I see there. It's unworthy of her. She has every excuse, with no one to take care of her, or to advise her." Just try advising Rose, my boy, and see what happens to you. "If she had a mother, or an aunt, or anyone at all that she could trust and rely on, she would select her company differently."

"What is wrong with her company?"

"Some of the men are unscrupulous. I know them well."

"She is not a child."

"She might as well be, so far as this kind of experience

234

goes. Before she came to France I think she led a very quiet life."

"Yes."

"I know she doesn't like my visits. She remembers that I was present when she heard the news of her lover's death."

Her lover! Burke said after a pause: "Has she spoken to you about that incident?"

"Of course not. How could she? I swore that I would never refer to it. A woman who is capable of such love is a pearl of great price. Don't you think so, Mr. Burke?"

"Yes, certainly, that is true."

A sitting duck, by all that's holy. Burke had scarcely believed that any of them still existed. Here was a solution to Rose, to set her up with this splendid, gullible creature, who would take care of her for the rest of her life. A pearl of great price – that's what he was himself. It was more than Burke had ever hoped for.

He said gently: "I hope to see Miss French this very day, or at latest tomorrow morning. May I give her your respects?"

"Of course."

"Does she come here sometimes?"

"I think she has outgrown this company."

This was said apparently without irony. Why should she come here? Madame FitzGerald was the one who had said she was up to no good. Her moral sense had never been strong, if you counted in her petty thieving, but with a respectable husband who visited this staid family occasionally, she would be forced back on to the straight and narrow path. The constant reminder of Ireland would be good for her too, the ghost of old Sophie Brien rising up now and then to wag a finger at her. It was not at all certain that Rose could be tidied away so neatly but it was worth a try.

The evening dragged on. Burke was almost yawning, which would have been unforgivable considering that the subject of the conversation was the freedom of Ireland. It would never do to visit Rose until he was certain of being a match for her. Even at her lowest she was like an eel. With good food and housing and nothing to do, she was probably in fighting shape now, at the top of her form. The old monastic idea was the one that Burke favoured, especially with women – catch them after a spell of misfortune and fasting and you can wipe the floor with them.

He was the first to stand up. The rest of them looked as if they would go on yapping all night. Old age – that must be it – bitter old age, else he could never think of them in those terms, these good, idealistic people who had never seen the sights that he had seen, nor been confined in a smelly little room for a month with no company but ghosts and devils.

They saw him to the door and he promised to come again the next evening. No one except Jules Dorval had mentioned Rose's name. Burke got her address from him, very quietly. Tomorrow, after a good night's sleep, he would go to see her.

Waking in the familiar bedroom of his usual lodgings was not a pleasant sensation. Last night he had been so happy to be taken in by his old landlady that he had not anticipated this. It was a ghostly feeling, as if he were watching himself from the outside, as he had sometimes imagined himself observing his own funeral. His mood had changed. Now he feared that his good resolutions were going to take all the joy out of life. He would miss the element of excitement. There had always been a bit of the gambler in him. From now on he would have to make do with the gamble of farming, which is a gamble everywhere in the world, the juicy, miraculous earth sometimes responding to loving care, sometimes thumbing its nose at your best efforts and refusing to yield at all. The most frightening sensation this morning, reminding him of yesterday's reflection on his lost love for Louise, was the recognition that he had lost Paris too. He would never have believed it possible. When he stood at the window, the noises and smells of the street no longer delighted him. Instead he felt a painful longing for the old farm-house in the quiet fields near Saint Jacques d'Ambes. Once there, old age would leave him and he

236

would live again in peace and contentment. Not that he had ever had too much of either of those things when he had lived there before, but that was his own doing. This time he would know better. No politics, no plotting, no women. Who would cook for him? Anna, perhaps. There was always someone. He might even watch his son grow, from a civil distance, though that was probably too much to hope for.

While he was drinking his coffee his eye fell on the bundle of increasingly ragged papers that he had placed on the table the night before. The journal – what would he do with it now? It was part of the past life that he was rejecting. If he were truly sincere, he would burn it. For the moment it seemed enough to make the decision to destroy it eventually. Prudence. One lesson he must learn thoroughly was that he should give up writing. It was the most dangerous habit in the world. It had never been one of his, until he was in the College. It would be painful to destroy this little master-piece, with all its homespun wisdom, but it would be madness to keep it.

He doubted if his landlady could read, and she certainly could not read English. Nevertheless he concealed the journal in the wardrobe, under his rolled-up nightshirt, in case anyone – Rose? – happened to come snooping.

The moment for calling on her had to be carefully chosen. If he came too early, he might not get past the maid, a forward piece according to Madame FitzGerald. If he came too late he might find himself among a throng of Rose's admirers and patrons. Somewhere in between lay the perfect moment. And there would be a lull between her morning session and the late afternoon when she might entertain more formally. Even now he could not believe the slanders against her. Surely she would be too fastidious to endure the humiliations of the trade she was said to be following. She had no need of money. If it turned out that she would like to be married, everything would be easier. He could make no decisions until he saw her, and spoke to her.

At the thought of that meeting a shiver of terror ran

through him, like the terror he had felt when he was about to face Lacombe in Bordeaux. It was ridiculous – what could she do to him? He knew. She could look at him, with those large, clear eyes of indeterminate grey, slightly narrowed at the corners, expressing all her scorn for him and his kind. Could he possibly be misjudging her? She had never said a single discourteous thing to him in all the months when she had lived in his house. They had circled each other like a couple of intelligent dogs of different breeds, each respecting the other's qualities. He realised that he had trusted her in certain things – not in petty thieving of course but that kind of weakness was unimportant, almost endearing. The night in the dark kitchen, when she had helped him to baptise the baby – that was the real key to Rose. All the same, he doubted if he would ever really know her. There was no need. Like a good doctor, he only needed to understand her illness. If he cured her of that, he need never see her again. A light would go out in his life but it was high time for all such lights to go out.

Prodding himself forward, he walked to her street, a short one of well-kept houses off the rue des Feuillantines. Her taste had been good, as usual. Her apartment was on the second floor. The maid who opened the door was well-dressed. If he were still under the jurisdiction of a bishop he would probably be suspended just for knocking at this door. Wise old Mother Church never left her sons alone with a woman for any purpose other than business, if she could avoid it. Well, it was business that took him here.

The maid's eye was too bright to be wholesome. She admitted that Rose was at home and inevitably asked for his name. After all his trouble, to be turned away from the doorstep would be intolerable.

He said: "Just say I'm an old friend from Ireland."

It worked, but when he found himself standing before Rose, the look of shock and horror on her face infuriated him. He realised that his anger was a healthier emotion than the sentimental rubbish that had been dancing on the fringes of his brain a few minutes ago. Even if she had been expecting someone more appetising, surely there was no need for this violent reaction. She didn't even observe the decencies of greeting him, but kept her hands clasped in front of her as if she were resisting the temptation to attack him. Once he had thought she was about to do that but fortunately she had fainted instead.

He said: "I'm afraid I took you by surprise. You look as if you had seen a ghost."

To his amazement she laughed, not an amused sound but almost hysterically. Then she said: "I thought I had. I was told you died in Ireland."

"Who told you that story?"

"Edmund."

"When?"

"Last June."

"I might have, but I didn't."

"Have you been in Paris long?"

Somehow she had managed to call up the tone that she used for social purposes, the typical hostess's question.

He said: "I got here yesterday, from Hamburg."

"You must be tired."

That meant he had aged. Dorval had made that same comment.

"Yes. I went to the FitzGeralds' last evening."

"Oh. I never see them now. How are they?" Without waiting for an answer she turned away and went on: "Please sit down."

Was this progress? It was hard to say. She seated herself in what was obviously her usual chair, a high-backed one of carved chestnut wood with claw-shaped arms on which she rested her beautiful hands carefully. All of her furniture was substantial. He took a large chair a few feet from her, and wondered whether she hid a smile as he placed himself in it without a single creak. She never missed anything.

He said: "So Edmund told you I was dead. Did he say where he had heard that story?"

"I think he said he had heard it from Ireland."

239

"He came to Paris?"

"Yes."

"If he had gone to Dr. FitzGerald's he would have heard the truth. They knew about me there."

"Edmund doesn't care a pin for Ireland now."

It would be indecent to try to discover how she had felt when she had heard the news. He asked: "What had he to say about Jeanne?"

"She was well. They have a child."

"I heard that, in Ireland."

"And René is well and growing big and strong."

"Does he live with them?"

"Yes. Bernadette looks after both children. She and Jean-Paul are married."

"None too soon. When did that happen?"

"Early summer, just before Edmund came."

"That was the last time you saw him?"

"Yes. He said he would not be coming again."

"When the weather gets warm, perhaps you'll pay them a visit."

"Mr. Burke, nothing would induce me to visit them. Edmund made it quite clear that he has finished with me. Don't you remember?"

That story, of course – Burke had made it up himself – that Edmund did not want his former governess living in the house. It was a monstrous thing to have done, to have cut her off forever from people who might eventually have become her friends. If she ever found it out, she would kill him. Get her married: that was always the great Irish recipe.

He said:

"Are you enjoying life in Paris, then? Plenty of friends and company?"

The look she gave him would turn a horse from his oats. All she said was: "Yes."

He could see that it was not true. His carefully worked out plan had not made her in the least bit happier. Independence was not what she needed, after all. He said gently: "I think I know why Edmund made that mistake about me. It was poor Colman Folan who died in Ireland."

She said sharply: "'Too zealous for the Nation's good.'"

"But he was no 'cringing knave' and well you know it," Burke said angrily. "He died in battle. Sometimes I think you know your Swift too well."

"I suppose that is possible. I never cared about politics, as you should remember."

"This was not politics. It was bloody war. I was there, at the edge of that battle. Colman rode a big bay horse that he had got from one of the Wexford farmers. He looked splendid. He cheered everyone on. If he had survived that battle it would have been a miracle. He died thinking we had won it."

"I'm glad of that, at least. He always had courage."

Was that an apology for her dismissal of him a moment ago? Whatever about politics, she had never cared about poor Colman. A Frenchman would be different. She might have a bit of respect for him.

He said: "I met Monsieur Dorval at the FitzGeralds' last evening. He said you have an elegant salon."

"That was kind of him."

Her tone was bored but she was watching him now in a different way. It was reasonable to risk a question.

"Do you have special days?"

"Sometimes I send invitations but most days people just drop in for an hour or two."

"So you have plenty of escorts for the Opéra?"

"Yes. It's very useful."

And I know that innocent tone of yours, old friend. Don't think you can fool me with it – this or something like it was in her mind. It was a stone wall. He stood up saying: "Well, I must go. I have some things to do. By the way – I almost forgot – can you lend me some money?"

"Money!"

Amusement showed on her face now. He had known she would be pleased to find him gone down in the world but it stung him all the same. He said: "I had barely enough to get

241

me here. I didn't want to borrow from the Irish in Hamburg, though the place is hopping with them. I knew I could get some easily in Paris. If it's any trouble – "

"No, no, of course not. You always have first claim on me. I don't forget how good you were to me when I turned up like a tramp in Bordeaux. Where are you staying?"

"At my old lodgings."

"I'm often there. Her daughter is one of my dress-makers. Was it she who gave you my address, or Madame FitzGerald?"

"No. I had it from Monsieur Dorval."

"You seem to have seen a lot of him."

"I sat beside him last evening. I was tired, and there was too much talk – it gave me a headache to listen to them. I'm tired of politics too – I have no more patience with those carpet knights. I just want to get back to my farming as soon as possible."

"To the Château?"

"Of course not. To Saint Jacques, to the old farmhouse. It's too big for me but that doesn't matter."

"I've never seen it."

"It's rather like an Irish manor house, big square rooms and a kitchen with a flagstone floor and a fireplace where you could roast an ox, and a vegetable garden. Perhaps I'll do some gardening in my old age."

"That's women's work. I can't imagine you at it."

"I'll always be a farmer – I could never give that up, unless my bishop demands it, but I don't think he will."

"Bishop?"

She did not look very surprised when he said: "I'm going back to the Church at the first opportunity. This won't be a People's Republic much longer – in two shakes we could have the King back in the saddle."

"Will you continue to supply horses? The wars seem never to stop."

"If I supply them I won't organise the markets and the distribution to the Army. That wouldn't do for a priest."

"Sheep will soon be the great thing in France, I've heard.

You should think about them – Merinos for the wool and Larzacs for the milk and cheese. You could make Roquefort. Jean-Paul and Bernadette know a lot about sheep. They were always hoping you would get interested in them some day."

"Were they, indeed? They never said anything about it to me."

"They're terrified of you."

"That's the best way to have them."

"But I think they'll be glad to see you. They always said things went well when you were at home and began to go to pieces the moment you went away."

"Did you think things are going well with Edmund?"

"The opposite, he said. He works hard but he doesn't know enough about the land and the people to make a success of it as you did. Don't tell him I said so."

"Is Jean-Paul cheating him?"

"Probably, but Edmund didn't say. He just said his income has gone down. I think he has had some failures with the horses."

"That's the one thing he knows about. I must get back there at once."

Burke was afraid to look her in the eye. Edmund – that little wart, that sparrow-fart – of course when Burke's back was turned he got up to his mean tricks again. The suspicion that entered Burke's head now was so monstrous that he could scarcely believe it to be true. Perhaps it was for this that he had been saved from the gallows – to see to Rose, though he had assumed it was to give himself time to repent. He could almost hear his devil chuckle at the ease with which he had been trapped there. Imagine the egotism that could entertain such an idea – God following the wretched Burke around to save him from his own stupidity and foolishness.

His mouth was stopped. He was supposed to have known of Edmund's generosity, nothing more. But he could not be quite sure yet. His new idea could be wrong. He said again: "I must get back to Bordeaux at once."

She crossed to an elegant little desk by the window, saying: "I'll get your money."

"I had almost forgotten it. All your talk of sheep. You would make a good farmer."

"I like to see things done right."

"I hope that Anna will come back to me now. Jeanne got rid of her. I hope she still remembers all you taught her."

"She knew those things already. All I did was get her to make use of her knowledge. You could tell her that I said she should cook as she did when we all lived at the Château Rochechouart."

"You think she will do that for one old man?"

"Yes, if you don't invite Jean-Paul to dinner with you. She doesn't like to cook for him."

"Why not? Isn't he as good as herself?"

"That is the reason."

O wise young judge. And here was the penitent Burke, planning himself a first-rate cook in his retreat from the world. Not such a bad thing, if it would keep his mind off other subjects. He remembered that his life had been happy and settled, in some extraordinary way, after Rose's arrival.

She had taken some gold coins out of the desk drawer, opening it with a key that she kept in the pocket of her dress. Of course she would keep her money locked up, knowing the dishonesty of housekeepers and servants. Burke's way was better – anyone with a mind to do it can pick a lock. If he had been foolish enough to keep his money in a locked drawer in the Château, she would have found it and made off with some of it at once. The loose floor-board was old-fashioned but satisfactory, until he was able to move his gold to the bank in Bordeaux. Even if Edmund tried to get his paws on it there, they would never give it to him. Still he would be glad to see it and count it again. Nothing like gold, when you came down to it.

He said: "Ten louis will be enough. I'll send it back to you directly, from Bordeaux."

"When will you leave?"

"In a day or two. Perhaps I'll see you again before I go."

"Perhaps."

That was as good as an invitation. She gave him quite a friendly look. He had always wished her well. Perhaps she was able to see that now. Nothing was certain with her, however – one false move and she would be like a burned cat again. He had to ask: "Have you had a visit from an Irish bishop, Dr. Everard?"

"No. I don't know anyone of that name."

"When I was in danger in Ireland I asked him to inform you if I was captured and executed."

"Thank you. I heard anyway."

"It wouldn't have been much of a joke, I can tell you."

"When I heard the news I didn't think it was funny."

Tomorrow he might have the courage to ask her some straight questions about her way of life. Now he felt tired and old. He needed to rest and sleep – the thought of James Burke taking a nap in the afternoon sickened him.

Rose said: "You should go home and have a rest. I suppose you spent all the nights in the coach since Hamburg."

"Yes."

"You'll feel better tomorrow."

"I hope so."

"Will you go to FitzGerald's again tonight?"

"Probably. Would you like to come with me?"

"No, thank you. I don't think they approve of me now."

It was his chance, and he let it go. Instead he said: "They're dull people, though they mean well. All the people in that circle who had any fire in them are dead and gone. I don't care if I never see Paris again, after this."

"It's a sad place, in many ways. People are too nervous to enjoy themselves."

"You think that's it? I would have thought things should be better now than they have been for a long time. All that loot from the wars."

"Oh, yes. Life goes on, for people with no brains."

# _15_

DURING THE NIGHT THERE WAS HEAVY SNOW. BURKE AWOKE feeling disgruntled and uncomfortable. The whiteness from the roofs across the street annoyed him, penetrating the room to every corner, showing up the dust and the streaks of dirt on the walls and on the furniture. There was a disgusting line of grease near the table where the dishes were always placed before meals were served. This establishment was too high-class to have a common dining-room. Instead, food was served in the rooms by the landlady herself, or by one of her servants if the guest was not considered important. Burke always got the best treatment. If he didn't get up at once and go out to a coffee-shop, she would be in with a tray and half an hour's gossip.

The damp cold nibbled at him from the moment when he put his foot out of the bed and touched the floor. It would not be much warmer in Saint Jacques but he loved this season there, when he made his plans for the spring and summer and did his accounts for the year, and still had time for long hours of reading. A big fire of pine logs was an unheard-of luxury in Paris – charcoal was their idea of a fire, and the windows kept tightly shut. Rose always opened them and let in the air, even in winter.

Merino sheep, she said, and Larzacs for the milk and the cheese – where on earth had she learned that? Surely not in Paris. It was just possible. Some of her friends still had estates in the country and would be knowledgeable about ways of making money from farming. Her mind never stopped working. She was one of those people who pick up information and file it away for future use, without considering when they will really need it – the perfect farmer's

246

wife. Not too much of that, if you please – but if Rose had appeared on the scene before Jeanne, or if Jeanne had been detected in the cowshed and carted off with the rest of the family, who knows what might have been Burke's fate? Perhaps even more children. One thing was certain – it would have been a lot harder to repent of Rose than of Jeanne.

It was nonsense, of course, to think of her in this way. She hated his coarseness, his roughness, as he knew very well, though she admired his success and his thrift, and even his forthrightness, in certain circumstances. She had approved of his handling of Edmund and Jeanne but she despised his interest in Irish politics. She thought it a waste of time. So it was, for him, from now on. He had done all he could in that direction. And hatred was too strong a word, though it would not have been at one time. She might even come to tolerate him, or he might improve, if there were good reason for him to make the effort.

Building up fantasies at his time of life was a sign of advancing age but he had to admit that it was a pleasant occupation. He got out of the house without being seen and marched along, inches deep in half-melted snow and mud. The sharp air revived his spirits, as it always did, and a pot of coffee and a brioche improved them further. Last night at Dr. FitzGerald's he had sat with Dorval again and quickly turned the conversation in the direction he wanted. He said that he had been to see Rose and that she was as handsome as ever.

Dorval said: "I told you so. Was anyone else there?"

"No. It was early in the day."

"I see you know about our Rose's habits."

Restraining his sudden anger Burke said: "You told me yourself that she has a salon."

"You should go, some afternoon."

"I intend to."

Dorval had not used that sly tone yesterday. Burke sat quietly and waited for more. After a moment Dorval said: "Even when she's at her most cheerful there is always something sad about her, as if she never stops thinking about her misfortune. Had you noticed it?"

This was better. Burke said: "No. We're old friends, from Bordeaux. Perhaps she doesn't feel so sad when she is with me."

"Perhaps not."

But Burke remembered that Madame FitzGerald had said Rose now used a loud, satirical manner. What better butt of her humour could she find than the hairy-heeled lord of the Château Rochechouart whose roof she had been obliged to share before coming to civilisation in Paris? It was a nasty thought, and he did not quite believe in it. Her control and her remoteness from her company were her strongest characteristics. In any case it no longer mattered what she thought of him. He saw no harm in asking another question:

"When did you notice this air of sadness? Has she always seemed like that to you?"

"It was always there but it's more intense since last summer. She seemed more sure of herself at first."

"And now?"

"There are stories. I don't want to pass them on. You're an old friend of hers. You might be able to do something for her."

It was a good start. A pity that Dorval had this dull, righteous air about him but she would just have to put up with it. Beggars can't be choosers. If he consented to marry her, he would certainly keep her tail-feathers trimmed. Interesting that he had noticed the change in her from the time of Edmund's visit. Later in the evening he asked Madame FitzGerald about him.

She said: "I saw you sitting with him. He comes very often – he's lonely, since his wife died."

"He has no idea of marrying again?"

"No, though we've all tried to find him a wife. He's young enough, and quite well off."

Better and better. Dorval would accept the FitzGeralds as intermediaries. Burke would keep right out of the picture. She need never know that the whole idea was his, no more than she need discover that he had been the source of her income.

All of this had seemed satisfactory enough last night but today, with that white light all around him, he was not so sure. Rose would have to be warned of the possibility of a proposal of marriage from Dorval, and who better to warn her than Burke? It was all his idea, after all. But if he had been terrified of his first meeting with her, he was in a worse panic now at the thought of broaching that subject. He doubted if he even had the courage to mention the name of Jules Dorval, since she had reacted against it the last time. It seemed clear that she wanted to avoid him because he had witnessed her humiliation – but where could a husband be found for her if such finicky objections were made? Who did she think she was? Poor as a church mouse, a reputation that would frighten the crows, a temper fit to scald the paint off the door – she would be lucky to get anyone to take her.

So he was too weak to follow his conscience, after all. Had the months in Ireland, which he had believed had remade his mind, meant nothing? He knew it was not true. No harm at all in being frightened out of his wits so long as he went ahead and did what had to be done, in the end. Besides, it was too soon to name a possible husband. All he had to do was condition her mind to the notion of marriage with someone. The rest could be left to Madame FitzGerald. Women's work, as she had said herself. He would talk to her about it today.

Once his mind was firmly made up on this, he found himself looking for excuses not to visit her yet. The snow, and he had only one pair of good boots, and she had said herself that he was tired. Poor old man. None of it was any use. He was as strong as a horse, full of energy stored up since his confinement in Cashel, and on the ship, and in the coach from Hamburg. People said he looked tired but by tomorrow morning they would be saying the opposite. He would go in a *fiacre*, dressed for his mission, in buckled shoes, black pantaloons, a white shirt – that would impress her. It would bolster up his courage too. Paris always made him feel the need to dress more carefully. In Bordeaux he was just one of the country landowners who came in about their business and went home again in the evening, not caring much how the citizens spent their time.

So he would go at the same hour as yesterday, before any of her other guests arrived. That had worked well. There was nothing to fear. She had been pleasant and friendly. She couldn't eat him, after all. So he comforted himself as he dressed in his better shirt and shook out his clean black, and found clean stockings, and tied a decent black cravat. She would not be ashamed of him if any of her fine friends happened to drop in.

The maid recognised him at once, of course, and led him upstairs without asking his name. She let him into the salon saying: "Your friend from Ireland, Madame."

She was in her special chair, with her back to the light. She did not stand up, but stayed very still, with her hands on the arms of the chair in her typical position. He knew at once that she was in a different mood from yesterday but he was not prepared for her instant attack.

She said: "I wonder you have the nerve to come back."

"What do you mean?"

He moved forward into the room, making sure first that the door was firmly shut. He disliked standing in front of her, full in the snowy light, which sparkled on her china and glass cabinets, and on the gold of her chairs.

She said: "Of course you act the innocent."

"I don't understand."

"You would have met him on the stairs if you had come ten minutes ago. Mr. Burke, I do not like to have my private affairs discussed and arranged by third parties."

"What on earth are you talking about?"

"Don't play the innocent with me. It's written all over your face."

"Who has been here?"

"Your friend, Monsieur Dorval."

"He's not my friend."

"He would be sorry to hear that. He speaks of you with great affection."

"I've only met him a few times, at the FitzGeralds."

"You made good use of your time, according to him, talking about me."

The devil take Dorval, with his long tongue. No – take that back. Apart from the sin of cursing him, Burke should perhaps be thankful to him. Now there was less need for a devious approach, something that went against Burke's nature at any time.

Rose said: "I can tell by your face that you know exactly what I'm talking about. Can you deny that you told Dorval he should come and make me an offer of marriage?"

"Yes, by God, I can. I never said anything of the sort to him."

"You sound convincing. It's not the impression you gave him. Can you deny that you spoke to him about me?"

"I certainly did that, but he began it."

That was a black lie, but the other was not. The first would have to balance the second, before God. Rose drew in her breath with a long hiss through her teeth, a sound as frightening as a growling tiger. She said: "You should have stopped him. You would have, if you were a gentleman."

Burke said, bold as brass: "It would take a strong man to stop him."

"I believe you. That man has an obsession about me. I've tried every possible method of getting rid of him."

Go carefully. Don't let her see that she has just punched you in the wind. Burke said: "Why do you try? Why don't you accept his offer?"

"Mr. Burke," Rose said slowly. "Let me ask you a question. Would you like to spend the rest of your life with Jules Dorval?"

"That's not fair. It's different for a woman, when she's married."

"No, it is not. He is a bore, and a lecher, and a bully. I dislike his company. He will not change. He's thoroughly

251

pleased with himself. He disapproves of me but he wants me all the same. Being married to him would be the worst kind of slavery. I've told him a great many times that I will not marry him, and still he comes back as if I had said nothing."

A great many times! And Dorval, the rat, had said nothing about that, only talking sentimentally about how sad she looked. At the moment she looked about as sad as a hunting cat.

Burke said: "Have you told your maid to keep him out?"

"Of course I have. But she can't throw him downstairs. I think he gives her presents of money from time to time."

"How long has this been going on?"

"For at least six months."

"You can't afford to refuse an offer of marriage, Miss French."

"Exactly what do you mean by that statement?"

Too late he saw his mistake. He tried to recover himself.

"You would be independent, if you were married. Supposing Edmund were to stop your pension – "

"How do you know he has stopped my pension? Have you been talking to him about me too?"

"No. But I guessed what had happened," Burke said, turning away, taking a chair and seating himself with his back to the light. "It's a long story."

"I have plenty of time."

"It seems to me that Edmund stopped your pension when he thought I was dead."

"That is how it seems to me too." There was a rasp in her voice now, a sound he had never heard from her before. "What I would like to know is why the news of your death should have made such a change in Edmund. I can think of only one reason."

"Edmund is not generous by nature."

"That had occurred to me. So you suggested to him to pay me a pension, for what reason I can't imagine."

She had it wrong. She still thought the money came out of Edmund's pocket. If she found out that it was Burke's

252

money, she'd eat him down to his shoes. He began to sweat at the very thought of it. If Edmund ever told, he'd skin him. She was saying: "Worse still, I think you actually forced him into giving me a pension, which we now see he was not willing to do. I simply cannot understand why you should want to humiliate me in this way."

"I did not want to humiliate you – the reverse, in fact. Lord God, girl, I couldn't hand you over to that pair of skinflints without lifting a hand to defend you."

She was an ungrateful hussy, throwing his generosity in his face as if it were an insult. What was wrong with being given a pension to live on? She told him instantly, though he had not said it aloud: "You think I should be grateful for your interference in my affairs. Let me tell you that if you had not set me up in this apartment, with an income of my own, I should never have been the centre of a group of people like Jules Dorval. When my income was stopped they were able and willing to let me earn it from them."

He had hoped she would deny it.

"So you're blaming me for the loose life you've taken to."

"Where did you hear that I'm living a loose life? For all you know, I've been selling them knitted goods and embroidery."

Burke snorted.

"All the knitting and embroidery you could do in a year wouldn't pay your maid's wages."

"And you think I should have gone to live in an attic and earned an honest crust of bread?"

"Yes, I do. At least you would be your own woman then. You could show the door to anyone you didn't want around the place. Once you start the other thing they can do what they like with you."

"As you did to Jeanne."

"Jeanne has no cause to complain of me."

"You think not?"

Two could play that game. If she could read his mind, so could he hers. She was thinking of poor suffering Jeanne, taken advantage of by that coarse, rough clown, all her refined feelings outraged, forced into marriage in the end for Burke's convenience.

He said angrily: "Jeanne did well out of her association with me. I kept her head on her shoulders but there's more to it than that. She's a scheming little bitch, fornicating under my roof with one of my guests. Anyone else would have blacked her eye for her. Instead I gave her the husband of her choice, and my best house, though she had an idea that it was still hers. I dealt fairly with her and she knows it. You must have seen by now that not all French ladies are as delicate as they look."

He had scored well. He watched her for a moment, then added: "You'll understand her better when I tell you that it was her idea, not mine, to – to – "

Though he had begun so bravely, he could not bring himself to finish the sentence. She did it for him.

"To get into your bed?"

"Yes. I'm not saying the thought hadn't crossed my mind. I'd be a timber man if it didn't." When had he ever talked to anyone like this? She was a jewel indeed, a dear, deceitful jewel. Abruptly he asked: "Have you given up singing?"

"What on earth makes you ask that now? I haven't, in fact. I've even had some lessons."

He could not imagine how to continue, though her voice had softened. Perhaps there was someone else in her circle that she liked better than Dorval. He said: "Is there not some other suitor you fancy?"

Rose said: "Just get that idea out of your head. Monsieur Dorval is the only suitor, as you call him. The others are something else. In any case I'll never marry now. Most women would but I know I can never care for anyone now. You 're wasting your time."

"So you intend to go on like this?"

"I have no alternative."

"Of course you have. You could leave Paris, for a start."

"And go back to Ireland? From what I hear, it's not a very

254

comfortable country at the moment, even if I were to get a welcome home."

"I was not thinking of Ireland."

"Where, then?"

She knew. He could tell by her astonished expression, her mouth held firmly to cover her amusement at the idea. There was no backing out now. He would have to burn the journal at once, before she could get her crooks on it. The thought gave him a pang, in spite of his decision to destroy it. He might begin on another, after all, about sheep and horses and hens.

He said: "I'm thinking of Saint Jacques d'Ambes. I'm going back there to live for the rest of my life, as I told you. Anna will cook for me but she's no housekeeper. She'll do a bad job unless you're there to keep an eye on her. Yesterday I could see that you know exactly how to handle her. It's a big house. You could have your own rooms, all the rooms you want. You could advise me about sheep. You always talked sense about the farms. You could go to Bordeaux to shop, and to the Opéra, and to meet your friends whenever you wanted."

"I have no friends in Bordeaux. I don't know anything about sheep."

"You'll soon learn. And you would soon make friends, if you had a place where you could invite them."

"You mentioned your bishop yesterday. What would he think of all this?"

"The bishop won't be a problem for a long time, and then he won't make any objection. Plenty of priests have a distant cousin to live in the house, to give her a home and to do the housekeeping."

"So I'm a distant cousin now?"

"As distant as you like."

She was really considering it. She was looking him over. His clean shirt stood up well to it, and his buckled shoes.

He said: "I used to love Paris but now I find that the air oppresses me. I want to get back to my land at once and take over my old work again. Everything has changed. I'm

255

finished with politics and rebellions. I haven't lost my nerve but I'm just too old to be useful except in a very small way, and I don't like very small ways. I want to see the Irish College in Bordeaux opened again. If I manage that, no bishop born will squeak at me. You would be as free as air, and I'll leave you the farm-house in my will, for your lifetime."

Quick as a flash she said: "And after that?"

"To the College. Please come."

"We don't agree."

"Then we could disagree."

Better not to watch her. Give her time. She was on the point of accepting. If she did, she would never go back on it. Swift's lines ran into his head:

> They keep at Staines the old Blue Boar,
> Are cat and dog, and rogue and whore.

It would be the mercy of God if they were not in hers too. It was dangerous even to have thought of them in the same room with her.

He said: "I'm going to bring all my books together at Saint Jacques. We can make a library."

"I'll come," she said abruptly. "You don't have to tempt me. I'm sick of the stones of Paris. I'm a countrywoman. I'll come, so long as you can swear that you didn't send Dorval after me again."

"I swear it."

"And there are no strings?"

"Only one."

"What's that?"

"If you will close my eyes when I die. I don't want the devils looking in at the last moment."

"Certainly. I'll do that. But you should know that devils never look in. They always look out."